"HURRAH! I SHALL BE A GREAT MAN!"

—*With the Immortals.*

THE COMPLETE WORKS OF
# F. MARION CRAWFORD
*In Thirty-two Volumes* ✒ *Authorized Edition*

# With the Immortals

BY

## F. MARION CRAWFORD

WITH FRONTISPIECE

## P. F. COLLIER & SON
### NEW YORK

# THE COMPLETE WORKS OF F. MARION CRAWFORD

# WITH THE IMMORTALS.

## CHAPTER I.

THE southern shore of the Sorrentine peninsula offers a striking contrast to the northern side. Towards the north the mountain opens into a broad basin, filled to the brim with soft tufo rock, upon which the vegetation of ages has deposited a deep and fertile soil. The hills slope gently to the cliffs which overhang the bay of Naples and they seem to bear in their outstretched arms a rich offering of Nature's fairest gifts for the queen city of the south. The orange and the lemon, the olive and the walnut elbow each other for a footing in the fat dark earth; and where there is not room for them, the holes and crannies of the walls shoot out streamers of roses and thrust forth nosegays of white-flowered myrtle. Westward from the enchanted garden of Sorrento the rocky promontory juts far into the sea, so that only a narrow channel, scarcely three miles wide, separates the mainland from sea-girt Capri, towering up from the blue water and rearing his rocky crest to heaven like some enormous dragon-beast of fable. Far down in the deep mid-channel, lies the watch-tower bell stolen by the Saracen corsairs from the little fort upon the shore; on Saint John's Eve the fishermen, casting their nets in the orange-tinted twilight, hear the tones of the long-lost bronze ringing up to them out of the depths, and the rough men tell each other how, on that very night of the year, long ago, Saint Nicholas raised a fierce storm in the "Bocca di Crape" and forced the heathen pirates to lighten their craft by heaving overboard the bell and the rest of the booty they had carried off.

Doubling the point, and running along the southern shore of the little peninsula, the scene changes. The rocks, which on the other side slope gently down, here rise precipitously from the dark water, throwing up great rugged friezes of hacked stone against the sky, casting black shadows under every sharpened peak and seeming to defy the foot of man and beast. Here and there, a little town hangs like the nest of a sea-bird in a cranny of the cliffs, poised on the brink as you may fancy a sea-nymph drawing up her feet out of reach of the waves, facing the fierce, hot south-west, whence the storms sweep in, black and melancholy and wrathfully thundering. A mile away, but seemingly within a stone's throw of the cliffs, lie three tiny islands, green in the short spring months, but parched and brown in summer, dark and dangerous in the stormy winter. They are the isles of the Sirens; past them once sailed the mighty wanderer, bound to the mast of his long black ship, listening with delight and dread to the song of the

sea-women, his heart beating fast and his blood on
fire with the wild strains of their music. Ligeia and
Leucosia and Parthenope are not dead, though they
plucked the flowers with Persephone, and though the
Muses outrivalled them in harmony and Orpheus
vanquished them in song. Still, in calm nights,
when the waning moon climbs slowly over the distant hills of the Basilicata, her trembling light falls
on the marble limbs and the snowy feathers, the rich
wet hair and the passionate dark eyes of the three
maidens, and across the lapping waves their voices
ring out in a wild, despairing harmony of long-
drawn complaint. But when the storm rises and
the hot south wind dashes the water into whirlpools
and drives clouds of warm spray into the crevices of
the islets, the sisters slip from the wet rocks and
hide themselves in the cool depths below, where is
perpetual calm and a dwelling not fathomed by man.

But man visits the shore and the islands too, from
time to time, though he rarely stays long. It is too
unlike what man is accustomed to, too far removed
from the sphere of the modern world's life, to be a
sympathetic resting-place for most of our kind.
Hither people come in yachts, or upon skinny don-
keys from Sorrento, or in little open boats rowed by
lazy fishermen; and they gaze and say that it is very
classic, and they go away with their cheap impressions and tell their friends that it is hardly worth
while after all. That is what everybody does. My
tale concerns a little party of persons, not absolutely

like every one else, who one day said to each other
that it would be possible to live among those wild
rocks, and that they believed themselves sufficiently
interesting to each other to live a life of temporary
exile in an inaccessible region. Such a resolution
must at once brand those who entered upon it with
the stamp of eccentricity, with the Cain's mark
which society abhors, and it is necessary to say something of the circumstances which led those four persons to determine upon so desperate a course.

Three of the settlers were young. The fourth
was older by some years than any of the rest, but
possessed that quality of youth which defies time
and, especially, that little moiety of time which we
call age. The party then, consisted of a man and
his wife, of his mother-in-law and his sister. By
the silly calculations of social humanity they ought
to have quarrelled. As a matter of fact they did
not. This was the first step towards eccentricity,
and it can only be explained by an honest and dis-
passionate description of the four persons.

Lady Brenda was five and forty years of age —
with extenuating circumstances. A German wag
once remarked that money alone does not constitute
happiness, but that it is also necessary to possess
some of it. So years alone do not make age unless
one has some of the ills which age brings. No
woman has any right to be old at five and forty, but
it may be questioned whether at five and forty any
woman has a right to be taken for her daughter's

sister. Lady Brenda was in some respects the youngest of the party; for she had been young when youth was regarded as an agreeable period of life, and she had brought her traditions with her. In appearance she was of medium height but of faultless figure, slender and rounded as a girl. Her complexion was of the kind produced by avoiding cosmetics. Her thick brown hair grew low upon her forehead and was not supplemented by any artful arrangement of other women's tresses among her own. Her features were very straight, and her large, bright blue eyes, rather deep-set but wide apart, met everything frankly and surveyed the world with an air of radiant satisfaction which was as contagious as her own humour. She moved quickly, laughed easily and felt sincerely the emotions of the hour. Her voice was so fresh and ringing that people liked to listen to it, and the things she said were generally to the point. The basis of her mind was an intuitive comprehension of what was best to be done and said in the manifold situations in which she might find herself placed. Logic she had none, but she arrived at perfectly just conclusions by methods of thought which seemed absurdly illogical. As a matter of fact she did not really arrive at conclusions at all, but having determined *a priori* what she intended to believe, she thought any argument good enough to support that of which she was already convinced. On the other hand her experience of people was immense, and she understood human nature marvellously well. She had lived in every capital of Europe and had found herself at home everywhere, received into the intimacy of a society exclusive to all other strangers, and she had gathered a vast mass of anecdote and experience, by turns startling, tragic, dramatic and comic which would have sufficed to fill many deeply interesting volumes. With all this, she was a little tired of the great world and had gladly accepted her son-in-law's invitation to pass a year in the south of Italy.

Lady Brenda's only daughter had been married to Augustus Chard two years before this time, and had presented her husband with a baby which was universally declared to be at all points the most extraordinary baby ever born, seen, or heard of. Mrs. Chard's name was Gwendoline. Lady Brenda, in the secrecy of her own heart, knew that the combination of names, "Gwendoline Chard," made her think of a race-horse charging into a brick wall. Otherwise she liked her son-in-law very much. The Chards adored each other when they were married, which is usual; but they continued to adore each other after marriage, which is not. There were many reasons why their lives should be harmonious, however, for they were a pair well assorted to live together. Gwendoline differed from her mother in that she had dark eyes, and that her hair was of a reddish gold colour full of magnificent lights. Her skin was paler than her mother's, and her figure, perfectly proportioned and well designed, was a little slighter.

She was an inch taller than Lady Brenda and carried her beautiful head erect upon her shoulders with an air of dignity beyond her years. Gwendoline was a woman who thought much and who generally decided beforehand exactly what she wanted. When she had decided, she proceeded to obtain her wish, and when she had got it, she was perfectly satisfied. These qualities placed her entirely beyond the pale of ordinary humanity. Her feelings were strong and deep, and her nature was noble and elevated; her wishes were therefore good, and for good things. Though young, she had travelled much and had seen much that was interesting. Gwendoline's principal taste was for music, an art in which she attained to great excellence, for her playing was original, passionate and artistic. As has been said, she worshipped her husband, who in his turn adored her. She could not deny that he held highly original views upon most points, and that his ideas about things in general were a trifle startling, but he had a way of making himself appear to be right which was very convincing to any one who was already disposed to be of his opinion. Lady Brenda was very fond of Augustus Chard, but considered him more than half a visionary; Gwendoline on the other hand was willing to spend her time in helping him to demonstrate that all existing things and conditions of things, with the exception of domestic felicity, were arrant humbug.

Augustus used to say that the taste for the vision-

ary ran in his family. His sister, who had joined
the party, illustrated the truth of his statement.
Diana Chard had the temperament of a poet with the
mind of a lawyer. Philosophy may be defined to
mean the poetry of logic, and accordingly Diana's
nature had led her to the study of philosophy. She
had read enormously, and she argued keenly with a
profound knowledge of her subject. But the hypothesis generally belonged to the transcendental region
of thought, where, as the problems proposed are
beyond the sphere of all possible experience, the discussion also may be prolonged beyond the bounds of
all possible time. She enjoyed the pleasure of argument much more than the hope of solution; and life
never seemed dull when she could discuss the immortality of the soul with an unbeliever, or the existence
of the supernatural with a well-trained and thoroughly
prejudiced materialist. She was moreover a musician, and an accomplished one, like her sister-in-law,
but her playing differed so entirely from Gwendoline's that no one thought of comparing the two.
Each was perfect in her own way; but each raised
entirely different trains of thought in her hearers.

Of the three ladies Diana was the tallest. She
was very slender and very graceful, slow and even
languid in her movements, but animated in her
speech. Her skin was very dark and pale, her hair
abundant and of a dark brown colour, her eyes, a
deep grey with strongly marked eyebrows and black
lashes; her mouth large and expressive, smiling
easily and showing very beautiful teeth.

Last of the four to be described is Augustus Chard. Imagine a big, well-knit man of bronzed complexion, with colourless hair, neither fair nor brown, average-sized blue eyes set very deep under an overhanging forehead, possessed of a remarkable constitution and of unusual physical strength. That was all there was to be seen, and from the exterior no one would have been likely to guess at the man's queer mental tendencies. It would not have struck the observer that Augustus Chard's mind was a mixture of revolutionary and of conservative ideas, leavened with an absurd taste for mysticism and magic, tempered by a considerable experience of more serious science, in which his immense wealth has permitted him to make experiments beyond the reach of ordinary men — a man in love with his wife, and to some extent in love with existence; active in mind and body, but seemingly under the influence of some strange planet which causes him to think differently from other people, and sometimes not very wisely either. Augustus either talked not at all, or talked excessively. Habitually a silent man, when roused in discussion his naturally combative temper showed itself, and, though patient in argument, he could not bear to abandon his point and would prolong a discussion for hours rather than own himself vanquished. Lady Brenda knew this and took a fantastic delight in combating his visionary ideas. Nevertheless they were very fond of each other, as people must be if they can discuss without quarrelling. Augustus Chard would say he believed in astrology and declare his intention of having the baby's horoscope cast, without further hesitation. Lady Brenda would reply for the twentieth time that she could not see how the stars could possibly have any influence upon human beings, and thereupon the discussion would begin again. In the course of an hour Augustus would demonstrate that Lady Brenda could not decide upon taking an extra cup of tea without the direct influence of Jupiter and that the appearance of beings from another world was not a whit more remarkable than the production of the electric light, nor more incomprehensible than the causes of attraction. He easily showed that nobody knew anything and that, consequently, no one had the right to deny anything; and he ended by prophesying such dreadful and extraordinary things, which must occur in the world in the course of a few years, that Lady Brenda felt her breath taken away. But a quarter of an hour later, when it was discovered to be twelve o'clock, they all laughed and remarked that they had had a most delightful evening, as they separated and went to bed.

Of Augustus Chard it is only necessary to say that he had considerable powers of organisation, in spite of some eccentricities of mind, and that he generally succeeded in what he undertook. When, therefore, he suggested to his wife, his sister and his mother-in-law, that it would be very amusing to buy a half-ruined castle perched upon the wild rocks and overlooking the isles of the Sirens, to furnish the place luxuriously and to pass the summer in a pleasant round of discussion, music and semi-mystic literary amusement, varied by a few experiments on the electric phenomena of the Mediterranean, it did not strike those amiable ladies that the scheme was wholly mad. They agreed that it would be very novel and interesting and that if they did not like it they could go away — which is the peculiar blessing of the rich. The poor man sometimes finds it necessary to cut his throat in order to go away; the rich man orders his butler to examine the time-tables, and his valet to pack his belongings, dines comfortably and changes his surroundings as he would change his coat.

Augustus proposed his plan in January. Before the end of April the castle was bought, repaired and luxuriously furnished, the beds were made, the French *chef* had ordered the kitchen fires to be lighted and had established a donkey post over the mountains to the market in Castellamare; the great halls and drawing-rooms looked thoroughly habitable, and everything was ready for the new-comers, who were to arrive in the evening. Augustus Chard congratulated himself with the reflection that his whim had been gratified at a trifling cost of ten thousand pounds, and he subsequently discovered that a ducal title had been thrown into the bargain. He immediately determined to bestow the title upon the captain of his yacht, for the sake of being able to order a real Duke to "go about"; but Lady Brenda, whose mind took a practical turn, suggested that as times and governments change rather quickly nowadays it would be as well to keep the parchment and see what came of it.

The party arrived at the appointed hour and proceeded to survey their new dwelling. Augustus Chard had come over from Naples several times and had personally directed most of the repairs and improvements. The result did not fall short of his intentions. The huge, irregular mass of building had been made perfectly habitable. The tiled roofs shone red above the rugged stones of the towers and walls; great polished doors moved noiselessly in the old marble doorways; plate-glass panes filled the high Moorish windows; pleasantly coloured glazed tiles cunningly arranged in patterns upon the floor had taken the place of the worn-out bricks; soft stuffs and tapestries covered the walls and rich Oriental carpets were spread under the tables and before the deep easy chairs; massive furniture was disposed comfortably in the hall and drawing-room, while each of the ladies found a boudoir fitted up for her especial use, furnished in the colours she loved best; Vienna cane lounges stood upon the tented terraces and hammocks were hung in shady corners overlooking the sea; the newest books lay by vases of roses upon low reading-tables, shades of the latest patterns covered the still unlighted lamps, writing-paper marked "Castello del Gaudio, Amalfi" was ready in the boxes in every room, and Lady Brenda remarked with pleasure that there was ink in the inkstands. Bimbam, Chard's butler, a Swiss, watched his mistress's face with anxiety as Gwendoline passed from room to room, examining everything with the critical eye of a practised housekeeper. For Gwendoline believed that the bigger a house was, the more keeping it needed, and Bimbam stood in awe of her rebuke; but if Augustus ventured to make a remark concerning anything outside of his own rooms, Bimbam smiled a soft and pitying smile, as much as to say that amiable lunatics like Augustus should mind their own business.

The great hall of the house opened upon a wide terrace, by a row of tall windows which stood open on the sunny April afternoon when the party arrived. Earthenware pots of flowers were arranged along the parapet, pots of roses and of carnations — not common pinks, but great southern carnations — and long troughs of pansies and heliotrope; while from the garden below the vines grew up, wild and uncultivated, putting out their first spring leaves. Behind the castle, and on both sides of it, and below the garden, the vast grey rocks lay like an angry sea of stone petrified in the very moment when the rough crests would have broken into a flinty spray. Far below, the isles of the Sirens lay like green leaves floating on the sapphire water.

The whole party came out together upon this terrace, followed at a respectful distance by Bimbam.

"It is too beautiful for anything!" exclaimed Diana, gazing at the sea. Like all imaginative people she loved the water.

"A dream!" cried Lady Brenda, who was not given to dreaming.

Gwendoline laid her hand upon her husband's arm and stood silently surveying the scene, her face pale with pleasure. Augustus stared out into the distance.

"What are you thinking of?" asked Gwendoline at last.

"I was wondering how the experiment would succeed."

"It will succeed admirably," said Lady Brenda. "We are admirable people — this is an admirable place —"

"Then let us fall to admiring each other and our surroundings," answered Augustus. "But I was thinking of the experiment."

"Oh — your spirits and things!" exclaimed his mother-in-law. "Really, Augustus, I can't understand how a man of your intelligence —"

"Had we not better sit down?" suggested Augustus, smiling.

"No," said Lady Brenda; "I am sure we have not seen everything yet. Come along — let us explore."

Bimbam whispered to Augustus that he had taken the liberty of improvising a Swiss dairy, as it was hard to get any milk but that of goats.

"Oh! I want to see my dairy!" exclaimed Gwendoline, and away they went.

Lady Brenda sent for writing materials and began a letter, while Diana entered the great hall and tried the piano. Lady Brenda had a vast correspondence and she wrote well, which was the principal reason why she was able to live in the country. People were so real to her, that to write to them was almost as good as to talk to them. She did not care so much for cows as she did for people. It does not follow that Gwendoline preferred cows to human society; but when she began to see a place, she liked to see it all, whereas her mother contented herself with proposing further explorations and then sat down to describe what she had already seen.

On this occasion Lady Brenda sent for writing materials and established herself upon the wide terrace. She wrote a very interesting epistle in which she explained to her sister that Augustus had come to the Castello del Gaudio to try things with ghosts and mathematical electricity and so forth, but that the place was charming and Gwendoline looked so well in jerseys — and a real mediæval castle with a drawbridge somewhere and a Swiss dairy not far off — the great hall was hung with Rhodes tapestry which Augustus had got from a Jew in Asia Minor — so rare, they sold little bits of it in London — and by the bye, where was Lord Mavourneen going to? Augustus meant to ask him during the summer, when he was tired of the ghosts — Diana was certainly a most delightful girl — just Gwendoline's age, but so different — life was a dream of summer flowers — if only Lord Brenda could be with her — but then perhaps he would not enjoy it so much, though of course he would like it immensely, dear fellow. She did not quite know whether Brenda were in St. Petersburg or in India, but of course he would write.

Meanwhile Diana played soft dreamy harmonies upon the wonderful piano, taking delight in the idea that in all the ages before no such sounds had floated out upon the evening air to stir the echoes of the jagged rocks, unless indeed the tale of the Sirens were true, a matter concerning which Diana held opinions of her own. She secretly hoped that her brother's experiments might be successful, and she felt sure that if success were possible at all it must be possible in the wild region where he had at last determined to make his great trial of a new theory. While she played, her mind wandered away to strange regions, and she fancied she heard wonderful sounds answering the ringing chords of the piano. Just then Lady Brenda came in and looked briskly round the great room.

"Really, Augustus has very good taste. Don't you think so?" she said, appealing to Diana.

"Such a piano!" exclaimed Diana, rising. "I wonder where he got it!"

"You can get most things for money, my dear," said Lady Brenda. "Augustus will probably get his ghosts, too!"

"For money?"

"Oh, I don't know! why should not ghosts be bribed, like other people?"

"If money were of any use, where they live."

"It must be awfully funny to be in a place where money is of no use," said Lady Brenda.

"Awfully funny — indeed!" repeated Diana with a laugh. "I hope they see the humorous aspect of their situation, poor dears."

"Do you suppose there is really anything in it, my dear? For my part I think it is all ridiculous, you know."

"Ghosts? well —" Diana hesitated. "There is no particular reason for thinking them ridiculous, after all."

"Oh, of course they are ridiculous," said Lady Brenda with an air of conviction. "Can anything be more absurd than to suppose that one's great-uncle can get up out of his grave and walk into a room without opening the doors and rap underneath a table without your seeing him? Just think!"

"Yes — if you confine ghosts to spirit rapping and table turning. I quite agree with you. But there are —"

"Oh, I know just what you are going to say about mathematics and electric things — of course I don't know anything about them and so I never pretend to argue, but I am perfectly sure it is all quite nonsensical. Don't you think it would be a good idea to have some tea?"

"Delightful," answered Diana, looking dreamily

out of the great window and letting her hands run carelessly over the keys of the piano.  She had more than once reflected on the impossibility of ever convincing any one who first stated a firm belief and then refused to argue about it on the ground of ignorance.  She also reflected that Lady Brenda was a charming woman and that it made not the smallest difference whether she believed in ghosts or not.

Just then Gwendoline entered the room, followed by Augustus.  The latter spoke in a low voice to the solemn Bimbam, who retired.  In a few minutes tea and Turkish coffee were brought in.

"Mamma, the cows are too beautiful," said Gwendoline.  "It was such a brilliant idea to build the little dairy up there among the rocks.  Now tell us what you have been talking about."

"By all means," echoed Augustus, examining the details of the room and walking slowly from one point to another with his hands in his pockets.  "By all means, tell us what you have been talking about."

"I have been writing a letter—" began Lady Brenda.

"The novelty of your occupation is only surpassed by—" interrupted Augustus.  But Lady Brenda would not let him finish the sentence.

"I know—please don't make fun of me.  It's dreadful, I know I am always writing letters."

"We talked a little about ghosts," said Diana. "Augustus, if you really have any ghosts, do have nice ones."

"Yes," said Gwendoline. "Have people who would be pleasant at dinner — people who can talk. It would be so delightful to be able to ask ever so many questions of historical people. I could make such a beautiful dinner party. Whom would you have, mamma?"

"I, well — I think if I might choose — perhaps I would have Francis the First. Whom would you have, Gwendoline?"

"Dear me! — Oh — I think I would choose a musician — Chopin, for instance. Let us all say. Diana, whom would you like?"

"Lots of people," answered the young girl. "Heine for one — then Pascal, and Plato and — let me see, I think Pico della Mirandola would be nice and I should be curious to see Giordano Bruno —"

"A conceited, blaspheming fool!" exclaimed Augustus, speaking for the first time. "I would be quite satisfied with Julius Cæsar."

"Do you think he would be quite sympathetic?" asked Lady Brenda, entering into the discussion as though the invitation were a reality.

"Oh yes!" exclaimed Gwendoline. "He was a great dandy, and immensely refined. Besides, Augustus would not be happy unless he were asked. Julius Cæsar is his ideal."

"Won't you have anybody besides Chopin, Gwendoline?" asked Augustus. "You might have George Sand, for instance."

"Oh no!" protested Gwendoline. "They would sit in corners and talk to each other all the evening."

"Why is not it possible!" exclaimed Diana regretfully.

"Perhaps it is," answered Augustus, quietly.

"Augustus, I think you are quite mad!" cried Lady Brenda, laughing.

"My dear mother-in-law, you are probably right. It is quite certain that I am mad, if you are sane, but if I am sane you are undoubtedly mad. Happily it is often people of very opposite dispositions who best agree. In either case, mad or sane, you are the most charming woman I know and I hope you will not change at all."

Lady Brenda blushed faintly, as she always did when anybody made her a compliment, and she kissed the tips of her fingers and waved them towards Augustus across the tea-table with a pretty gesture.

"Oh, Augustus! How can you say mamma is more charming than I am?" said Gwendoline with a laugh.

"Or than I am?" echoed Diana, between two bites of a huge strawberry.

"With such women as you, my dears," answered Augustus, imperturbably, "the most charming woman is always the one who is speaking at the moment."

"We might all speak at once," suggested Lady Brenda, "then we should all be equally charming."

"No man could stand that," answered Augustus.

"You would take refuge in the fourth dimension, then, I suppose?" asked Diana.

"Like the bishop who said he travelled in the third class because there was no fourth!" suggested Gwendoline. "Let us return to the question of the dinner party. Shall I write invitations to the people we mentioned? Could we not perform an incantation and burn the notes upon the sacrificial altar?"

"We could," said Augustus. "It would be a comparatively cheap form of amusement. But in the course of time, if Julius Cæsar and the rest never came, the novelty of asking them would wear off."

"If they only knew what agreeable people we are, I am sure they would come," answered Gwendoline.

"I will see about it," said Augustus. "It will soon be time to dress for dinner."

## CHAPTER II.

AUGUSTUS CHARD believed that science had reached a point at which it was necessary to try entirely new experiments and to try them on a vast scale. It seemed to him that the problem of greatest present importance was of a practical kind — the production of electricity in a serviceable form and at a cost which should at once make it the universal source of heat, light and motive power for the whole world. After a careful examination he had come to the conclusion that the most convenient form in which the fluid could be produced was the voltaic, which also was unfortunately the most expensive. He accordingly set to work to ascertain whether any method existed, and could be guessed at, whereby the earth herself could be made to produce under the existing circumstances of nature a current of voltaic electricity. He argued that if such a current could be produced, and if the quality should prove satisfactory, the quantity as compared with the needs of mankind must be unlimited.

Acting upon his usual plan of beginning from first principles, he reflected that in the earliest experiments voltaic currents were produced by immersing two metals in a fluid. He naturally discarded all

the chemical theories of electricity as worthless,
basing his reasoning entirely upon fact and not fearing to give trial to any system which suggested
itself, regardless of all existing prejudices about
probability. Grotthuss's hypothesis had no charms
for him. The problem was, not how to explain the
chemical action of currents, but how to produce currents on an enormous scale at a trifling cost. It was
necessary to consult nature and not books. If he
succeeded in producing a vast quantity of electricity
he would find leisure to discourse upon its chemical
effects. The idea that the earth must be considered
to be a gigantic reservoir of electricity presented
itself to his mind under a practical aspect; and it
immediately struck him that in the shape of land
and water the earth contained the two elements of a
stupendous battery; acted upon at all points by a
uniform fluid agent, the atmosphere. The idea was
simple and grand. It would be sufficient to immerse
one conductor in the sea and to attach another to the
land. If anything were to result from the attempt it
must result immediately. No one had ever thought
of it before and the credit of the discovery would
belong wholly to him, Augustus Chard. If it failed
there was no one but Lady Brenda to say "I told you
so." Augustus accordingly set to work to convert
the earth into a battery, beginning with a prelimi-
nary experiment, to the success of which he attached
considerable importance and for which he had caused
special instruments to be constructed. Even if this

previous attempt should fail Augustus would not be discouraged. A great mathematician [1] has said that "a law would be theoretically universal if it were true of all cases whatever; and that is what we do not know of any law at all." All previous experiments on such a scale might fail and yet the final experiment, which nobody had ever tried, might be brilliantly successful.

Augustus therefore proceeded to construct an artificial world. This is a very simple operation, and it is unfortunate that the construction of the real article should be accompanied with such difficulty. It would be well worth while for the European Powers to construct two little supplementary worlds, one for Russians to live in and one for Turks. It has indeed been found theoretically possible to make much out of nothing at all, but hitherto all efforts to materialise the cosmic ether into human habitations and other practical conveniences have signally failed. Augustus made his world in a glass bowl with earth and pebbles and salt water, and tested its nature with a tangent compass of his own invention, very delicately constructed. His expectations were raised to the highest pitch and he hesitated to make the connection of the wire in the mercury cup. At that moment Lady Brenda entered the room, dressed in an exquisite spring costume, with a little straw hat upon her head and a wonderful parasol in her hand.

"Come and look at my ghost," said Augustus, smiling.

[1] Clifford.

"It does not look at all like my idea of a ghost," answered Lady Brenda.

"Neither is your idea of a ghost at all like mine," returned her son-in-law. "Look here, I am going to consult a kind of Egyptian oracle which I have reconstructed from original manuscripts rescued by Dr. Mumienschinder from a tomb in Thebes. The peculiarity of this oracle is that it tells the truth sometimes. It is a sort of teraphim —"

"Oh, I know. They eat teraphims in America. Brenda dotes on them."

"I said teraphim — you mean terrapin," said Augustus, gravely.

"I see," said Lady Brenda, "of course. Go on."

"Now I am going to perform a magic rite. I will put this bit of copper wire into this little cup of mercury. Do you see that needle? If the needle moves I shall be a great man — if it does not — well then we will see."

"Put it in. I am sure it won't move," said Lady Brenda, confidently.

"Here goes. One, two, three!"

Augustus and his mother-in-law fixed their eyes on the little needle. It trembled and moved, very little indeed, but visibly.

"Hurrah!" cried Chard. "I shall be a great man! I told you so!"

"How can you be so silly, Augustus!" laughed Lady Brenda. "Of course it moved — you shook it with the wire. Don't tell me you really put any faith in that nonsense!"

"I put a good deal of faith in it," he answered, quietly, still gazing at the needle, which remained deflected until he severed the connection, when it at once returned to its normal position. "Now that it is settled that I am to be a great man, let us go for a walk."

"Much nicer than pottering over such rubbish," said the lady. "I have just had such a delightful letter. Guess from whom it is?"

Augustus guessed, and so they went down towards the sea. He was not given to talking of his intentions until they were fulfilled, and there was yet much work to be done before the colossal battery could produce the phenomena he expected from it. But he had a large body of workmen in readiness, together with vast quantities of material, which seemed to consist chiefly of great sheets of zinc-coated wire netting, of endless coils of the same wire and of great heaps of cork floats, each as big as a man's head, like those used for setting tunny-nets in the Mediterranean. In a number of large deal cases which were yet unopened there were apparatus of all kinds for electric lighting, there were electric motors, electric heating stoves and ranges for cooking by electricity; not to mention telegraphic instruments for measuring currents, for varying the tension of the electricity produced and for ascertaining the tension of the charge in long cables.

The workmen began their labours under Chard's direction and in a week the sea was covered for a

considerable distance with a net-work of cables and
floats disposed in the shape of a huge fan, adapted to
the shape of the lonely little bay below the Castello
del Gaudio. All along the shore and half way up
the height every level bit of ground was covered
with wire netting, and pieces of the latter were
thrust into the deep crevices of the rocks and adapted
over the rocks themselves wherever these were smooth
enough; and the netting, again, was covered with
layers of mud and sand and pebbles to protect it from
the action of the sun. All these nettings were carefully joined to a system of thick, insulated copper
wires which ultimately converged into one cable and
led to a stone hut at some distance from the castle.
From the cables floating on the sea, endless spirals of
zinc-coated wire hung down to the depths, but did
not reach to the bottom. These spirals also were
connected and the connections all ended in a second
insulated cable which led up by high posts to the
little hut. The interior of the latter was now trans-
formed into a rough laboratory and some of the instruments were unpacked from the cases, cleaned
from dust and dampness and fixed upon heavy deal
tables. Thick glass pillars surmounted by massive
brass knobs and binding screws stood upon blocks
of wood, for Augustus had taken his precautions,
not knowing how far the mysterious element might
confine itself to the voltaic form, and fearing some of
those startling manifestations of statical electricity
which have puzzled and even terrified experimenters

ever since Franklin drew sparks from his kite and since Armstrong's workman was knocked down by an electric shock from his steam-engine.

Augustus shut himself up in his laboratory and cautiously began his operations. It was first necessary to ascertain whether the current would produce a spark, and if so, whether the spark were of such magnitude as to be dangerous. Carefully he connected the extremities of his cables with a large universal discharger and adjusting the points at a distance of four inches apart, he retired to the corner of the hut when the commutator was placed upon a separate stand. With intense anxiety he turned the lever that was to produce the connection, keeping his eyes fixed upon the universal discharger. Instantly a lambent flame shot across the space between the points and shed a strange blue light upon the objects near it, even in the broad daylight. Augustus breathed hard. He feared that he had produced a current of strong tension and small quantity. He broke the circuit and increased the distance of the points to eight inches. Again the same lambent flame leapt across as he turned the lever of the commutator. The tension must be enormous, equal to that of a Ruhmkorff inductorium of a hundred thousand metres secondary coil, at the very least. Confused by an appearance so familiar to him, Augustus then attempted to charge a Leyden battery by attaching separate wires to the pillars of the discharger and allowing the sparks to pass as before. No result fol-

lowed, and Augustus laughed at himself as he realised
his mistake. But at ten inches and a half the spark
ceased to pass between the points: even at that distance the tension in a constant current was almost
incredible. Chard wondered whether the galvanometer would indicate any great quantity of the fluid.
With such a tension a tangent compass was of little
use and he introduced a common galvanometer into
the circuit and watched it as he turned the key of
the commutator. He expected to see the needle
deflected to an angle of forty-five degrees, indicating
a comparatively very small quantity of electricity,
such as is frequently found in currents of very high
tension. To his surprise and delight the needle
moved quickly round through an angle of 180
degrees and presently remained stationary with its
north pole pointing to the south. The quantity was
therefore enormous, far beyond even what Augustus
had expected, and the tension was, after all, small
in comparison. The real world seemed likely to
carry out the promises of the artificial one. The
gigantic force developed was docile as a child.
There were no stunning and unexpected shocks from
the fittings of the apparatus, no sparks flying off
with a report like a pistol shot such as Augustus
had seen in the handling of large dynamo-electric
machines and other imperfectly controllable genera-
tors. Half an hour convinced him that the current
could be stored in common accumulators without
trouble or danger and that the tension could be

diminished by diminishing the quantity. These admirable properties Augustus attributed to the perfect balance between internal and external resistance which was maintained in his vast natural battery. The incandescent arc light worked admirably and the accumulators when connected with electromotors left nothing to be desired. A few experiments with the latter and a few rough calculations convinced Augustus that the force of his constant current was sufficient to run a train of two hundred tons at the rate of a hundred miles an hour. The idea was fascinating and he grew pale with excitement. If a few hundred yards of collectors could produce such effects, what might be expected from an apparatus covering a mile of sea-coast? Augustus resolved to illuminate the mountains that very night, in honour of the discovery, and he lost no time in setting his men to work. Lamps were hung upon the jutting rocks, upon the walls and terraces of the castle, upon posts set upright upon the narrow shore below, and high upon the tower a truck bearing half a dozen lamps together was hoisted and connected with the rest.

## CHAPTER III.

IT was a warm evening in the latter part of May. Augustus had said nothing of the result of the experiments he had been making during the past weeks, intending to surprise the three ladies by showing them the astounding results of his work all at once. The party sat at dinner in the vaulted hall and talked upon indifferent subjects.

"You seem to be revolutionising this part of the world, Augustus," said Diana. "I was walking on the rocks this afternoon with Gwendoline and it seemed as though you were preparing an immense show of fireworks."

"Nothing to speak of," answered her brother; "I will show you after dinner."

"You have not succeeded in getting those people to dinner whom we were talking about the other day, have you?" asked Gwendoline. "I thought the fireworks might be in their honour."

"No, I am afraid they won't come for my asking. Perhaps if they got a word from you, my dear—"

"What oppressive weather!" remarked Lady Brenda. "I am sure there is going to be a thunderstorm."

"I think so too," said Gwendoline. "I always

feel the thunder before it comes. Is not it very warm for May? We might almost go out after dinner."

"By all means, let us go out," assented Augustus. "I have something to show you. It is singularly oppressive, as you say — and yet the weather seems fine enough."

"Did it never strike you that your experiments might have an effect on the weather?" asked Diana.

"If one could find a means to affect the weather," Augustus replied, "one might produce rain and drought at will. No — I do not believe it has gone as far as that. If the currents I have produced were being discharged through the air their action might make some very slight local change. But they are not. Just now they are running off into accumulators like water into a cistern."

"I hope it is not you," said Gwendoline, "but there is certainly a very strange feeling in the air — very strange indeed. I never felt anything like it before."

Bimbam just then entered the room and whispered something to Mrs. Chard, bending low with the respectful air of a trained elephant.

"It is very odd," said Gwendoline. "Tell him to send something else. Just fancy," she continued, turning to the others, "Célestin has sent word that the ice-cream won't freeze — he says 'he is at the despair but that congeals not.' It is very provoking — the first time I have ordered it."

"Don't look at me like that," said Augustus, laughing, "it is not my fault."

"I believe it is," said Gwendoline, making a little face and then laughing too.

"Do you seriously suspect me of having put Nature's nose out of joint?" asked her husband.

"Never mind, dear! It is not the least matter," said Lady Brenda to her daughter. "Those things will happen sometimes, you know. Célestin will turn the ice-cream into something else, of course. Dear me! I feel as though the room were full of people — it is very warm."

"Open that window," said Augustus to Bimbam, the butler. The servant obeyed and a gust of hot air blew in, almost stifling in its oppressiveness, but the stars shone brightly in the dark and there seemed to be no clouds in the sky. The party sat in silence for some time, going through the form of eating, but the sultry weight in the atmosphere increased with every minute until it seemed as though the simoon of the desert had broken into the dining-room.

"I cannot stand this a moment longer," said Gwendoline, rising to her feet. "I cannot breathe."

"Let us go out," said Augustus. "I will amuse you with my new fireworks. It must be cooler outside."

The three ladies left the table, and Augustus sent for a lantern. He meant the surprise to be complete, produced by a turn of his fingers, in the twinkling of an eye. Bearing the lantern in his hand he left the house with his three companions and began to ascend a short steep path which led to the stone hut where he had centralised his apparatus.

"It is weird — almost ghastly," said Diana in a low voice.

"One feels afraid to speak," answered Gwendoline.

"Does not it sometimes feel like this when there is to be an earthquake?" asked Lady Brenda.

"Exactly like this," said Augustus, reassuringly.

"Good gracious! You don't think there is going to be one?"

"No, I never heard of an earthquake on this peninsula. There will very probably be one in Naples to-night. Take care — the stones are loose. Here we are. Now take a good look. I want you to stand here — so — facing the sea and turning a little towards the castle. Don't move or turn your eyes away — it will be very curious. You are not afraid? I must go inside the hut to do it."

Augustus entered the low door, carrying his lantern with him, and leaving the three ladies outside in the dark. He went straight to the commutator and having assured himself that the connections were properly made he laid his hand on the switch.

"Ready," he called aloud. "Look where I told you — now!"

The key turned under his fingers and almost at the same instant a cry of surprise and delight broke from the little party outside. Augustus went out and joined them, and gazed on the wonderful effects of his discovery.

The rocks ·and the shore were as bright as day.
High on the castle burned a beacon which must have
been visible thirty miles away at sea; from every
point of rock a little sun shed a broad circle of daylight, and from deep fissures and crevices straight,
broad shafts of light beamed upwards to the dark
sky like radiant ladders to heaven. The frightened
quail, at that season just settling on the southern
shore after their flight from Africa, flew whirring up
towards the lights, uttering their peculiar short cry.
White gulls shot from the rocks and sped in huge
circles like gigantic flakes of snow whirling down to
the dark, placid water. The rocks threw weird and
unimagined shadows under the light which had
never shone on them before. The four spectators of
the wonderful scene looked out, and held their
breath, and then looked at each other.

"How did you do it, Augustus?" asked Gwendoline.

"I suppose they are electric lights," said Diana,
"but the effect is like magic."

"Perfectly wonderful!" exclaimed Lady Brenda.
"I never saw anything like it. There is some real
practical use in this sort of thing."

"You did not seem to think there was much use
in my glass bowl oracle the other day," remarked
Augustus.

"No — that was ridiculous," answered his mother-
in-law.

"It was the same thing on a smaller scale. I was

only teasing you — it was an experiment with electricity; it was not an oracle at all."

"How could you make fun of me in that way?"
asked Lady Brenda, half hurt, half laughing.

"Only to see what you would say," replied Augustus. "Come, let us take a walk among the lights
and see the effect from different places."

"It is hotter out of doors than it was at dinner,"
said Lady Brenda. "It is like a sirocco in August
— it burns one's skin."

It was quite true; as they moved along the narrow
paths, puffs of burning air blew from the rocks on all
sides, unexpectedly, and so violently that it seemed
as though the party were struck by clouds of hot
whirling feathers. The wind seemed palpable and
thick. One would almost have said that the gusts
cast shadows in the brilliant light of the countless
lamps. At the same time, in the dark distance
above the illumination, the stars were dimmed and
went out one by one. Then as the four persons
emerged upon a little platform of rock from which
they could view the wild scene, the blasts of scorching wind suddenly ceased and the air settled down
upon them like a thick warm blanket. They panted
for breath, and by a common impulse they all sat
down upon the blocks of stone to rest.

An indescribable awe seized upon them all, like
the creeping shadow of an event to come. Gwendoline sat by her husband's side and laid her hand
upon his clasped fingers. Lady Brenda chose the

place where the light was brightest, while Diana,
sitting a little apart, leaned her cheek upon her hand
and stared out into the strange mixture of daylight
and darkness, half startled by a feeling of weird
horror, half delighted by the delicious sense of confused reality and dreamy illusion which her brother
had conjured up.

The four sat there for nearly a quarter of an hour
without exchanging a word.  There are times when
the most loquacious being alive must be silent; moments when the unwonted consciousness of the limit-
less unknown lies heavily upon the little body of our
poor knowledge, as the weight of some huge beast
that stretches its vast bulk across a tiny trail of toil-
ing ants.  The ants are too small to be all crushed
by anything so big and rough, but they lie paralysed
and helpless till it pleases the giant to relieve them
of his burden and let them move again.  The mind
sticks like a fly in a pot of honey when transported
to an atmosphere not its own, and seems to struggle
with an element in which its consciousness is re-
doubled while its activity is destroyed.  No one of
the four could have given a reason for the silence,
nor can any one find explanations for such things
without assuming a theory which one half of the
world considers absurd and the other half believes to
be dangerous.  The fact that for thousands of years
man has been trying experiments with a view to
finding out something about himself, and that his
efforts have uniformly resulted in failure, has not

made him more lenient to beliefs which he dislikes,
nor more willing to admit his own well-demonstrated
ignorance.  He still explains as accident that which
he knows not how to explain by law, and rocks himself to sleep in the security of self-deceived vanity,
until he is roused from his slumber to tremble at
those terrors which his fatuous self-satisfaction has
so deservedly incurred.  Science, what follies are
committed in thy name!  What blind faith is placed
in thy feeble utterances, which might more worthily
be fixed on higher and truer things!

Silently the four sat together and looked down
upon the scene, breathing with difficulty in the hot
thick air.  The wind had entirely ceased and the
silence was so profound as to be almost terrifying.
Then, suddenly and without the smallest warning, a
fearful crash of thunder burst above their heads and
struck the rocks, and echoed back in horrible rever-
beration, peal upon peal, rolling to the distance, as
though the great earth had struck upon a mountain in
the smooth grooves that guide her course, and, jolt-
ing heavily, were grinding the mass to pieces beneath
her resistless weight.  Then all was silent again.

Even Augustus started slightly from his reverie,
and the ladies sprang to their feet.  There was something in the suddenness of the explosion that struck
them all as unnatural and horrible.

"Let us go home — I am sure it is going to rain,"
said Lady Brenda, but her voice sounded hollow and
weird.

"Look at the lights!" exclaimed Gwendoline.
"What is that moving round them?"

"I don't know," answered Augustus. "It is very
extraordinary."

"It is beautiful," said Diana, her eyes fixed on the
strange phenomenon.

As they looked, faint clouds of rosy haze moved
between them and the lamps, pausing suddenly and
then shooting on like wild figures with streaming
drapery of impalpable fineness, tinged with unearthly
hues, that left a luminous track in the dark air between. And the figures, or clouds, multiplied till
there were myriads of rosy streamers, chasing each
other like fire-flies in a wood, intertwining and
mingling and shooting away again, but rising higher
and higher still, as they soared and leaped into a
broad arch through the night sky, emitting a radiance of their own; and the rose colour deepened to
red, and the red to purple, and again from time to
time a great golden flash flew higher than the rest and
trembled in the perfection of a faultless curve and
fell again into the night beyond.

Then again the thunder crashed and pealed and
echoed as though a Supreme Power were shaking the
mountains like pebbles in the hollow of a bowl, and
the hot wind puffed like the fierce blast of a furnace
from the face of the bare rocks.

The four stood close together, pale and trembling.
The ground shook beneath their feet as though it
would give way and dissolve in the convulsion of

the elements. The far-springing arches of streaming light blazed higher and higher, and struck wide
circles in the black air, eclipsing in their matchless
radiance the bright lamps below, and piercing the sky
with scimitars and spears of light, symmetrical, terrible, and glorious, leaping from a sea of rosy and
golden flame which thickened and surged about the
castle and down to the shore, hiding everything in
its fiery waves.

A blinding white flash, an explosion as of a thousand cannon bursting together — the four fell back
against the face of the cliff, half stunned, unconscious with horror and fear. The thunderbolt had
struck the rocks not fifty yards below them and in
the din of the elements they could hear the great
masses of stone bounding down the precipice to
plunge into the sea below.

Augustus was no coward, neither were the three
women of the timid kind who tremble in ordinary
danger. But it was clear that to stay where they
were was death, certain and sudden.

"Unless I can reach the hut, we are lost," said
Chard.

"Go," said Gwendoline, firmly. "We will wait
here." But as she spoke a third peal of thunder broke with deafening crash upon the hills
above.

"I cannot leave you here," said Augustus. "You
will be safe on the other side of the cliff upon the
sandy shore — if anywhere."

And so, under the awful light of the wild streamers, amidst the howling of the dry and scorching wind and the pealing of the thunder, the four began their descent, not knowing at what step they should meet death nor which of them should reach the shore alive. And when they were on the sand Augustus left them and fled up the height again through the very midst of the flaming air, where indeed there was no heat to burn, but such whirlpools of hot wind as made him stagger in his race; and ever and again the dreadful thunder cracked and burst and roared, so that his senses reeled and, but for the loved ones below, he must have lost all consciousness and fallen a victim to the convulsion of the elements he had roused. For he knew that it was his work now, as he sprang up the rocks towards the hut; he had roused the mainsprings of nature and disturbed her rest so that he doubted whether any effort of his could lull the storm. The hut itself was in a blaze of purple and rosy light; but he rushed boldly in and groped for his instruments in the luminous hot mist. He could not find it, and his heart sank, but he searched still and at last felt the cold enamelled key of the switch beneath his hand. In convulsive triumph he grasped the lever and gathering his senses of remembrance by an effort, he turned it half round.

At first there was no change. His heart beat fast with terror, as he stood holding the tiny thing by which he hoped to direct and subdue such mighty forces. But gradually the colour faded from the room, the mist disappeared and the light of the lantern which he had left there an hour before shone out quietly and illuminated the scene. He took it and then he went to the door. All was changed. The sea of flame had disappeared, leaving but a phosphorescent suggestion of light behind. In the sky above the wild streamers flashed convulsively and died away, one after another. The lamps were extinguished, and in the clear sky the stars shone brightly. But far to the south-east a soft light was in the sky, and as he looked he saw that the moon was rising. The low and distant rumblings of the thunder grew fainter and ceased. Augustus began his descent, reflecting on the awful peril from which he had escaped.

As he reached the shore the scene was inexpressibly beautiful. The May moon, but a day past the full, rose softly over the low range of the Basilicata. The placid sea. lapped the dusky shingle and caught the reflection of the moonbeams as one might toss handfuls of diamonds upon a mantle of dark velvet.

The three women stood together on the shore, their lithe and graceful figures just outlined in the moonlight. All was peace and calm, the storm was ended, and Nature, like a tired child, drooped and slept, soothed by the lullaby of the rippling moonlit sea.

"It is all over," said Augustus, quietly.  But he took his wife in his arms and kissed her.

As they all turned together they were aware of a man in grey clothes who sat upon a worn boulder at the water's edge, his head supported in his hand, gazing to seaward.

## CHAPTER IV.

THEY all came forward by a simultaneous movement of curiosity and approached the solitary
stranger. As they came near he slowly turned his
head, looked at them and rose to his feet. He was
below the middle height, slightly made and graceful, dressed scrupulously in the fashion of five and
thirty years ago, save that the linen collar was less
close about the throat than men wore it then, and
loosely bound with a black silk cravat; he wore
yellow nankeen trousers, the waistcoat was buttoned
across and fitted tightly to his slender waist, and
the long grey coat, narrow chested and tight in the
sleeves, was unfastened and thrown back, while one
small and delicate hand grasped a dark mantle which
would have fallen to the ground as he stood up. It
was a wonderful face upon which the moonlight
fell; a face pale and thin and spiritual, from the
smooth broad forehead about which the short fair
hair grew in abundant thickness, to the sensitive,
half sarcastic downward curve of the lips, visible
distinctly between the drooping moustache and the
pointed beard. The fine and slightly aquiline nose,
delicately modelled and long in proportion to the
face, enhanced the mournful expression of the feat-

ures.  The eyes, veiled by the drooping of their lids,
seemed to speak of such sadness as is distilled from
the secret and melancholy visions of a poet's soul,
rather than of that hopeless misery which prolonged
and acute suffering stamps upon the face of an unfortunate man.

The stranger looked coldly at the party as though
he were ill pleased at being disturbed in his reverie.

"Do you see me, that you look at me thus?" he
asked, as they came quite near to him.  The question was a strange one indeed, and there was a pause
before any one answered it.

"We mean no discourtesy to you, sir," said
Augustus at last.  "Seeing a stranger so near our
house, in this desolate region, we naturally desire to
offer you such hospitality as we may."

"And I, sir, am most ready to thank you," said
the other, a strange smile passing over his face as he
frankly held out his hand.  Augustus took it, willingly enough, but he started as he touched the long
white fingers.

"You are very cold," he said.  "Pray come with
us to the house."

"No," answered the stranger, "I am not cold — at
least I do not feel cold," he added, smiling again.
"I am past feeling those things."

The ladies stood together in a little group.
Augustus and the unknown gentleman were not two
paces from them.

"I think it is a little rash of Augustus — asking

him to the house," said Lady Brenda in an under-
tone.  "He is so very oddly dressed!"

"Oh, Augustus is always right about those things,
mamma," answered Gwendoline.

The stranger apparently overheard the remarks
exchanged by the mother and daughter, for he moved
forward a little and spoke to Augustus so that they
could hear what he said.

"I feel," he said, "that upon accepting the kind
offer you have made me, I must tell you my name."

"Mine is Augustus Chard," said the host, not
wishing to be outdone in courtesy.

"And mine needs a word of explanation before it
is told," rejoined the stranger, "a word of explanation which may save many misunderstandings in the
future.  Do not be startled at what I say.  There is
nothing supernatural in it.  Nor must you imagine
that I am a madman.  You have been doing dangerous things with Nature, Mr. Chard, you have caused
some of her laws to act for a time in a way not familiar to you.  I supposed so from what I felt before
you approached me.  When I realised that you saw
me, I understood that I had become visible, and I
was greatly surprised, as no one has seen me for a
long time — not since I died, in fact —"

"Not since you died?" exclaimed the three ladies
at once.

"No, not since I died," continued the speaker,
calmly.  "By your experiments you have made dead
men visible for a time.  I have been dead thirty and

odd years, and if there is anything left of my bones I am not curious to see it. This, that you see, is what is left of myself. I am Heinrich Heine. You see I did well to give you a word of explanation. I am quite harmless; indeed, I always was."

"My dear sir," said Augustus, "I have too long been accustomed to expect the unusual in nature to be startled at it when it appears, especially when it procures me the pleasure of meeting one whom I have so sincerely admired as yourself. My wife, my mother-in-law, Lady Brenda, my sister, Miss Diana Chard. We have so often spoken of you that I will answer for the satisfaction these ladies must feel at this meeting."

"Yes indeed!" said Gwendoline and Diana together.

"This is all very queer and — astral — that sort of thing," said Lady Brenda. "But I suppose it is all right."

"Madam," answered Heine, "whatever brings me into such company must necessarily be right. Clearly, Mr. Chard's experiments were not for his own benefit but for mine."

"If you are not really cold," suggested Diana, "we might stay here for a while. It is so hot in the house this evening."

"No," objected Gwendoline, "I must go and see the baby — poor little thing, I don't believe it could possibly have slept through that frightful storm. Then we can sit upon the terrace in the moonlight."

As they all moved slowly towards the house, Lady
Brenda glanced curiously at the graceful form of the
dead poet as he walked beside her.  She was very
far from being persuaded that he was really a dead
man, but she was by no means far from believing him
to be a dangerous escaped lunatic.  Under the circumstances the doubt was very reasonable.  But
Gwendoline and Diana felt that delicious thrill of
excitement which every one experiences on being
suddenly brought into the company of a person long
admired and studied.   On reaching the castle it was
found that the model baby had slept soundly through
the disturbances, and that the servants, having been
at dinner during the whole time, had noticed nothing but the thunder.  Augustus breathed freely, for
he had feared that his electric storm might produce
a serious convulsion in the prosaic mind of Bimbam.
That catastrophe was averted, and the immediate
prospect presented no difficulties.

A quarter of an hour later the whole party were
seated upon the terrace in the full light of the May
moon, looking over the placid southern sea.  Heine
sat in the midst of the group.  Saving his antiquated
dress, there was nothing in his appearance to distinguish him from his living hosts.  Augustus alone
had felt the icy chill of his hand.

"This is almost as good as life," said Heine in his
dreamy voice.  "You have the advantage of me still,
however."

"Are you really dead?" asked Lady Brenda, in-
credulously.

"As dead, dear madam, as the little Veronica — as dead as Doctor Saul Ascher, who died an abstract death from reason-poisoning before his wizened little legs finally refused to carry about the over-loaded, over-packed, over-hardened thing he called his head."

"I never heard of Doctor Saul Ascher," said Gwendoline.

"Nor I," echoed Augustus and the rest, all together.

"He was much talked of in his day, especially by himself," said Heine. "His reputation suffered a mortal blow when he died. I only mentioned him as an illustration. If you like it better, I will say that I am as dead as a door-nail. I have passed from the condition of life to the condition of existence. By a happy accident I am now alive for purposes of conversation, a pastime in which I always found an unreasoning delight, provided I was not required to play an important part in it."

"I don't think it is at all unreasonable to like conversation," said Lady Brenda. "When people have ideas they ought to exchange them."

"Yes — when they have any. I once wrote a book about ideas, and I took the definition of the idea, not from Plato, but from a Berlin cab-driver — he said ideas were a lot of stupid stuff that people got into their heads. The cab-driver evidently knew what he was talking about. I am more convinced of that now than I ever was before."

"Why?" asked Diana.

"I used to have ideas about death, before I died. I used to think one must sleep too soundly when one was dead. Death is the end of sleep. There is no more sleep for us, for ever, it seems — and alas, there are no more dreams either! I regret the sadness of life, for the sake of the contrasted sweetness of its dreams. I regret my bitter-sweet emotions, my joy in being sad and my delicious imaginary sadness in being joyful. I was made up of contradictions when I was alive. Now I know too much even to contradict myself. Our conversations now are tame. All conversations are, unless we speak of our hopes; and though we have plentiful material for reflection here, we have but little ground for anticipation. Our discussions, such as they are, cannot be better defined than as a perpetual comparison of our past experience. You will readily conceive that with our unlimited command of time such subjects may be exhausted."

"But of whom does your society consist?" asked Lady Brenda. "I can imagine that you might form a most delightful circle out of such elements."

"The elements are a little mixed," answered the poet in his soft, slow tones. "We have formed a little society almost as exclusive as a faculty of professors in a university — also a little more witty, for there are no professors among us, either ancient or modern."

"You never liked professors. I have noticed it in your books," said Diana.

"No — and professors never liked me; a fact which was of vastly greater importance to me than my liking or disliking them. We have only one of each of a certain number of classes. For instance we have only one conqueror."

"Who is he?" asked Augustus.

"A certain Julius Cæsar. His soul does not inhabit the body of a schoolmaster as I once supposed. I was greatly relieved when I met him here. Perhaps he is the most unique in his way. I have not heard that any one has died recently who greatly resembles him. He has taken the place of Bonaparte in my estimation, since I made his acquaintance."

"Perhaps you will change your mind again," suggested Lady Brenda, hoping to make the dead man say more.

"No," he answered, sadly. "We are terribly consistent after death. We shall never change our minds again, now. We are the bronze of which our lives were but the clay moulds. We are new things indeed, but the impression is fatally true, for we are no longer subject to illusions — alas! there are no delicious self-deceptions for us now. We modelled ourselves in our lives and, as we modelled, so we are cast in this imperishable essence of the soul. But we are still fated to receive impressions, all true, and therefore commonplace and detestable, because when one sees nothing but fact one ceases to fabricate fiction. Moreover, the knowledge that we cannot write down what we think and sell it to

newspapers and poetry-mongers for money is sadden-
ing to industriously-minded little poets like myself.
The poet is accustomed in his lifetime to earn his
living by forcing words to fit the bed of Procrustes,
squeezing the poor sensitive feet into the iron boots
of verse, ramming down the whole into couplets —
very like strings of sausages in which mauled and
chopped meat is forced into skins and tied up into
appropriate lengths for quotation — I mean for the
breakfast of an average strong man, and then hung
up in long strings in the bookseller's window to
attract the hungry. Words are words, even in verse
— and pig is pig, even in sausages, but I doubt
whether the pig would recognise himself after the
transmigration. It is the proud privilege of the pig
to be made into sausages after his death, and if he is
a lucky pig his sausage form may even serve as an
ornament and be decorated with laurels in the pork-
butcher's shop at Christmas-tide, which is better
luck than happens to most poets. For the poet eats
himself up in his lifetime, and misses his daily
search for rhymes, as well as the daily price of them,
when he is dead; just as an Italian donkey on Sunday misses being kicked up hill with a load on his
back before dinner; just as a business man who takes
a holiday misses the delight of doubling himself up
all day upon his desk and letting the delightful,
crabbed, money-getting figures tickle his nose and
his heart from morning till night. The poet after
death is like the business man on a holiday, the

Italian ass on Sunday and the pig before he has been
made into sausages — he has no *raison d'être*, no reason for existing, he is out of his sphere, lost in the
labyrinths of everyday fact, uncomfortable as an
antelope strolling on the Boulevard des Italiens, as
a tragedian in the solitudes of the steppes, as a cat
in a country where the houses have no roofs, so nice
and romantic to howl upon at night. No one pays
me for howling now, nor if any one would, could I
find a roof. Perhaps I could not even find a subject
for my lamentations, except the absence of such a
subject, which indeed is a very serious matter for a
poet."

"How can you speak of poetry in such a way —
you who wrote such exquisite things?" asked Diana.

"You may be sure," answered Heine, with that
wonderful smile which drew strange angles about
his sensitive mouth, "that if it were still in my
power to make verses I would not laugh at my old
trade. But the grapes which hang too high are
eternally green — as perpetually sour as unrealised
hope."

"Which is very sour indeed," remarked Augustus.
"Nevertheless, you must have realised most of your
hopes during your lifetime. You were brilliantly
successful."

"In exile," answered the poet, sadly.

"In a perfectly voluntary exile, I believe?" returned Augustus.

"No — a fatal exile," said Heiné, almost passionately. "In Germany I was a Frenchman, in France I was a German — among Jews a Christian, among Christians a Jew, with Catholics a Protestant, with Protestants a Catholic. I was always in contradiction with my surroundings, I was in a perpetual exile. Had I been made like some people, full of raw fighting instincts, I would have fought. As it was, I was unhappy, sick in soul and ill in body, and so I became a poet and wrote verses. You say they were good? Yes, I believe they were, for I took pleasure in writing them; but had I possessed Mr. Chard's sanguine constitution I would have been a leader of men instead of a writer of lyrics. I used to think I might play a political part — indeed, I often fancied that I did. Since I died I have learned what stuff is needed to play a part in the world of nations."

"Broad shoulders and a rough fist," said Augustus. "Soldiering is girl's play compared with it."

"You may well say that. Broad shoulders, a rough fist and a hard heart. I think my heart was never very hard. Even when I abused people it did not hurt them much. My shoulders are not broad and my fist — you see," said the poet, glancing with a pathetic pride at his delicate fingers, "I have the hand of a woman, I was not made for a politician."

"It is strange," said Gwendoline, "that great poets so often believe themselves to be statesmen, or have opportunities of becoming statesmen thrust upon them."

"Yes," replied Heine, "there was Goethe, to begin with. Dante was another. Milton had the strongest political tastes. Victor Hugo was a type of the politician-poet. Horace refused to be political private secretary to Augustus. Catullus began as a writer ⸱of political squibs against Cæsar. Mickievicz was a furious patriot. Even Byron aspired to political fame and sacrificed his life heroically for an idea. Perhaps I should say for a principle, I do not like the word idea."

"If you will pardon me, I think that is one of your amiable eccentricities," remarked Augustus. "The great fights — or the great struggles of history, have either been fought for material advantage or for ideas. It seems to me nobler to fight for an idea than to fight for money — or for what practically results in money."

"By all means," answered Heine. "In my mind the word idea is associated with certain philosophical theories which I consider absurd, but if you use the word in the sense of a principle, and enthusiasm for that principle, I agree with you. That is what the sickness of modern times means. It is too long since the world has fought for a pure principle. Individual nations have had their struggles, chiefly internal, about what they considered right or wrong, but it is long since the joint enthusiasm of all humanity has been roused to shed blood and spend it in attacking and defending a purely moral cause. At present the thinking world is divided into two

very distinct classes — those who say that principles
are worth fighting for, and those who say that there
should be no fighting and that the principles will
take care of themselves.   Neither party has the full
sympathy of the masses."

"I always think," said Lady Brenda, "that the
world depends entirely on the thinking people.   The
masses are not of so much importance.   They always
follow, you know."

"You and I, madam," replied the poet, "may
design a very good pyramid, as big and symmetrical
as the pyramid of Cheops.   But however perfect the
design may be, we cannot build it unless the masses
help us.   Without the concurrence of the masses the
noblest political schemes must fail."

"Their failure does not make them any the less
noble," objected Lady Brenda.

"No.   But it makes them less useful and therefore
less important.   The successful people are those
who induce many to follow them, and that can only
be done by presenting the many with ideas which
they can understand.   The thoughts of great poets
are generally noble, but not easily understood by the
masses.   The poet, however, aims at elevating the
people to his own level, and being carried away by
the grandeur of his plans he thinks it a simple matter to make a poetic commonwealth of the whole
world.   He is of course disappointed; he dies fancying his life a failure, and after he is dead he is surprised to find that nobody ever thought anything of

his political capabilities, whereas he has earned immortality by his verses. The great man of the future will be he who shall discover the idea — as you call it — for which mankind shall be willing to take up arms. If his idea succeeds he will be a very great man and will probably be murdered, like a gentleman; if he fails he will be the last of humanity and will most likely be hanged, like a thief. After all, it is better to be a poet. If people only knew and understood how much better it is to live out one's life naturally! There is so little of it, and the remembrance of that little must serve one so long!"

"It is certainly best to be a poet," said Diana, leaning back in her chair and looking from the moon to the dark water, and dreamily again from the water to the silver shield above. "But it is not everybody who can. They say there is but one good poet in a thousand million human beings."

"The proportion is truly discouraging," answered Heine. "It is even worse when you reflect that there is not more than one good poet in a thousand million poets of all kinds, any more than you will find two wise men in a milliard of puckery, peppery, self-satisfied scientists. It must therefore be difficult to be very wise or to be a very good poet — but be careful never to tell people so, for as yet nobody has found it out."

"It cannot hurt people if they try to be either," said Lady Brenda.

"The ultimate disappointment of being convinced

of failure in the nine hundred ninety-nine million
nine hundred ninety-nine thousand nine hundred and
ninety-nine cases is hardly ever felt in practice by
poets, never by scientists. It follows that, at a comparatively small cost, thousands of millions are made
perfectly happy in the belief that they are great.
Even when idiots do not obtain appreciation, which
rarely occurs, they find pleasant consolation in attributing their lack of success to the stupidity of others.
There are more ways of believing oneself great than
by obtaining praise from one's contemporaries, or
money for one's works. I received forty copies, free
of charge, as sole and entire payment for my first
book of verses, after another publisher had refused to
print it altogether; but when I was correcting the
proofs I felt that I was a much greater man than
before, and I have never since felt so great as on
that day. I had a considerable reputation when my
excellent uncle remarked of me to a friend that 'if
the silly boy had ever learned anything he would
not have needed to write books.' I had reputation,
I say, and yet I was so much struck by the truth of
the remark, that I would have accepted the post of
theological adviser and attorney-general to the king
of the cannibals, had it been offered to me — anything for a respectable profession, as I said to myself. But the last theological adviser had chanced to
disagree with the king about an hour after the Sunday meal, and on taking medical advice and consult-
ing the family butcher I lost confidence in myself

and did not apply. Uncle Solomon Heine also
thought there was truth in his saying and repeated
it frequently. I was then a man of one book, but he
was a man of one joke. I afterwards wrote other
books, but my uncle's jest did not multiply. Still,
that one joke elevates him; he stood upon it as on a
pedestal; and the pedestal bore to him about the
same relation as the Vendome column bears to the
statue of Napoleon."

There was something so good-natured in his story
of the facetious uncle Solomon, that all the party
laughed a little, except Diana, who was dreaming of
something very far away. Heine noticed her silence.

"What were you thinking of?" he asked, turning
towards her.

"I will not tell you — you would be angry," she
answered.

"I? angry?" exclaimed the poet in some surprise.
"Dead men are never angry. Anger is an emotion,
and there are no emotions of that kind for us. We
have lost the power of influencing our surroundings,
and we perform no actions which can be influenced
by them. We shed tears sometimes, and sometimes
we laugh a little — but we are never angry. What
were you thinking of?"

"I was thinking — wondering about the dead
Maria," said Diana in a low voice.

"Yes," resumed Heine, softly, "I wonder too — I
wonder why I suffered as I did. But no one knows
the story. I regret the suffering now that it is gone,

and I wish it were with me again.  When I was
alive I used to think that she came back from the
dead in the silent evenings — evenings like this —
and that she sat with me and spoke with me as she
used to speak.  Now that I am dead I cannot find
her — I have long given up the search.  I sometimes
fancy I hear her voice singing — it is a strange,
sweet voice, like a nightingale's last notes, full of
silky tones that make me tremble with a sort of
creeping fear, tones that seem to come from a bleed-
ing heart, that wind and spin themselves among my
thoughts like soft, beseeching memories.  And her
dear face that seemed modelled by a Greek master
out of the perfumed mist of white roses, delicate as
though breathed into shape, noble beyond all thought
— and the passionate eyes illuminating the classic
splendour of her beauty — I remember all.  Her
hand, too!  There were little blue veins under the
polished, high-born skin.  It was not like a little
girl's vegetable-animal hand — half lamb, half rose
— thoughtless and fair; there was something spiritual in the white fingers, something that suggested a
story of sympathy, like the hands of beautiful persons who are excessively refined or have suffered terribly — and yet it had a look of pathetic innocence,
and if I touched it, it shrank delicately under the
gentlest pressure.  She was dead when I saw her
last — she was so beautiful when she was dead, so
terribly, so fascinatingly beautiful, as she lay among
the roses on her bed.  She died before I could reach

her, but I saw her dead. She loved me once — I
thought she loved me in the end, though she took
another. They respected me — they left me alone
with her. Old Ursula looked at me once, strangely
I thought, and she went out. The shaded lamp
stood on a table. A purple flower drooped in a glass
beside it, and gave out a faint unnatural perfume.
I stood by the bedside. I thought of the dark-robed
knight who would have kissed his dead love to life
again. I gazed long, and at last I bent down and I
pressed my lips on her cold mouth. Suddenly the
lamp was extinguished — it must have been the breeze
from the open window, for I know I was alone —
I felt cold, icy cold, arms go round my neck — I
heard a name spoken. It was her voice, it was not
my name. — The rest? I do not know the rest, for
I fled from the house, from the town, from the country. They told me she was not dead. She was dead
to me — dead as I am now. To me she is always
dead, always, always! These are not tears, the
moon casts queer lights on dead men's faces."

His voice trembled and ceased, and silence fell
upon the little company that sat in the May moonlight over the sea. The story of human suffering is
ever old, yet ever new — the dead man who had been
telling his long-dead tale had himself said so, and it
is true. Each of those who heard him, heard him
differently; yet each felt in the story the whole
depth of the pain for him which they could have felt
had they stood beside him nearly seventy years ago

when it all happened, when the woman he loved was suddenly restored to life with another's name upon her lips, when he himself was wounded in the first spring of his youth with a wound that never healed.

But it was not his manner when alive to excite sympathy for his own sufferings, nor was he now willing to let his tale end thus.

"You are silent," he said, "and you are sorry for me. I thank you. Sympathy exists in the human heart, unexplained by learned treatises about the pursuit of happiness. We shudder at the sight of a ghastly wound, and the tears rise to our eyes as we listen to the story of a broken heart. It is not for me that you are sad — it is for what I have told you. There are many sad stories — not all mine."

"Tell us a sad story," said Diana. "I love sad stories."

"I saw a beggar die upon the high road. His story was sad enough. He had seen many misfortunes, many troubles; many pains had had their will of his racked body, many days and years of suffering had piled their load upon his aching shoulders; grief knew him and tracked him down, and sorrow, the pitiless driver of men, had stung each galled wound of his soul with cunning cruelty, goading and sparing not as he came near to the end. The silver hairs were few which hung straggling from beneath the torn brim of his battered hat, and the furrows were many and deep upon his colourless face. His dim eyes peered from their worn and

sunken sockets as though still faintly striving, striving to the very last, to understand those things which
it was not given him to understand. Feebly his two
hands clasped his crooked staff, road-worn and splin-
tered by the flints; upon one foot still clung the
fragments of a shoe, the other had no shoe at all,
and as he stood he lifted the foot that was bare and
tried to rest it upon the scanty bit of dusty leather
which only half covered the other, as though to ease
it from the cruel road, while he steadied himself
feebly with his stick. Had there been the least
fragment of a wall near him, a bit of fence, even a
tree, he would have tried to lean upon it; but there
was nothing — nothing but the broad flinty road,
with the ditch dug deep upon each side, nothing but
the cold grey sky, the black north wind that began
to whirl up the dust, scattering here and there big
flakes of wet snow, and, far away behind, the barking of the dogs that had driven him from the gate
while the churls who lingered there after their day's
work laughed and made rough jokes upon him. A
little boy, the son of one of those fellows, had taken
a stone and had thrown it after the old man — the
missile had struck him in the back and he had bowed
himself lower and limped away; he was used to it —
people often threw stones at him, and sometimes they
hit him. What was one blow more to him, one
wound more? The end could not be far.

"So he rested his naked foot upon the other, now
that he was out of reach of harm. He could hear

the dogs barking still, but dogs never chased him long; they would not come after him now. The boy could not throw stones to such a distance either, and would not take the trouble to pursue him, though one of the men had laughed when the old man was hit, and another had said it was a good shot. He might rest for a while, if it were rest to lean upon his staff and feel the bitter wind driving the snow-flakes through the rents in his clothing, and whirling up the half frozen flint dust to his sore and weary eyes. The night was coming on. He would have to sleep in the ditch. It would not be the first time — if only he could get a mile or two farther he might find some bit of arched bridge across the ditch which would shelter him, or a stone wall; or even perhaps, a farmhouse where he should not be stoned from the door and might be suffered to sleep upon the straw in an outhouse. Such luck as that was rare indeed, and the mere thought of the straw, the pitiful dream that if he could struggle a little farther he might get shelter from the wind and snow, was enough to bring something like a shadowy look of hope into his wretched face. With a great effort he began to walk again, bending low to face the blast, starving, lame, and aching in every bone, but struggling still and peering through the gathering gloom in the vain hope of finding a night's resting-place."

"I would have killed the boy who threw the stone, if I had been you!" exclaimed Lady Brenda in ready sympathy.

"Alas, dear madam, I was dead myself," said Heine. "It was only the other day. Well, as I said, he struggled on; but the end was at hand. The road grew worse, for it had been mended and the small broken stones lay thick together, rough and bristling. He could hardly drag his steps over them. In the darkness he struck his naked foot against one sharp flint that was larger than the rest; he stumbled and with a low cry fell headlong upon the jagged surface. His hands were wounded and the blood trickled from them in the dark, wetting the stones more quickly than did the falling snow; his face, too, had been cut. For some moments he struggled to rise, but he was too weak, too utterly spent; then he rolled upon one side and rested his bruised face upon his torn hands and lay quite still, while the wind howled louder and the snow-flakes fell more thickly upon his rags and his wounds, upon the sorrows of his soul and the pains of his body. One long breath he drew — it was more than an hour since he had fallen.

"'God be merciful to me!' he murmured, and again, 'God be merciful to me, for I think it is the end.' And the Angel of the Lord came in the storm and the darkness and touched his forehead; and it was the end. The snow buried him that night and the north wind sang his funeral dirge."

"How terribly sad!" exclaimed Diana in deep sympathy.

"To think that such things happen!" said Lady Brenda and Gwendoline in one breath.

"Do you think it is the fact, or the way the fact is told, which brings the tears to your eyes?" asked the poet. "If I had stated the fact thus: an old beggar died in a snow-storm; shortly before he died a little boy hit him with a stone — I say, if I put the thing in its simplest expression, would you feel as deep a sympathy? I believe not. I told you a long story — a true one, if you please — to show you that your sympathy could be commanded, could be excited, by my words. You asked me of a thing concerning myself — I was not willing to state it as a fact, I was obliged to state it with such accessories as should make you feel uncomfortable in my favour, so to say. All of which proves that man, living or dead, is a detestably selfish creature, and not very strong at that. When he has command of his audience he uses it unmercifully to rouse sympathy in others. When his audience has command of him, he generally makes a fool of himself. I once visited Goethe. In half an hour I could find nothing better to say to him than that there were good plums on the road from Jena to Weimar and that I was writing a Faust. I got no applause for my plums and no sympathy for my Faust; I never wrote the Faust, but I never ate plums from that day. So much for knowing how to manage one's hearers."

"I wish you would not talk in that light way, after what you have been telling us so earnestly," said Gwendoline.

"I cannot help it, dear madam," answered Heine.

"I have a particular talent for being easily moved; and when I am moved I shed tears, and when I shed tears it seems very foolish and I at once try to laugh at myself — or at the first convenient object which falls in my way. For tears hurt — bitterly sometimes, and it is best to get rid of them in any way one can, provided that one does not put them beyond one's reach altogether."

"People talk a great deal of sweet pain," remarked Augustus. "I do not understand how anything which hurts can be sweet at the same time."

"Can you understand how a thing sweet at the time may hurt afterwards?"

"Perfectly," answered Chard.

"Then can you not understand how when the thing hurts it is pleasant to remember that it was once sweet? It is very simple. By no means all pains are sweet, but on the whole there are enough of the sort to supply poets for many years to come. There are men among us here, whose sufferings are bitter still — very bitter."

"Shall we ever know any of your companions?" asked Lady Brenda.

"They would be delighted, I am sure. We rarely have an opportunity of exchanging words with living people — it has never happened to me before. Mr. Chard has discovered a rather dangerous way of making it possible, and I am delighted to see that you are not in the least nervous. That shows how greatly ideas have changed in thirty years. When

I was alive there was something that made one's
flesh creep in the idea of talking with a dead man.
You have overcome all that.    If Mr. Chard will only
continue his experiments there is no reason why we
dead men should not play a real part in society."

"I see no objection whatever," said Lady Brenda.
"I am sure, if they are all like you, it would be
most charming.    But, after all, you may only be
some one who knows all about Heine and talks
delightfully about him."

"Will you let me look at your hand?" asked the
poet, bending forward and taking Lady Brenda's
fingers in his.    "What a beautiful ring, I always
loved sapphires — "

But Lady Brenda turned pale, and after a moment's
struggle with her convictions she nervously snatched
her hand away.

"Oh you are — you are really dead — I can feel it
in your fingers," she cried.    After that, Lady
Brenda ceased to be sceptical.

"There is only one point upon which I must warn
you in regard to my friends," resumed Heine, smiling at Lady Brenda's discomfiture.    "They wear the
dress of their age — as I do.    You must trust to
them to avoid your servants, who might be surprised
— or else you must warn your servants that some
friends are coming to stay with you who wear the
costumes of their country."

"I will manage that," said Augustus, confidently.

## CHAPTER V.

THE moon rose higher and higher in the cloudless sky, bathing the terrace in silver and lending in her turn to men the light she borrowed from heaven. For some minutes no one spoke, and it was as though all nature lay in a trance while the visions of heaven passed by. It was the hour when in eastern lands the lotus unfolds its heavy leaves, to take up the wondrous dream broken by the scorching day; it was the hour when in the laurel groves of Italy the nightingale raises her voice in long-drawn weeping for her sister's murdered son, in passionate sorrow for the blood she has shed and can never more wash away; the hour when the mighty dead come forth from their tombs beneath the dark cathedral aisles and kneel before the high altar where the transepts meet the nave, and where the moonbeams from the stained windows of the lofty dome make pools of blood-red light upon the marble floor.

All the party were silent, realising perhaps in that moment the whole beauty of the scene. Heine leaned back in his chair and looked steadily at the moon, resting his elbows on the carved arms of the seat and clasping his delicate white fingers before him.

Suddenly and without the least warning a wonderful strain of music broke the silence. Some one was playing on the piano in the great hall, and through the open windows the sounds floated out to the terrace. No one dared to speak, though all started in surprise. It was a wild Polish mazoure, fitful, passionate and sad, woven in strange movement, now sweeping forward in a burst of fervid hope, full of the rush of the dance, the ring of spurs, the timely measured tread of women's feet, the indescribable grace of slender figures in refined yet rapid motion — the whole breathing a reckless delight in the pleasure of the moment, a defiant power to be glad in the very jaws of death. Then with the contrast of true passion the pace slackens, the melody sways fitfully in the uncertain measure and sadness, waking in the harmony, trembles despairing for one moment in the muffled chords, while even love hardly dares to breathe sweet words in the ear of tired beauty. But again the dance awakes, the stronger rhythm breaks out again and dashing through the veil of melancholy, seizes on body and soul and whirls them down the storm of wild, luxurious, and wellnigh unbearable delight.

"That must be by Chopin!" exclaimed Diana. "But I never heard Gwendoline play it — "

She stopped short in surprise. She had imagined that Gwendoline had slipped away to the piano during the silence, but as she looked she saw her in her place.

"It is by Chopin," answered Heine with a smile. "It is Chopin himself."

All rose to their feet and hastened to the drawing-room; Gwendoline reached the door first.

At the piano sat a man with a fair and beautiful face, dressed much as Heine himself but with far greater elegance. There was about him a wonderful air of distinction, an unspeakable atmosphere of refinement and superiority over ordinary men. He had the look which tradition ascribes to kings, but which nature, in royal irony, more often bestows upon penniless persons of genius. His fair hair was fine and silky as spun gold; his skin transparent as a woman's; his features delicately aquiline and noble, and in his soft eyes there shone a clear and artistic intelligence, a spirit both gentle and quiet, yet neither weak nor effeminate, but capable rather of boundless courage and of heroic devotion when roused by the touch of sympathy.

He rose as the party approached him, and they saw that he was short and very slender. He smiled, half apologetically, and made a courteous inclination.

"Perhaps the introduction of a dead man is hardly an introduction at all," he said in a muffled voice, which, however, was not unpleasant to the ear. "I will save my friend Heine the trouble — I am Frederic Chopin."

Gwendoline, in her delight at meeting her favourite composer, would gladly have pressed him to remain at the piano, but hospitality forbade her.

She sat down and the others followed her example. The two dead men glanced at each other in friendly recognition and took their places in the circle. They looked so thoroughly alive that it was impossible to feel any uneasiness in their society, and perhaps none but Augustus and Lady Brenda, who had touched Heine's icy hand, realised fully the strangeness of the situation. But Chopin was perfectly at his ease. He did not seem to admit that his presence could possibly cause surprise. He sat quietly in his chair and looked from one to the other of his hosts, as though silently making their acquaintance.

"What an ideal life!" he exclaimed. "If I could live again I would live as you do — in a beautiful place over the sea, far from noise, dust and all that is detestable."

"It is a part of fairyland," answered Heine. "Do you remember? It was only last year that we came here together and sat on the rocks and tried to think what the people were like who once lived here, and whether any one would ever live here again. And you wished there were a piano in the old place — you have your wish now."

"It is not often that such wishes are realised," said Chopin. "It is rarely indeed that I can touch a piano now, though I hear much music. It interests me immensely to watch the progress of what Mozart began."

"It sickens me to see what has grown in literature from the ruins of what I helped to demolish," answered Heine.

"Believe me, my dear friend," returned the musician, "without romance there is neither music nor literature."

"What do you mean by romance, exactly?" asked Gwendoline, anxious to stimulate the conversation which had been begun by the two friends.

"Heine will give you one definition — I will give you another," answered Chopin.

"I never really differed from you," said his friend. "But give your definition of romance. I would like to hear it."

"It is the hardest thing in the world to define, and yet it is something which we all feel. I think it is based upon an association of ideas. When we say that a place is romantic we unconsciously admit that its beauty suggests some kind of story to our minds, most generally a love-story. Such scenery is not necessarily grand, but it is necessarily beautiful. I do not think that a man standing on the summit of Mont Blanc would say that it was a romantic spot. It is splendid indeed, but it is uninhabited and uninhabitable. It suggests no love-story. It is hugely grand and vast like Beethoven's Ninth Symphony, or like the great pyramid. But it is not romantic. There is more romance in a Polish landscape — with a little white village in the foreground surrounded by flat green fields and green woods, cut symmetrically in all directions by straight, white roads, and innocent of hills — one may at least fancy a fair-haired boy making love to a still fairer girl, just where the

brook runs between the wood and the meadow. No
— Mont Blanc is not romantic. Come down from the
snow-peaks — here for instance, where the wild rocks
hang and curl in crests like a petrified whirlpool, but
where the walls of this old castle suggest lives and
deeds long forgotten. You have romance at once.
From the grey battlement some Moorish maiden
may have once looked her last upon the white sails
of her corsair lover's long black ship. The fair young
Conradin may have lain hidden here before Frangi-
pani betrayed him to his death in Naples. Here
Bayard came, perhaps, after the tournament of Bar-
letta. Here Giovanna may have rested — she may
even have plotted here the murder of her husband — ”

“ I did not know you were such an historian,” interrupted Heine with a smile.

“ I have learned much since I died,” answered
Chopin, quietly. “ But I am encroaching on your
ground. I only want to prove that it is easy to see
the romantic element in a place which we can asso-
ciate with people. If none of those things really
happened here, it seems very simple to imagine that
they might have happened, and that is the same
thing in history.”

“ Absolutely the same,” assented Augustus, whose
favourite theory was that nobody knew anything.

“ Very good,” continued the composer. “ Romance
is then the possibility of associating ideas of people
with an object presented to the senses, apart from

the mere beauty of the object. I say that much magnificent music pleases intensely by the senses alone. Music is a dialogue of sounds. The notes put questions, and answer them. In fugue-writing the second member is scientifically called the 'answer.' When there is no answer, or if the answer is bad, there is no music at all. The ear tells that. But such a musical dialogue of sounds may please intensely by the mere satisfaction of the musical sense; or it may please because, besides the musical completeness, it suggests human feelings and passions and so appeals to a much larger part of our nature. I do not think the great pyramid suggests feelings and passions, in spite of all its symmetry. It may have roused a sympathetic thrill in the breast of Cheops, but it does not affect us as we are affected by the interior of Saint Peter's in Rome, or by Westminster Abbey, or by Giotto's tower. These are romantic buildings, for they are not only symmetrical, but they also tell us a tale of human life and death and hope and sorrow which we can understand. To my mind romantic music is that which expresses what we feel besides satisfying our sense of musical fitness. I think that Mozart was the founder of that school — I laboured for it myself — Wagner has been the latest expression of it."

"I adore Wagner," said Diana. "But it always seems to me that there is something monstrous in his music. Nothing else expresses what I mean."

"The 'monstrous' element can be explained,"

answered Chopin. "Wagner appeals to a vast mass
of popular tradition which really exists only in Germany and Scandinavia. He then brings those traditions suddenly before our minds with stunning force,
and gives them an overpowering reality. I leave it
to you whether the impression must not necessarily
be monstrous when we suddenly realise in the flesh,
before our eyes, such tales as that of Siegmund and
Siegfried, or of Parzifal and the Holy Grail. It is
great, gigantic—but it is too much. I admit that I
experience the sensation, dead as I am, when I stand
among the living at Bayreuth and listen. But I do
not like the sensation. I do not like the frantic side
of this modern romantism. The delirious effects and
excesses of it stupefy without delighting. I do not
want to realise the frightful crimes and atrocious
actions of mythological men and beasts, any more
than I want to see a man hanged or guillotined. I
think romance should deal with subjects not wholly
barbarous, and should try to treat them in a refined
way, because no excitement which is not of a refined
kind can be anything but brutalising. Man has
enough of the brute in him already, without being
taught to cultivate his taste for blood by artificial
means. Perhaps I am too sensitive—I hate blood.
I detest commonplace, but I detest even more the
furious contortions of ungoverned passion."

"But you cannot say that Wagner is exaggerated
in his effects," argued Diana.

"No—they are well studied and the result is

stupendous when they are properly reproduced. He
is great — almost too great. He makes one realise
the awful too vividly. He produces intoxication
rather than pleasure. He is an egotist in art. He is
determined that when you have heard him you shall
not be able to listen to any one else, as a man who eats
opium is disgusted with everything when he is awake.
I believe there is a pitch in art at which pleasure becomes vicious; the limit certainly exists in sculpture
and painting as well as in literature, just as when a
man drinks too much wine he is drunk. The object
of art is not to make life seem impossible, any more
than the object of drinking wine is to lose one's senses.
Art should nourish the mind, not drown it. To say
that Wagner's own mind, and the minds of some of
his followers were of such strong temper that nothing
less than his music could excite them pleasurably, is
not an answer. The Russian mujík will drink a pint
of vodka in the early morning, and when he has drunk
it he is gayer than the Italian who has taken a little
cup of coffee. You would probably think his gaiety
less refined than that of the Italian, though there is
more of it. It will also be followed by a headache —
but the headache, the moral headache after an orgy
of modern art is worse than the headache from too
much vodka. It is like Heine's 'toothache in the
heart.' He used to say that the best filling for that
was of lead and a certain powder invented by Ber-
thold Schwarz. Romantism can go too far, like
everything else. The Hermes of Olympia was de-

scended from a clumsy but royal race of Egyptian granite blocks; but he is the historical ancestor of the vilest productions of modern sculpture. Modern art is drunk — drunk with the delight of expressing excessively what should not be expressed at all, drunk with the indulgence of the senses until the intellect is clouded and dull, or spasmodically frantic by turns, drunk with the vulgar self-satisfied vanity of a village coxcomb. Ah, for Art's sake let poor art be kept sober until the heaven-born muses deign to pay us another visit! "

"Amen!" exclaimed Heine, devoutly. "The same things are true of literature. But I admire Wagner, nevertheless, though his music terrifies me. I think Mozart was the Raphael, Wagner the Michel-angelo of the opera. Any one may choose between the two, for it is a matter of taste. But in music the development from the one to the other seems to me more rational than it has been in literature."

"How do you mean?" asked Gwendoline.

"I think music has advanced better than literature. They were both little boys once, but the one has grown into a great, dominating, royal giant — the other into a greedy, snivelling, dirty-nosed, foul-mouthed, cowardly ruffian. There are bad musicians and good writers, of course. The bad musicians do little harm, but the good writers occupy the position of Lot in the condemned cities — they are the mourn-ers at the funeral of romance. The mass of fiction makers to-day are but rioters at the baptismal feast of Realism, the Impure."

"What a sweeping condemnation!" exclaimed Augustus. "I thought that you yourself were a supporter of realism, or declared yourself to be, though your lyrics are certainly very romantic."

"I was the renegade monk from the monastery of the romantists," said Heine. "A Frenchman once told me so. But when I grew old and married, I hankered for the dear old atmosphere, and my little French wife helped me to breathe it again."

"Our great modern realist, Ernest Renan, says of himself, half regretfully, that he feels like a *religieux manqué*," said Augustus.

"I can understand that," answered Heine. "But when I was young the word romance stunk in my nostrils. It meant Platen."

"And what does it mean to you now?" inquired Gwendoline, who wanted to lead the dead poet back to the point.

"You would have a definition, madam?" he replied. "Romance is a beautiful woman, with a dead pale skin, and starry eyes and streaming raven hair, and when I look into her sweet dark face I could wear a ton of armour on my back and cleave a Saracen to the chine with my huge blade for her sake, or go barefoot to Jerusalem, or even read Platen's poetry all through. But she looks so strangely at me with her great black eyes, that I am never quite sure whether she is quite real and quite serious. I only know that she is very, very beautiful, and that I love her to distraction."

"That is a definition from fairyland," said Chopin with his soft sweet smile.

"And you want one from the library of a student, I suppose," answered Heine. "Romance is the modern epic. I forget who said so, but it is true in a limited way. The romantic languages were those Latin tongues which were not Latin, but Berlinish."

"In other words — slang," suggested Augustus.

"Slang — exactly. *Latinus grossus qui facit tremare pilastros*, as the Roman schoolboy calls it —"

"Please translate!" exclaimed Lady Brenda.

"If it means anything it means the Romantic dialect — a coarse rough Latin that would make columns shake. The words are not all in the dictionary, madam, but metaphorically they are in most people's mouths. It afterwards became the most elegant language of its age and has given the name of romance to the school of literature it founded. The first romantic writings were in that language — the love-songs of the troubadours, and I have seen in an old library in Siena a very beautiful manuscript collection of them with the original music and words by Jehan Bretel."

"What were they like?" asked Gwendoline, eagerly.

"I can remember a stanza or two:

> "'Mi chant sont tout plain d'ire et de douleur
> Pour vous dame ke je ai tant aimée
> Que je ne sai se je chant u se pleur
> Ainsi m'estant souffrir ma destinée

Mais se Dieu plaist encor verrai le jour
Kamour sera cangie en autre tour
Si vous donra envers moi millo r pensée
Chanson vatent garde ne remanoir
Prie celi ki plus jaime pour ke souvent par li soiez cantée.' [1]

" The spelling is very curious, but the sentiment is unmistakable and the language is Provençal. There is the origin of romance in the Romansch language. Those songs preserved the customs of those times, the troubadour with his lute below the castle wall, the obdurate lady behind the lattice in her tower, the life-and-death seriousness of love in the eleventh century — it is all there, and we call it romance. The literature of love-songs continued to spread after the customs of those days had passed away, but it did not move with the times, though it increased. The knight in armour, the lute, and the lady with her scarf were preserved like curious zoological specimens in spirits, and are the foundation of all romance. Then we had Germans and Englishmen who wrote long epic romances in other languages, such as Wolfram von Eschenbach and Sir Thomas Malory, who got his *Morte d'Arthur* from the French. A modern poet owes much of his fame to his treatment of the same theme, which shows that the subject is not even yet worn out. But though the old songs still stir us, they are not enough for us nowadays. The frantic

[1] From a fine illuminated manuscript in the Municipal Library of Siena — a part of two long songs copied by the writer with the music in 1878.

fighting, the melancholy tragedy, the black-and-white magic which appealed to the imagination of a Black Forest freebooting baron of the tenth century, do not appeal to ours. The French pastoral romances were an attempt to change the form of the solemn chivalric epic of earlier times into something lighter and more gay. But unlike the chivalric epic the pastoral had no foundation in real life and consequently disappeared almost without a trace. The modern romantic novel is a prose epic, generally founded on modern life."

"And what is the modern realistic novel?" asked Diana.

"It is the prose without the epic," answered the poet. "It is therefore the opposite of romance in every respect. It sets aside all invention, and takes for its standpoint the principle that a hero is not necessary to a story, and that every-day life, with such episodes as it may chance to bring forth, should be of sufficient interest to everybody, to make everybody ready to dispense for ever with imagination. The realists say that a man may learn more from being shown what he is than from being told what he should be. The romantists say that if a man will study the ideal he can to some extent imitate it. When I was a young man romance stood on a low level. The mechanically correct and spiritually feeble performances of our little poets did not please me. Goethe was a realist, and I determined to be a realist. I did not perceive that Goethe was also a

romantist, and that while he was well able to paint
men as they are, he had a surpassing gift for describing them as they should be.   I believe that literature
without realism cannot last.   But I believe also that
literature without romance cannot interest."

"Nor life, without romance, either," said Gwendoline.

"Oh! Do you think so?" exclaimed Lady Brenda.
"I am sure I know many people who are not at all
romantic but whose lives are very interesting to
themselves."

"People who make money an object," answered
Augustus.   "But they have a romance nevertheless,
and a very pretty one — the story of the loves of
the pound, the shilling and the penny, told in
many manuscript volumes with a detail worthy of
M. Zola."

"Yes," said Heine with a smile, "the love of a
Hamburg banker for a dollar is wonderful, passing
the love of women."

"The sense of romance must be instinctive," said
Diana.   "We distinguish at a glance between what
is romantic and what is not, as we distinguish
between black and white.   For instance Alexander
the Great is a romantic character; Julius Cæsar is
not.   I do not see that in those cases the explanation is true which ascribes romance to the traditions
of knights-errant, troubadours and tournaments."

"That is true," said Chopin.   "Just as the prime-
val song of the Arab or the Hindoo peasant is romantic, while Chinese music is not."

"Judas Maccabæus was a romantic character," put in Heine. "Moses was not, though he was a greater man. Judas Maccabæus was the Cromwell of the Jews, and it is impossible to read his history without a thrill of enthusiasm. I suppose that is why the early Church instituted the feast of the Maccabean martyrs, on the first of August, though they were Jews, put to death before the birth of Christ for the Jewish faith by Antiochus Epiphanes — a mother and her seven sons. Judas Maccabæus was undoubtedly a hero."

"Then our whole theory of romance falls to the ground," said Lady Brenda.

"I think not," answered Augustus. "It is enough to extend it a little, and to say that all men and women who have acted nobly under the influence of strong and good passions have been romantic characters."

"That is not enough, either," objected Heine. "I do not think that they need have acted nobly, nor necessarily under the influence of good passions. Alexander, burning Persepolis under the influence of Thaïs's smiles and Timotheus's song is a romantic character enough. But the action was not noble, nor the passion good."

"But was he romantic in that case?" asked Lady Brenda. "It was rather like Nero burning Rome, you know."

"Perhaps there is a doubt on the subject," replied the poet. "It may be a question of individual taste.

Take another instance, out of more recent times. Was Giovanna of Naples, the first — the daughter of Robert — a romantic character or not?"

"Of course," answered Lady Brenda.

"Was her love for Luigi of Taranto a romantic passion?"

"I suppose so," admitted the lady.

"Then the murder of her husband, Andreas of Hungary, which she planned and caused to be executed out of her love for Luigi, her cousin, was romantic. There is no doubt of it. Many murders have a strong romantic colour. Christina of Sweden causing Monaldeschi to be killed at Fontainebleau, is another instance. There was nothing noble or good about either of those cases."

"I yield," said Augustus. "Then suppose we say that men and women acting under the influence of strong passions are romantic characters."

"There is more truth in that," replied Heine; "but it does not include enough."

"It does not tell me why I feel that the Arab is romantic while the Chinaman is not," remarked Chopin.

"My dear friend," said the other, "we know very little about Chinamen, and their appearance does not suggest romantic thoughts."

"True. But why?" insisted the composer, who felt that there was something in his question.

"It appears," said Augustus, "that some races are fundamentally excluded from all connection with our

ideas of romance. But I believe that is because we
cannot get so near to them, being by nature so different from them, as to be able to understand their
feelings and passions."

"I have heard that Chinese music has sixty-six
keys," remarked Chopin. "That would account for
their music not being comprehensible to us. Then
it follows that unless people and their feelings come
readily within our understanding we cannot connect
them with any idea of romance."

"Yes," answered Heine, "and the more we know
them, the more we appreciate the romantic element.
No schoolboy thinks Achilles half as romantic as Rob
Roy. And yet Achilles is one of the most romantic
characters in all epic poetry."

"Then the *Iliad* is a romance?" inquired Gwendoline.

"It is the big romance, with a big hero, in big
times, which we call an epic," replied the poet.
"And it is written in magnificent verse. The modern romance is an infinitesimal epic of which Tom is
the hero, Sarah Jane the heroine, and a little modern
house with green blinds and an iron railing is the
scene of the action. But Tom and Jane love each
other almost as much as Achilles and Briseis and are
a great deal happier; and if the little house catches
fire when Tom is out, and he comes back just in time
to plunge through the flames and carry off Sarah Jane,
with the loss of his eyebrows and beard and at the
risk of his life, he is just as much of a hero as Achilles

when he put on his new armour and went to kill
Hector and the Trojans.   For a man cannot do more
than risk his life with his eyes open for the sake of
what he loves, whether he be Achilles or Tom.   The
essential part of the romance is something which shall
call out the strongest qualities in the natures of the
actors in it; because all strong actions interest us,
and if they are also good they rouse our admiration.
And if those strong actions are done for the sake of
love, or of what we call honour, or to free a nation
from slavery they strike us as romantic."

"Because all those things," remarked Augustus,
"are closely associated with modern romance from
its beginning.   The mediæval knight was the imper-
sonation of love, honour and patriotism."

"Also, because those are the feelings most deeply
felt by the human heart, and in spite of all that realism can do, stories of love, honour and patriotism will
always and to the end of all time, appeal to every one
who has a soul.   The realists, of course, say that there
is no soul, and that love, honour and patriotism are
conventional terms, as right and wrong are conventional conceptions.   That is paltry stuff.   But the
actions may be bad and yet be romantic, where love
is the subject, and as that is the most usual subject
for romance, it follows that men have endeavoured
to treat it in the greatest variety of situations.   Bad
or good, it always interests.   Our sympathy for fair
Rosamund is at least as great as that we feel for
Anne Boleyn."

"I fancy it is not certain whether the most romantic characters excite the most sympathy," said Lady Brenda.

"After they are dead they generally do," answered the poet, with a smile. "When we think of a romantic character we always fancy to ourselves that it must have been very charming to be the hero or heroine of all the thrilling scenes in which he or she took part. In fiction the romantic character has been worn out, partly because fiction is never so extraordinary as reality; the result is that in modern books we are often most drawn towards some minor character of whom we feel at the end of the book that we have not seen enough, simply because we have not been bored by him. But the romance of history does not wear out. There is the same difference between people in history and people in fiction which exists between a real king and a stage king with a tinsel crown. It is easy enough to dress an actor in royal robes, and to tell people that the crown is of real gold, eighteen carats fine; it is quite another matter to find words for the sham king to speak, and kingly actions for him to perform. For the construction of a good epic you must have both, or must find both; and that is a little hard when one has but a little acquaintance with kings. It is not everybody who can say with Voltaire: 'I have three or four kings whom I *coddle* —j'ai trois ou quatre rois que je mitonne.'[1] But history presents us with the real king, in flesh and

[1] In a letter to Tronchin.

blood; his actions are harmonious, because they have actually been performed by the same man. Few writers of fiction nowadays have the combined imagination, accuracy and versatility necessary to invent and describe a series of actions, thoughts and words, so harmonious as to make the reader feel that one man could really have spoken, thought and acted as the author makes his hero act, speak and think. The writer then separates himself from romantism altogether. and confines himself to describing things he has actually seen and of which he is positively sure. But he finds it hard to make his books interesting with such materials. Failing greatness, he sees that there is a short cut to popularity. If a writer cannot be sublime, he can at least be disgusting; and to excite disgust is, he thinks, better than to excite no notice at all."

"I think you are unjust to the realists," said Gwendoline. "I do not think that realistic books are always disgusting, by any means."

"No," answered Heine. "But they are more likely to be. With the genius of Goethe one may be realistic without being repulsive. But Goethe himself said that to call a thing bad which is bad does no good, whereas to call a bad thing good does immeasurable harm. Many realists call bad things good."

"So do many romantists," objected Gwendoline. "And I do not see that we are any nearer to knowing what romance really is. Your beautiful woman with the starry eyes does not satisfy me. That is poetry, but it does not explain my feelings."

"I believe I can define romance, after listening to you all," said Chopin, who had not spoken for some time. "My own definition only applied to music, but it can be extended. In the first place romance consists in the association of certain ideas with certain people, either in history or in fiction. The people must belong to some race of beings of whom we know enough to understand their passions and to sympathise with them. The ideas must be connected with the higher passions of love, patriotism, devotion, noble hatred, profound melancholy, divine exaltation and the like. The lower passions in romance are invariably relegated to the traditional villain, who serves as a foil for the hero. Shorten all that and say that our romantic sense is excited by associating ideas of the higher passions, good and bad, with people whom we can understand, and in such a way as to make us feel with them."

"I do not think we shall get any nearer than that," said Augustus Chard. "It explains at once why we think that Alexander was a romantic character, whereas Julius Cæsar was not. Alexander was always full of great passions, good or bad. Cæsar was calm, impassive, superior to events. Alexander burnt a city to please a woman. Cæsar found in a woman's love a pretext for conquering her kingdom and reducing the queen who loved him to the position of his vassal. Cleopatra was a romantic character, but she was unfortunate in her choice of men. Cæsar was murdered, she murdered her husband, Antony killed himself for her and she concluded the tragedy by killing herself for Antony, after her son and Cæsar's had also been put to death. There is material for a dozen romances in her life, but if she were a character of fiction we should say her story was absurdly impossible. As it is, her history is a romance of the most tremendous proportions."

"I think Cæsar was romantic too," said Diana. "He had outgrown romance when he conquered the world. He must have been very different when he was young."

"Very different," said a placid voice from one of the tall windows.

A man stood outside in the moonlight, looking in. His tall and slender figure was wrapped in a dark mantle of some rich material; the folds reflected the moonbeams with a purple sheen, circling the straight neck and then falling to the ground behind the shoulder. On his brow a dark wreath of oak and laurel leaves sat like a royal crown above his high white forehead. The aquiline nose, broadly set on at the nostrils, but very clearly cut and delicate, gave to his face an expression of supreme, refined force, well borne out in the even and beautifully chiselled mouth and the prominent square chin. His eyes were very black, but without lustre, of that peculiar type in which it is impossible to distinguish the pupil from the surrounding iris.

"It is Cæsar," said Augustus, under his breath, as he rose to greet the new-comer.

"Yes, I am Cæsar," answered the calm voice of the dead conqueror. He came forward and stood in the midst of the party, so that the lamplight fell upon his grand face. "You spoke of me and I was near and heard you. You are not afraid to take a dead man's hand? No — why should you be?"

The hand he held out was long and nervous and white, looking as though the fingers possessed the elastic strength of steel.

"Are we in a dream?" asked Diana in low tones, turning to Heine. The poet sighed.

"You are but a dream to us," he said, softly. "We are the reality — the sleepless reality of death."

"Yes: we are very real," said Cæsar, seating himself in a huge carved chair that might have served for an imperial throne, and looking slowly around upon the assembled party. "You were speaking of my life. You were saying that I was not a romantic character. Do not smile at my using the word. In nineteen centuries of wandering I have learned to speak of romantists and realists. I was not romantic. Could Homer himself have made an epic poem about my life? I think not. Homer had traditions to help him, and Virgil had both Homer and the traditions. The purpose of my life was to overthrow tradition and to found a new era for the world. I was a modern. I was a source of realism. There was nothing mythical about me. Romance grew out of the decay of what I founded. I do not think that the romantic sense existed in men of my day, though the popular respect for the ancients was even then immense, and Rome was full of traditions. It is only by extending the term that anything can be called romantic which happened earlier than ten centuries after my death."

Too much awed to speak as yet by the strange presence, the living members of the party held their breath while Cæsar was speaking, and the smooth inflexions of his calm voice filled the quiet air. A few moments of silence followed his speech and it seemed as though no one would answer him; but at last Chopin lifted his delicate face and spoke.

"Nineteen centuries!" he exclaimed. "Ah, Cæsar, why could you not have lived on through all those years? Poland would still have been free and the Poles would still have been a people."

"The world would have been free," rejoined the dead conqueror, sadly. "I believed in unity, not in partition. I meant to build, not to destroy. My heart sinks when I see the world divided into nations, of which I would have made one nation."

"'Every individual man is himself a world,'" said Heine. "'A world that is born with him and dies with him, and under every gravestone lies the history of a world.'" [1]

"That is true," answered Chopin, "and my world was Poland and is Poland still."

[1] Heine, ii. p. 53.

"Mine is the whole world of living beings," returned the poet.

"Yes," replied Chopin, with a fine smile. "I know it. But the world according to Saint-Simon would not resemble the world according to Julius Cæsar."

"And yet," said Cæsar, "I watched the development of Saint-Simon's doctrines with interest. They failed as all socialist movements have failed and always must fail, to the end of time, until they proceed upon a different basis."

"Why?" asked Lady Brenda, taking courage.

"The usual mistake. The followers of Saint-Simon, or the stronger part of them, tried to abolish marriage and they tried to invent a religion. Religions are not easily invented which can be imposed upon any considerable body of mankind, and no considerable body of civilised mankind has ever shown itself disposed to dispense with the institution of matrimony. The desire to obtain wealth without labour, the negation of religion and the degradation of women have ruined all socialistic systems which have ever been tried, and have undermined many powerful nations. It is impossible to govern men except by defending the security of property, upholding the existing form of religion and exacting a rigorous respect for the institution of marriage."

"That is true," said Heine, thoughtfully. "The object of the Saint-Simonists was to create a common property, to be shared equally for ever, and to incul-

cate a form of religion which they had invented.
They might have succeeded in that. But Enfantin
had the unlucky idea that free love was a good thing,
and that ruined the whole institution just when it
was at the point of success."

"It could never have succeeded," answered Cæsar,
"even if he had let marriage exist, because the perpetual division of property is an impossibility. But
the abolition of marriage would alone have been
enough to ruin the scheme. I see in the modern
world many nations, and each nation has its own
very distinct form of government. Apply as a test
to each the question of the stability of property, of
religion and of marriage, and you will have at once
the measure of its prosperity. I see in Europe a new
empire, vast, strong and successful. The government
protects wealth, marriage and religion; but religion
is the least stable of the three, and there is no country in the world where there are so many who deny
religion as there are in Germany. Look closer. You
will see that there is no country in the world where
there are so many anarchists, and these anarchists
are perpetually sapping the sources of the nation's
wealth and trying to undermine the institution of
marriage. They are doing their work well. Unless
there is a religious revival in Germany, she will soon
cease to preponderate in Europe."

"That is a novel idea," said Augustus Chard.

"I think not," answered Cæsar, with a quiet smile.
"I think it is as old as I am at least. But look at

Europe again.   Of all European nations, which is
the most prosperous?   England.   In spite of many
political mistakes, in spite of many foolish and expensive wars, in spite of the many incompetent statesmen and dissolute monarchs by whom she has been
often governed, in spite of civil wars which have
overturned her government and religious wars which
have changed her dynasties, in spite of the narrow-
ness of her original territory, the inclemencies of her
climate, the barrenness of her Scotch mountains and
the indolent misery of her Irish peasants — in spite
of all these, England is the most prosperous country
in modern Europe.   Apply my test.   Is there any
country in Europe where property is better protected,
where religion is a more established fact, where the
marriage-contract is so scrupulously observed?   Certainly not.   Look at her neighbours — even at France.
Why did France grow prosperous under Napoleon
the Third?   Because he protected religion, fostered
the growth of commerce, and never so much as
thought of attacking marriage.   Now the existing
government is opposed to religion of any kind and
has introduced divorce, which in France is a very
different matter from divorce in England.   France is
less prosperous than she was.   Italy comes next with
her cry of freedom.   Religion is tolerated, marriage
is respected, but the property of the individual is eaten
up to pay the debts of the government.   The country
is not prosperous.   Italy as a nation is a failure, not
by her own fault, perhaps, but by force of circum-

stances. How can a man be healthy whose head is
buried in ice while his feet are plunged in hot water?
You must cool his feet and warm his head, but you
must not apply leeches to every part of his body at
once. When a man needs blood you must not bleed
him in order to show him that his veins are not yet
quite empty."

"Nations suffer at first when any great change is
made, even when it is a change for the good," remarked Heine.

"That is a maxim which has been made an excuse
for much harm," replied Cæsar. "I do not think it
is always true. A nation certainly ought not to
suffer for twenty years because it has been unified.
In twenty years a new generation of men grows up,
and if the change has been for good, these young men
should find themselves in better circumstances at
twenty than their fathers were before them. I have
watched the world for nearly two thousand years, and
I think the history of that period shows that whenever
a change for the better has taken place in a nation's
government it has been followed almost immediately
by a great increase of prosperity. Within a very few
years after my death the empire of my nephew had
eclipsed everything which had preceded it and in
some ways, also, everything which has been seen since.
The second unification of the empire under Charlemagne gave a fabulous impulse to the growth of
wealth. Even the foundation of the present German
Empire was followed in a short time by a great de-

velopment. England became powerful from the time of William's conquest. She increased in wealth and importance under the great changes made by Elizabeth. She made another stride under the reign of William Third; and she reached the highest point of wealth and influence shortly after the inauguration of Free Trade, which was one of the greatest changes ever introduced into the administration of any country. There is a gigantic republic in America which but a few years ago was struggling in a great civil war, but which is now probably the most prosperous nation in the whole world. No. I believe that great changes, if they are good are followed very soon by an increase of prosperity. This has not taken place in Italy, and there are no signs of it. On the contrary, her lands are ceasing to be cultivated, her men are emigrating in enormous numbers, and those who remain are obliged to pay the taxes, in order to maintain the fictitious credit of an imaginary importance. The best king, the best statesmen, even the best disposition of the people cannot turn thousands of square miles of barren rock into a fertile garden, nor force a small and poor country to maintain the state of a great empire."

The dead man spoke calmly and sorrowfully of his country. He alone could realize the vast gulf that lay between his day and the present, and though he was Cæsar yet the rest could hardly believe him. There was silence for a time in the hall, and the great moon rose outside and her rays made the tiles of the terrace gleam like snow, while far down upon the sea the broad path of her light glittered like a river of pearls on dark velvet.

Then a cool breeze sprang up and the three dead men rose silently and went out from among the living into the wonderful night.

"We have been dreaming," sighed Lady Brenda, rising from her chair and looking out.

## CHAPTER VI.

THE little party sat by the open window of the hall on the next evening. Since the extraordinary events of the preceding day they had talked of nothing else. Augustus was endeavouring to explain his theory that by a gigantic experiment upon nature he had accidentally upset some fundamental but wholly unknown law, and he promised that if his mother-in-law would not be frightened he would cause another electric storm and produce even more extraordinary results.

"But I am quite sure it was all a dream," objected Lady Brenda. "Only when I think of that man's hand, I really shiver. Anything more awfully clammy!"

"I am sure they will come back to-night," said Gwendoline, in a tone of profound conviction. "It was all very odd, but I know it was quite real."

Diana was seated at the piano, running her fingers over the keys in an idle fashion, striking melancholy and disconnected chords and then pausing to listen to the conversation.

"Yes," she said presently, "I am sure they will come back."

"The question," remarked Augustus, "is whether

such a disturbance is likely to outlast a day unless the forces which produced it are — " he stopped, starting slightly. Lady Brenda dropped her fan, Gwendoline rose swiftly from her chair and drew back, while Diana's fingers fell upon the keys and made a ringing discord. In the dusky gloom of the long window stood two men. The one was Cæsar; the other a man taller than he, with a long white beard and wrapped in a cloak. Cæsar came forward, followed at a few steps by his companion.

"I have come back," said the dead man, quietly. "You do not grudge us poor ghosts an hour's conversation? It is so pleasant to seem to be alive again, and in such company. We left you too soon last night, but it was late."

"But where are the rest?" asked Gwendoline, disappointed at not seeing Chopin, and glancing curiously at the old man who stood by Cæsar's side.

"Chopin is at Bayreuth to-night. There is a musical festival and he could not stay away. Heine is sitting by the shores of the North Sea talking to the stars and the sea-foam. But I have brought you another friend — one perhaps greater than they when he lived, though we are all alike here."

Cæsar led his companion forward, and in the short silence that followed all eyes were turned upon the new-comer.

He was a man of tall and graceful figure. The noble features were set off by a snowy beard and long white locks that flowed down upon his shoulders and contrasted with the rich material of his mantle. The wide folds of the latter as he gathered them in one hand did not altogether conceal the dress he wore beneath, the doublet of dark green and trunk hose of scarlet, the tight sleeve, slashed at the elbows where the fine linen showed in symmetrical puffs, the black shoes and the gold chain which hung about his neck. He was old, indeed, but his walk had a matchless grace and his erect form still showed the remains of the giant's strength. His dark eyes were brilliant still and emitted a lustre that illuminated the pale, regular features, too deathlike to convey any impression of life without that glance of the sparkling soul within.

He paused before the group and courteously bent his head. All rose to greet him, and if there was less of awe in the action there was perhaps more of reverence, than any had felt when the greater guest had entered.

"I am Lionardo," he said in a low and musical voice. "Lionardo, the artist — 'from Vinci' they call me, because I was born there. I have joined you and the rest — these dear friends of mine who have made me one of them, and you who have conferred on us the privilege of once more exchanging thoughts and grasping hands with the living."

"There is none whom we will more gladly honour," said Augustus, gravely. "The privilege is ours, not yours. Be seated — be one of us if you will, as well as one of these — whom you have known so long."

"Long — yes — it seems long to me, very, very
long. But I have not forgotten what it was to live.
I loved life well. Men have said of me that I wasted
much time — I have been laughed at as a blower of
soap-bubbles, as a foolish fellow who spent his time
in trying to teach lizards to fly. Perhaps it is true.
I have learned the secret now, and I have learned
that I could not have attained to it then. But it
was sweet to seek after it."

"I have read those foolish stories," said Diana,
whose eyes rested in rapt admiration on the grand
features of the artist. "No one believes them —"

"Here in Italy," said Cæsar, in his placid yet dominating tones, "people may say of you as the English
said of their architect — *si monumentum quæris, cir-
cumspice.*"

"They would have needed to bury my body by
the sluices of the Lecco canal, to give the same force
to the epitaph," answered Lionardo, with a soft laugh.
Then with the courtesy natural to him he turned to
Diana who had been speaking when interrupted by
Cæsar's quotation.

"I appreciate the kindly thought that makes you
say that, Lady Diana — your name is Diana? Yes, it
suits your face. I used to think I could guess people's names from their faces. Another of my foolish
fancies. However, I am obliged to say that there is
some truth in the report concerning the soap-bubbles.
I had a theory that they were like drops of liquid —
that each drop had a skin and that I could make

drops of air and find out how they would act, by giving them artificial skins like those of other liquids. Something has been produced from the idea by modern students. The mistake I made was in attempting to work out my theory before proclaiming it. That is impossible. Modern students make a fat living by proclaiming their theories first and omitting to demonstrate them afterwards, taking for granted that no one will deny what persons of such importance as themselves choose to suggest."

"I have never heard that you were so cynical," said Lady Brenda.

"Nor in your presence could I be so long," rejoined the old artist, with a smile. "But I was not cynical in my time. I am cynical in yours. Save for such company as these gentlewomen, I would not choose to be alive to-day."

Cæsar sighed and looked away from the rest, his nervous white hand tightening upon the carved arm of his deep-seated chair. It was a long, deep breath, drawn in with sudden and overwhelming thought of returning vitality and possibility, swelling the breast with the old imperial courage, the mighty grandeur of heart which had ruled the world; then relinquished and breathed out again in despair, deep, inconsolable and heart-rending, in the despair which the dead man whose deeds are all done and whose life-book is closed for ever feels when he gazes on the living whose race is not yet begun.

"Yes," said Lionardo, looking kindly at the con-

queror's averted face, "you are right — for yourself.
We are not all such as Caius. If I were to live again
I should waste more time in disproving theories to-
day than I ever wasted in trying to prove them four
hundred years ago. We were all for progress under
Ludovico Sforza. Borgia understood progress in his
own way — but it was progress, too, for all that. He
could have given lessons in more than one thing to
many of your moderns. Even Pope Leo understood
what progress meant, in spite of his ideas about my
methods of painting. But nowadays everything goes
backwards. A bag of money is paraded through the
world bound on an ass's back, and everybody wor-
ships the ass, and men lie down and let him walk
over them, thinking perchance that the beast may
stumble, and the sack burst open, and that haply
they may scrape up some of the coin in the filth of
the road. We were more simple than the moderns.
We had less money, but we knew better how to
spend it."

"Is it true, I wonder," put in Augustus, "that the
amount of money in circulation indicates progress
while the way in which men spend it indicates civilisation ? "

"No," said Cæsar, answering for the rest. "The
nation which has the greater wealth may not have
progressed further than others, save in power. Power
is not progress — it depends on other things. It is
the result of a combination of strength and discipline
under an intelligent leader. The highest power is

generally reached by a people when the spirit of
organisation has attained its greatest development in
military matters but has not yet spread to the civil
professions.　The army is then held in the highest
esteem and is the favourite profession.　When the
passion for order has extended to mercantile affairs,
the nation's actual power as compared with other
nations begins to decline.　Interests of all kinds
become vested in the maintenance of peace, and the
warlike element falls into disrepute.　It becomes
the nation's business to lend money to other nations
who are still in the military stage, herself meanwhile
giving and receiving guarantees of peace.　But
though a people may be rich by commerce they may
not have progressed; and again whole nations may
be made fabulously wealthy by seizing the wealth of
others.　We Romans did that.　We did not pretend
to the culture of the Greeks; we certainly did not
possess their skill in making money — but we possessed
them and their country, and gold flowed in our
streets.　It did us very little good.　We got it without progress, by force, and we spent it recklessly in
paying men to tear each other to pieces.　No — a large
amount of money in circulation does not indicate
progress, though it may be the result of it."

"Money is very uninteresting," said Gwendoline.
"It always seems to me that the world would be
much nicer without it."

"When you are as old as I am, you will appreciate
your advantages, my dear," said Lady Brenda.　"It

is good to be rich, and I fancy it must be very disagreeable to be poor."

"But I know quite well how it feels to have
money," objected Gwendoline.  "I would like to
know how it feels to have power—power such as
you had," she added, looking at Cæsar.

"Not many have known what it is," he answered,
with a curious smile.  "Each one who has possessed
it has probably felt it in a different way.  For my
part, though I was accused of not being serious in my
youth, like Lionardo here, I think I grew more than
serious under the responsibility.  Perhaps, however,
it made less difference to me than it has to others.
I was born to wealth, if not to power, and I resolved
to make the most of my money.  I made use of it
by spending it all and then borrowing largely on the
security of what I had squandered.  They said I was
not serious—but they made me leave the country
nevertheless."

"I imagine," said Gwendoline, "that to have
boundless power suddenly put into one's hands must
make one feel as though one were to live for ever."

"Living for ever is a sad pastime without it,"
returned Cæsar.  "I am not of Lionardo's mind.  I
would live again."

"To die again as you died?" asked Diana in a low
voice.

"Yes," answered the dead conqueror, "to die again
as I died, if need be, but to have power once more.
And I know what I say—you cannot know.  For

death was horrible to me.  Not the physical pain of
it, though they were clumsy fellows; they were long
in killing me — I thought it would never end.  I
could have done it better myself, and indeed I was
more merciful to them than they to me.  Not one of
them died a natural death, for I pursued them one
by one when I was dead.  I have never seen them
since; they are not here.  But none of them suffered
as I did.  I knew that my hour was come when I got
that first wound in the throat, and as I struggled,
the horror of it overcame me.  Visions rose before
my eyes of the things I had not yet accomplished,
but of which the accomplishment was certain if I
lived.  It was such a disappointment — more that than
anything else.  Such a heart-rending despair at being
cut down before my work was half finished, before the
world was half civilised.  People forget that I invented civilisation — I, the dead man who am speaking to you.  But it is true.  And in that moment I
felt that I was dying without having realised in practice the theory which was to change the world.  That
handful of low assassins cost the world fifteen centuries of darkness, and I knew it even then.  Had I
lived, I would have kneaded the earth as a baker
kneads dough, and the leaven I had put into it would
not have rotted and fermented for lack of stirring.
As I felt one wound after another, I felt that my murderers were not only killing Cæsar, they were killing
civilisation; every thrust was struck at the heart of
the world, making deep wounds in the future of man-

kind and letting out the breath of life from the body of law. That was my worst suffering, worse even than the death of my ambition. I had done enough already to be remembered, and I knew it. I was satisfied for myself to die. But I˙had conceived great thoughts which had grown to be a new self apart from the old, vain, ambitious Cæsar, having a separate and better life — and that they slew also. Augustus did much, but he could not do what I would and could have done."

"No," said Lionardo, thoughtfully, "you were the greatest man who ever lived."

"That is saying too much," answered Cæsar in quiet tones. "I meant to be. That is all. My fortune deserted me too soon. The greatest men, after all, are poets. They are also the most justly judged, for what they leave is their own. They leave themselves to mankind in their own words. We statesmen and soldiers are at the mercy of historians. I meant to have written the history of my whole life in the form of annual reports such as I made upon my wars in Gaul."

"Could you not do it now?" asked Lady Brenda. "We know so little of the history of your youth, and I am sure it must have been most interesting."

Cæsar smiled. "If I were able to write at all," he said, "I would not choose my youth as a subject upon which to make a report. My youth was a trifle over-full of movement, besides being very ostentatious. My first object in life was to become popular, for I knew that popularity was the surest way to power. I led the popular party for eighteen years before I ever attempted to lead an army, and when I turned soldier I was already a finished statesman. That is the reason why I knew what to do so soon as I had got the whole power into my hands. I had conquered the most important part of my world by art before I found it necessary to subdue the remainder by force. I was beginning to amalgamate a new world out of my two conquests when I was murdered."

"Do the dead forgive?" The words were spoken by Gwendoline in a low tone and as though no response could be expected to such a question. But there were those present who could answer it. Lionardo da Vinci turned his soft eyes upon the questioner.

"Yes," he said, "we do forgive, and very freely too."

"Yes — and no," said Cæsar.

"Both?" asked the artist. "How can we both forgive and not forgive, illustrious friend? There must be caprice in that — there must be an uncertain vacillation between two thoughts. You never vacillated, nor stood long choosing between two paths, nor, having chosen, looked back and regretted."

"The sum of man's works," replied the greater spirit, "is composed of his intentions taken together with his deeds in such a way as the Greek geometer would have expressed it. The sum of his life is largest when the deeds are as great as the intentions which prompted them, for of four-sided figures the square, with equal lines, encloses the greatest space. But if the intentions be ever so great and the deeds few, the figure is long indeed, but narrow and of small area; and again if the deeds are numerous though the intentions small, then the deeds are the result of accident and must not all be imputed to man for good. My intentions were my own. I forgive them that said they were unworthy, or little or bad, for I know what they were. But my deeds were the world's, and those I left undone should have been the world's also. Wherefore I forgive not those men who cut them short, who clipped the sum of my life and made my square smaller than it should have been. For my life was the world's health, and though my nephew was a cunning physician, all his medicines could not cure the gangrene in the wounds my slayers made in the world's skin, nor could all his cleansing arrest the deepening darkness of the stain that spread from my blood over the body of the nation I sought to make clean and great. For my life was not sacrificed boldly for good in a great cause. I did not fall in the front of the fight at Pharsalus. I did not sink when the skiff overturned at Alexandria; I was not caught by the enemy in Germany when I slipped through their lines in a Gallic dress; I did not lose heart when my soldiers lost their way in the trenches at Dyrrachium, though I lost the place itself. I risked my

life often enough to have deserved to lose it finally
in some nobler way than by the hands of such
butchers as made an end of me — fellows who knew
not where to strike to kill — who in three and
twenty thrusts could strike but one mortal blow.
I stabbed Cassius in the arm with my writing point,
but what could I do against so many? I saw a sea
of faces around me, cowardly pale faces of men who
got courage cheaply from their numbers. I saw
myself hemmed in by a hedge of steel knives and I
knew that my hour was come. I saw their faces,
but I would not let them see mine in death. I covered my head and my body with my garments and I
died decently, since there was nothing left but to
die. But I saw each one of those faces once more
and in the instant of death, within three years, and
I heard the lips of each dying man curse the hour
in which he had slain Cæsar. Even then I could
not forgive them, for the sake of the world that
might have been. I can pardon them for murdering
me as a man. I will never pardon them for murdering my unborn deeds. Therefore I say we dead men
both forgive and forgive not."

The conqueror's calm voice ceased and his dark,
thoughtful eyes fixed themselves as though staring
back through the mist of nineteen centuries to that
morning when he had entered the curia, laughing at
Spurinna's prophecies and unconsciously grasping in
his hand the unread note which might have saved
him from his fate. The look was sad, but the sad-

ness had long passed from the stage of present despair to regret for the past, and again to a melancholy curiosity to see what should yet become of the world.

The gentle Lionardo bowed his head gravely, as though admitting his companion spirit to be right.

" I understand that," he said. " We should not forget that you, the dictator, have not only to pardon the injuries done you in your person, but you have to forgive also the injuries done in your person to the world, or as we should say, to history. In my little way, had I been foully murdered I could more easily have forgiven my murderers than I could forgive one who should wantonly destroy my painting of the Last Supper. It is but an artist's vanity — that is to say, it is the satisfaction of the artist in his work. I cannot say what I might have felt had I been violently prevented from finishing that picture. It is unfinished still — it would be so had I lived until to-day. I think it is a part of the temperament of some artists not to finish, though they work for ever. They search after that which never was nor ever can be ; or, at all events, we searched in our day. I think it was better. We pursued the ideal. Modern painters pursue the real. I was not a realist because I painted grinning peasants for a study, and modelled heads of laughing women for my pleasure. We did not know what realism meant in those days, though people call us the founders of the realist school. We sought to represent nature's meaning ; men now try to copy what nature is. You, Cæsar, tried to make of men what heaven meant them to be, orderly, happy, prosperous within reasonable limits. Napoleon, like Alexander, ruined himself in attempting to create an unlimited empire out of unreasoning and often unwilling elements, believing that to command men's bodies was to command men's souls. You succeeded in spite of failure, for though you were killed at the most critical moment of your existence your work survived you; Napoleon failed in spite of success and survived to see the destruction of the greater part of his work, which followed almost immediately after he was conquered and taken prisoner."

"It was not his fault," said Cæsar. "Any more than my poor young general Gaius Curio was to blame when he was defeated by Juba. Napoleon's plans were admirably laid. He did not admire me. I admire him. If his work did not survive long, that is due to the fact that he was brought up as a soldier and had a soldier's instincts. I was trained as a statesman and attached more importance to the stability of the State than to extending its boundaries. I am called a conqueror; had I lived I should have been called a civiliser, and I would have earned the name. People do not reflect that Napoleon conquered a great extent of territory and rose to be emperor, with what at first were very inadequate means, and from the humblest beginnings. Charlemagne's conquests were more extended than mine,

far wider than Napoleon's, and yet he is not called
a conqueror. He is called the Great. He accomplished his work, which on the whole was a work
of civilisation, and much of it remains to this day;
at least his influence remains. The resuscitation of
the German Empire is largely due to the imperial
traditions which he founded; but the invention of a
French Empire was not due to his influence. It was
the spontaneous invention of an astounding individuality, tremendous in its immediate effects, formi-
dable so long as a personality could be found worthy
to be invested with the halo and attributes of Bonaparte, and bearing his name; but, on the whole it
was not a circumstance in the world's history to
which any great mass of popular or national tradition
will ever be attached, for the Napoleonic supremacy
was the impression of an individual upon nations;
it was never the expression of the nations by the
individual. The title, German Emperor, was sometimes in the Middle Ages a very empty word as
regards the man who so designated himself. I have
sometimes laughed to think that a dignity expressed
by my own name should degenerate to such a
mockery. But the thing meant by Cæsarism — Im-
perialism — was never to be despised. There was
always present in the minds of the chief nations a
consciousness of the force of a mighty tradition and
of a mass of traditions which they sought to embody
in the person of a leader, chosen for his qualities
and invested with the supreme power in virtue of

them. If he failed to make good his rights he was despised, but it was long before the belief was extinguished that at any moment, if he so chose and so laboured and fought, the German Emperor might again rule the world, even as Charlemagne had done. There was nothing dynastic in my conception of the Imperator, but the circumstances of the times made the institution a military one. I never meant that it should be that. I would not submit to a council of generals or a mob of guards, though when I could not persuade the people I was willing to submit to them. The empire which my nephew founded began to go to pieces when the soldiers outgrew the people in strength, and outranked them in social consequence — it fell because it was a military institution. The empire of the Germans — the Holy Roman Empire — was shattered on the death of Charlemagne, because it was intended to be dynastic, and his sons tore each other to pieces. It revived temporarily when some strong individuality rose to the surface; it alternately decayed and revived with the decadence of each old imperial family and the investiture of each new one. My empire — I never used the word in the modern sense — my command, was intended to be that of a democratic monarch, an expression now used emptily to flatter a king who is at the mercy of his rabble."

Cæsar laughed softly, as he had laughed many times in the nineteen centuries which had elapsed since his death, and there was something in the mirth of the great spirit that froze the conversation. Lady Brenda wished she were quite sure that it was Cæsar who had been talking and who sat there by her side with the golden laurels on his broad brow, his nervous white fingers playing constantly with the border of his purple mantle. Augustus was pondering on the words he had heard, while Gwendoline half wished to put another question. Diana leaned back in her deep chair and gazed at Lionardo's beautiful face from beneath her drooping lids, and she wondered inwardly whether it would not be better to be the quiet spirit of a great artist than the regretful ghost of a murdered conqueror.

## CHAPTER VII.

It was late in the afternoon and Lady Brenda was seated alone upon the terrace of the Castello del Gaudio. A little table stood beside her, on which lay some writing materials and a couple of sealed letters, ready for the post. The rest of the party had gone upon a distant excursion on the water, but Lady Brenda had stayed at home to attend to her correspondence, which was one of her chief amusements and occupied much of her time. She had not ventured as yet to speak in her letters of the remarkable things which were occurring in her son-in-law's house. She was too much puzzled and at the same time too much interested as yet to explain to herself what happened. The strange thing, in her opinion, was that the apparitions did not strike her as supernatural, nor startle her so much as she would have supposed that ghosts should have done. There was an ease, a simplicity, and a perfect naturalness in their appearance and manner that disarmed prejudice and forbade fear. She wished to see more of them, and as she sat looking out over the water, while the freshness of the evening crept up to the terrace, her mind dwelt on the subject and she thought of the characters she would most like to see.

In history, Francis the First of France was one of her favourites. If she had a rather modern tendency to laugh at romance, she had also, far down in her nature, a profound admiration of romantic characters in the past. Francis appealed to her taste. His courage, his beauty, his adventures, his victories, his tournaments and his love-affairs pleased her, and she had often said that if she had her choice of an historical person whom she might meet, she would choose him. She thought so now, and it seemed so possible, in the light of what had already happened, that she spoke aloud as though of a living person.

"Yes," said she, "I would choose Francis the First. I wonder whether I could not send him an invitation by one of the others?"

Almost immediately, she was aware that some one was on the terrace. She looked round and she saw that she had her wish. The king was advancing slowly towards her, his velvet cap in his hand. She was not startled now, and she smiled when she thought how easily and quickly her wish had been realised. Whether it was a dream or not, she was determined to enjoy it, and this particular dream was very pleasant. She knew now how much she had really wished to see the man who stood before her.

Lady Brenda was somewhat surprised, and somewhat disappointed at the looks of her visitor. King Francis was undoubtedly imposing in appearance, of a fine presence and altogether a most noticeable man. He was taller than other men, broad-shouldered and straight-limbed, erect and evidently of great strength. His short, jet-black hair and pointed beard of the same hue set off his brilliant colouring and piercing black eyes; his forehead showed a good capacity of mind, and his strong nose argued ambition and personal courage. But there was in his manner and looks a lack of that refinement which especially characterised the other dead men Lady Brenda had known at Castello del Gaudio. He wore the dress of his time, as did each of the others — long hose of grey silk, with embroidered shoes, and a close-fitting doublet of maroon-coloured velvet, his only ornament being a heavy gold chain hung about his neck.

Lady Brenda rose to receive her royal guest, and studied the details of his face and dress, illuminated by the glow of the setting sun, and thrown into relief against the cold background of the grey hills. Francis made a courteous salute and motioned Lady Brenda to be seated, himself taking the vacant armchair by her side.

"It is so good of you to have asked me here," he said, fixing his eyes upon her and speaking in clear manly tones.

"It was most kind of your majesty to take pity on my solitude," answered the lady, smiling.

"I never allowed a lady to be alone when it was in my power to bear her company," returned Francis.

"No," said Lady Brenda, rather nervously. "Your majesty was always fond of women's society. How can you live without it?"

"I can hardly be said to live at all — though it seems that I am practically alive now, within the circle of your son-in-law's enchantments — I should say perhaps that I only live in your smiles. Existence in our circumstances is very monotonous."

"You were so fond of brilliant changes, too," suggested Lady Brenda.

"Change! Ay — indeed I was. As a compensation I have not changed any clothes since the spring of 1547. That was three hundred and forty years ago. It is true that from what I have seen of more recent costumes I do not often regret the durability of my imperishable garments. As for the present fashions in the dress of ladies, something might be made of them by using respectable materials. I confess, however, I am surprised beyond measure at the stuffs you all wear — forgive my frankness — I seem to feel the affectation of too much simplicity in your appearance. Women as beautiful as you are could surely afford to dress better than women who are ugly."

"Your majesty is very flattering," said Lady Brenda, with a slight blush of pleasure. "But in regard to dress I beg to differ from you. It is much more the thing to be simple nowadays — one is much more respected. And for that matter, the ugly women could dress gorgeously, too."

"An ugly woman is ridiculous," said Francis. "The more she bedizens herself the more ridiculous she grows. But a beautiful woman can dress in cloth of gold and diamonds, and the richer her clothes, the more her beauty will shine."

"You loved to see beautiful women richly dressed — it is true. I have read of it in your majesty's life. But the times have changed since then. I imagine the sudden appearance of Madame d'Etampes, in full court dress — "

"Heaven forbid!" ejaculated Francis, crossing himself devoutly.

"I thought your majesty was much attached to her," said Lady Brenda, calmly.

"So I was — as the horse may be said to be much attached to the cart," answered the king. "I could not get rid of her. She drove me to distraction — but she drove me, nevertheless. There was nothing I could call my own, from the king's justice to the king's jewels. I verily believe that Anne did more harm than I did, which is saying something. The difference was that she did it with premeditation, whereas my evil deeds were chiefly of the lazy kind — sins of omission, perhaps of wrong conviction."

"Your majesty did not omit to burn alive a number of persons belonging to my religion," said Lady Brenda, stiffly.

"Madam," replied the king, "with your permission we will not discuss religious matters. I will only say that the Protestants with whom I had to do were Calvinists and that their church resembled yours about as nearly as a cellar resembles a court drawing-room — and I will take the liberty of point-

ing out that your Queen Elizabeth destroyed more
Catholics than I ever destroyed Protestants, and
that she did it in a more cruel way. I will not
speak of my fickle friend Henry of England. His
example adds too much weight to the argument.
Madam, I would rather speak of Mádame d'Etampes
than of religious matters — but I would infinitely
prefer to talk of neither."

"If your majesty will select a subject for conversation — " suggested Lady Brenda.

"Let us talk of yourself — "

"No — of yourself."

"Very well," said the king, leaning back in his
easy chair which his broad shoulders overlapped on
each side. "Let us talk of myself — though I suspect
that means that you wish to talk of the women I
loved. Does it not?"

"Their names are well known to history," said
Lady Brenda.

"Better than their characters. I do not think
people generally have any clear conception either of
Madame de Châteaubriand, Madame d'Etampes or
Madame de Brézé — "

"Your majesty loved Madame de Brézé?" inquired
Lady Brenda, with sudden curiosity.

"Diane was a beautiful woman — she was four and
twenty years of age when she came to beg for her
father's life and I was but five years older. We were
made for each other, and she was a wiser woman than
Anne d'Etampes, as Catherine found out. I could

have loved her, but I loved another — then. One whom I have long regretted."

"Françoise de Foix," said Lady Brenda in a low voice, for the king seemed moved.

" Yes — Madame de Châteaubriand. I can see her now with her fair gentle face, her golden hair, her soft blue eyes, her small graceful figure. Poor Françoise ! I can never forget her last look when she said good-bye in the garden. I thought little enough of it then and I called back Primaticcio as though nothing had happened. On my faith ! It was very heartless ! I hardly know how I could do it. Had I known how she was to die I would not have done it — no ! on my faith as a gentleman ! I would not have done it."

"Indeed," said Lady Brenda, " it would have been better for France had you treated Madame de Châteaubriand less cruelly. She might have wearied you a little, but she would not have betrayed you to the emperor."

"It is easy, when once you are dead — or if you live three centuries after an event — to say that a deed was cruel. Living people who read history look at it much as a character of the time looks at it after his death — coldly. It is impossible for you to realise exactly how matters stood, nor what I felt. I was bored, my dear madam — do you understand? Bored — "

"As most people are by what is too good for them," put in Lady Brenda.

"You are severe, but there is truth in what you say. I am only a dead king, after all, and I daresay I do not judge my own life much more leniently than you do, now that it is over. But pray reflect that when a woman bores a man, the case is serious indeed."

"Very," answered Lady Brenda, gravely. "It has recently been said, however, that only people who themselves are bores are bored by others. I mean no disrespect to your majesty; but I believe that if your majesty's mother, of blessed memory, had not conceived the idea of presenting to you Mademoiselle de Heilly, you would not have wearied poor Françoise as you did, till she began to weary you."

"Yes, madam," said the king. "It is also true that if the serpent had not talked of apples to our mother Eve, Paradise would have continued to be a terrestrial institution. But the serpent was a great busybody, and Eve liked apples."

"It seems to me that your majesty then plays the part of Eve," remarked Lady Brenda.

"Can you doubt that if the serpent had addressed himself to Adam instead of to his consort, he would have been equally successful?"

"No," said Lady Brenda. The king laughed.

"It would be very singular if you did," he answered. "Madame d'Angoulême treated me with the politics of the serpent — and I must say in justice that a more beautiful apple was never selected by the devil himself. It amused me at the time. Unfortunately, when we are dead the heart begins to live."

"How strange!" exclaimed Lady Brenda. "I should have thought that it would be the reverse!"

"You would have supposed that after death the affections are wholly destroyed? No. That is not my experience. I was heartless in my lifetime. I treated Françoise abominably, and I made Anne de Heilly's miserable husband Duc d'Etampes. I made Françoise return the jewels I had given her, because Anne wanted them. She broke all the monograms out of the settings before she sent them back, and I remember being glad that she did it. I knew that Anne was betraying me, and betraying France daily, and yet I let her power increase, because I disliked the annoyance of another separation — and during all that time Françoise was languishing in her dungeon. No one told me of that, however. But when I was dead I found that I had a heart, and my heart persecutes me. I love Françoise. — Faith! madam, I do not know why I tell you these things!"

"Pray go on," said Lady Brenda, sympathetically. "Your majesty is not the first person who has made me confidences."

"I am sure of that," answered the king. "You have a sympathetic face. Women with blue eyes can feel for others. Françoise de Foix had blue eyes — Anne's eyes were dark."

"Are they both here?" asked Lady Brenda.

"No," said Francis, listlessly. "I shall never see them again. Anne loved me for the gifts I gave her, and there are no gifts here. Françoise loved me for myself. That was not much, was it? I took myself from her and she never forgave me. She was right, I deserved not to be forgiven, but I did not find out how sorry I was until I came where I have time to be sorry for ever. I am tormented with a new sense which in life I did not possess — the sense of an undying affection for that lady."

"How very sad!" exclaimed Lady Brenda.

"It is horrible. Men should not suppose that while they are alive they can be heartless with impunity. When they are dead the heart will awake and cause them bitter anguish — all the more bitter because it is a pain to which they are not accustomed. People have called me perjurer because I would not go back to Madrid. There is less reason for that accusation than for the reproach of heartlessness I incurred. Charles knew well enough that the treaty he imposed upon me could never be carried out, unless my chivalric instincts made it possible. He reckoned on my stupidity — or rather on my stupid adherence to the details of an antiquated code. What he really wanted was my marriage with Eleonora. He got it. I more than atoned for refusing to return to captivity by letting him go freely through my kingdom on his way to Ghent. Anne advised me to put him into the Bastille. If I had been the perjured wretch people have since described me I would have followed her advice. I was a better gentleman than Charles. Perhaps that is not saying much. In my lifetime I aspired to be the first gentleman in

France, or in the world. My faults were such as his majesty, Charles the Sour, could not well comprehend. But he comprehended my virtues in such a way as to attempt to play upon them to his own advantage on every possible occasion. I generally chose those occasions to lapse from virtue — as when I broke my Madrid promise. He had no right to expect me to sacrifice my kingdom and the welfare of my people to my personal convictions concerning the code of honour."

The king laughed, and in his laughter there was a coarse element which struck very disagreeably upon Lady Brenda's refined ears.

"You say nothing?" continued the king, as he noticed her silence.

"I do not understand politics," said Lady Brenda, wisely.

"I fear I did not understand them either," laughed Francis, good-humouredly. "The lady who ruled my son and my son's wife always said so. I was persuaded that I understood everything when I was alive — and when a man holds such an opinion of himself he will always find fools to agree with him and women to govern him. Had I known more of myself I might have avoided many complications — and poor Françoise would not have died in the vaults of a Breton castle."

"Perhaps there need never have been any Françoise for your majesty in that case," suggested Lady Brenda.

The king looked at her curiously as though not fully understanding her, or fancying that she was jesting.  But Lady Brenda was grave and serious.

"You mean, madam, that I should have loved the queen, because she was queen — first Claude and then Eleonora?  That is a very singular notion, but I presume that ideas have changed since my day."

"Perhaps not so much as they ought to change," returned Lady Brenda.  "There was a publicity in those days — "

"We were more honest."

"You had less to fear."

"We were more in earnest," said the king.

"Then you were worse — because you were more in earnest in doing wrong."

"Perhaps; but we were misguided by bad example — "

"Which your majesty strengthened by doing openly and ostentatiously what ought not to be done at all."

"I think we were bolder," objected Francis.  "If we did wrong we were not afraid to do it in the face of the world."

"That is not a high form of courage," replied the inexorable lady.

"Nevertheless, it was courage," laughed the king.  "But I will not discuss the question.  I am sufficiently persuaded of my own badness without further argument.  On the other hand a man is never so much in need of a word of encouragement and appreciation as when he is conscious of not deserving it."

"Am I to pay you compliments?" asked Lady Brenda, laughing in her turn. "It would not be hard. History has found much to say in praise of your majesty's reign. You were generous on many occasions — and you did much for the arts."

"By employing jewellers to make trinkets for Françoise and Anne. When any of those things are found nowadays they bring good prices, because they belong to the epoch of Francis the First. Yes — my name is connected with the arts. I meant it should be that of a conqueror and I am most famous for a phrase I did not pronounce when I was conquered. Fate, madam, is ironical. Perhaps I am more famous for having lost the day at Pavia than I should have been had I won it. If Bayard had been with me, instead of Bonnivet I should have had the victory. But Bayard was dead — poor Bayard! He was the truest friend I ever had."

"Have you found men truer friends than women?" asked Lady Brenda.

"Women have the qualities which attract without retaining affection — men have the faculty of retaining without attracting."

"What does that mean?"

"It means that I always expected to find friends in the women I loved and was always disappointed; and that, though I was not attracted to seek the friendship of man, yet the few men who were my friends were on the whole very faithful to me. Bayard was one — poor Lautrec, Françoise's brother, was another. Louis de Brézé was faithful —"

"He received a poor return," said Lady Brenda.

"Madam," returned the king, with much suavity, "he was old. His wife was young. My son Henri was very wild. What would you have? Diane did very well."

"It was abominable," exclaimed Lady Brenda, hotly. "Diane de Poitiers might almost have been your majesty's son's mother!"

"It was precisely because she was older than he that she had such an influence over him," explained Francis. "Beware of reading histories in which everybody is abused for doing in one age what is considered immoral in another; in that way you get a very imperfect idea of the times. It would be as sensible to say that you think me very vulgar for wearing this dress instead of a coat and a tall hat. I cannot get rid of this dress — for I lived in it. In the same way, we of my time cannot get rid of the ideas of our epoch. We were brought up in them, we lived in them and we died in them. Indeed I think we were already improving. In a moral way, I daresay I do not compare badly with Henry the Eighth of England, with Roderigo Borgia, with Giovanni Maria Visconti, or even with my old enemy Charles Quint."

"Perhaps," admitted Lady Brenda. "The difference would have been greater had you prevented the attachment of your heir to Diane de Poitiers, and had you had no such affairs of the heart as caused the destruction of Madame de Châteaubriand — and your majesty's destruction by Madame d'Etampes."

"As for Diane," said the king, "Catherine did not object to her husband's attachment, as you call it. Honestly, would you, in her place, have thought it worth while to be so particular?"

"I? Indeed I would never have spoken to him again — though he was my husband!"

"Really?" exclaimed the king, with a rough laugh. "Are you so severe as that, madam?"

"I cannot understand loving a man who does not love me," replied Lady Brenda, firmly. "It is enough to make one severe."

"But suppose that you had never loved him at all—"

"I would not have married him, even for the honour of being your majesty's daughter-in-law. If I had been married to him, supposing that he loved me, and if he afterwards showed me that he did not — in such a way as that — I would never speak to him again."

"Consider what would have been the difficulties of Catherine's position had she refused to pardon Henri," objected Francis. "She must have led a miserable life. Diane was powerful. She ruled France after my death."

"I would have been divorced from the king, and he could then have married Madame de Brézé."

"Divorce in those days was not easy. We had prejudices which did not permit us to imitate our brother of England. We still regarded matrimony as a bond — a view of the rite which seems nowadays to be falling into disrepute."

"Oh! I do not think so at all," exclaimed Lady Brenda, in a tone of conviction.

"No? And yet divorces can be had very easily. It appears to me to be only an ingenious method of legalising the very faults with which you reproach me."

"On the contrary it is a human mode of escape for women who are ill-treated by their husbands. I am sure, if Brenda treated me as you — your majesty — treated Queen Claude and then Queen Eleonora, I would get divorced at once."

"But then there would be many men who would be certain to be divorced from every wife they married. A man loves a woman; he marries her; he tires of her and begins to love some one else; his wife at once divorces him and he is then at liberty to marry the next woman. She, in her turn, divorces him — and so on, so long as he can persuade any woman to accept his hand. It is convenient for the man. It will also lead to fraud, for people will only have to say, by agreement, that they are maltreated and they are instantly at liberty. It is bad, madam, very bad. It is better that a few individuals, like myself, if you please, should be sinful, than that in order to legalise sin for the few it should be legally placed within reach of the many."

"I do not think that is the case at all," said Lady Brenda, who was puzzled by the king's argument, but not convinced. "I mean that if a man really and truly treats his wife badly she ought to have some redress."

"She has. I believe that a woman may bring a suit against her husband ; she may obtain a legal separation, and he is obliged to support her. Why should she wish to marry again?"

"If she is young, why should her whole life be ruined by being tied to a brute? Why may she not be happy with some one else?"

"Because if you make it possible for her, you make it possible for the next woman, who perhaps was treated badly, but less badly than the first — and then it is possible for another who has hardly suffered at all, and at last it is possible for every man or woman who chances for a moment to prefer some other person to his or her wife or husband. It is not that in some cases it would not be a positive good ; it is that the remedy you provide for such cases soon ends by creating cases in very great numbers, because the remedy is an agreeable one."

"Yes — but it is very hard for the woman who is ill-treated, all the same," said Lady Brenda, unwilling to relinquish her defence.

"Very —- I agree with you," replied the king. "I made many women unhappy in that way myself. If the whole world, in regard to marriage, were directed by one sublimely wise individual, who should be really able to judge when divorce is just and necessary and to dictate the terms of it, the institution would be a good and wise one. All government is but an attempt to combine the best faculties of the many into such a working shape as may represent the

imaginary action of one sublimely wise individual.
Hitherto the attempt has never wholly succeeded.
The government of the many has never been so good
as that of one or two exceptionally good and talented
autocrats who have really lived. Owing to the rarity
of such individuals it is found that, as a whole, it is
better to adopt the form of government by the many,
where at least there is some sort of balance maintained
between the bad and the good sides of human nature.
I myself believed in myself so much that I founded
the autocratic despotism of the kings of France,
when the Parliament gave their verdict in accordance
with my instructions against Charles de Bourbon. It
was the first thoroughly autocratic act accomplished
by a French monarch, and but for Louis de Brézé,
Diane's husband, it would not have been brought
about, as you probably know. It was no wonder
that I pardoned her father, when her husband saved
me from destruction. I pardoned almost every one
concerned in the conspiracy except the Constable
himself. Fortunately he was killed in the storming
of Rome, or he would still have given me trouble.
He had the devil in his body, and would have given
me no peace. Madame d'Etampes would have helped
him, and did, as she afterwards helped the emperor,
out of sheer hatred for Madame de Brézé."

"So I have heard," said Lady Brenda. "It is an
instance of the advantages your majesty obtained
from the connection with Madame d'Etampes."

" To carry out your theory, madam, I should have

divorced Eleonora, and married Anne in the face of the emperor. The result would have been startling."

" Yes. Madame d'Etampes would have been satisfied and you would have had her for a friend instead of an enemy. Only — according to my theory, the divorce should have been demanded by the queen, and not by your majesty. At all events the treaty of Crespy would never have been signed."

" It would have been a pity if it had not been signed, though no one could have foreseen that," answered the king. " Madame d'Etampes wanted to make a great man of my poor boy Charles at the expense of his brother, out of spite against Diane de Poitiers, by marrying him to the emperor's daughter or niece, as the emperor pleased; and to obtain this she persuaded the emperor to relinquish finally his claims upon Burgundy. Charles died, and the marriage never took place, but Burgundy remained French, and Henry ultimately overcame the emperor in at least one campaign, though he failed in others. Had he taken my advice about the Guise he might have done better. His prospects were not injured by anything I did, nor by the peace of Crespy. It is not fair to impute his failures to Madame d'Etampes, however much she tried to do him injury. She was not successful, or she would not have been obliged to leave the court after my death."

" Poor woman ! " exclaimed Lady Brenda. " It must have been very hard for her to leave it all! However, she had laid up a very pretty fortune."

" An she never loved me in the least. She was not to be pitied, for she got all she wanted in this world."

" No. I pity Françoise far more," answered Lady Brenda. " You say you never see her now ? "

" Never — I have sought her long," said the king, sadly. His whole manner changed from a tone of half cynical, half buoyant good-humour to the expression of a profound sadness, as indeed occurred every time he mentioned the ill-fated countess. " You cannot imagine," he continued, " how the thought of her dominates me, nor how hopeless is the passion of a dead man for a dead woman. It is a result, such a love, and it is irreparable, as results most often are. You who live and love cannot know what it is to love only when the body is in the grave, long crumbled into dust, and to love without hope. You who can still repair your mistakes, you cannot realise what it is to exist where there is no reparation. You who lightly forget, or remember only when it is convenient, you cannot guess at the agony of a state where you must perpetually remember everything and be conscious of the shame of a fault for centuries at a time."

" Would it be any relief for you to see her now ? "

" Yes," answered Francis, thoughtfully, " I think it would be a relief. I may be wrong, but I fancy I should be more peaceful if I could hear her say she forgave me. Perhaps she would not say it."

" I don't know," said Lady Brenda. " I think

she would. It may be possible to bring about a
meeting now, owing to these astral things, or whatever Augustus calls them. I will ask him."

The king was silent and seemed deep in thought.
The sun had long disappeared and as they talked the
twilight deepened into night, the broad water turned
black and grey in streaks and bands, and then at last
all black, while one by one the stars shone out above
as though angels were lighting the candles at the
altars of heaven. The soft land breeze floated down
from the mountains and whispered over the terrace,
and stirred the thin lace which Lady Brenda had
thrown over her head and about her neck. The dead
king sat motionless by her side, his head sunk on his
breast, his great white hands clasped together upon
one knee. Lady Brenda was thinking that the party
stayed long upon their excursion and was wishing
that they would return; and then her thoughts came
back in ready sympathy to the being by her side, to
his sufferings and regrets, his overwhelming memories
of the past and his slender hopes for the future.

As they sat there side by side a woman in a black
mantle came slowly towards them across the terrace,
her long mourning garments trailing noiselessly
behind her. The dark hood had fallen back from
her head, and the light from the open windows of
the drawing-room fell full upon her fair and pale
young face. Slowly and noiselessly she came forward, but though the king did not look up, he
seemed to feel her presence, and his hands twisted

each other, while his broad chest heaved with excitement.

She came and stood before him, a frail, fair, blue-eyed woman with a sorrowful face and dishevelled golden hair, and she looked down on the dead king's bent head.  Suddenly he sprang to his feet and threw out his arms as though he would have clasped her in them.  But she drew swiftly back from him and faced him, looking sadly into his eyes.

"Ah, sire," she cried in a strange, heart-broken voice, "why were you so unkind, so cruel to me?"

"Françoise, for the love of Heaven forgive me!" groaned the wretched spirit, stretching out his white hands towards the woman.

"Forgive you?" she echoed, sadly.  "Is that all?  I forgave you long ago.  It is not all — to forgive, even when we are dead, you and I."

"It is not all, Françoise — there is more — more than I can say.  I love you still," cried the king, springing forward.

"No — no — no!  You never loved me — it was only I who loved, and loved to death, too well, too long, too sinfully!"

With streaming eyes the dead woman looked despairingly at the dead man, and then with a cry she turned and fled through the soft dusk into the darkness beyond.  But Francis stood still, looking sorrowfully after her, his hands hanging listlessly by his sides, his eyes moistened with tears.  Then he turned to Lady Brenda.

"And so it is," he said, "that our sins pursue us for ever and cannot be forgotten. I tell you, I love her — I never really loved another woman, and I know it now. But she can never know it, until all this is over. The sin of loving her pursues me even in death — ah, madam, it is all too great and deep for me to understand."

"I am sorry she came — indeed I am," said Lady Brenda. "She has made you more unhappy than you were before."

"Yes," answered the dead man. "When we are alive we often long for something that is not good, and when we have it, we are disappointed. But when we are dead we are doomed to long for the same things, and when they are given to us they are more bitter in one moment than all the pains of ten lifetimes. If pain could kill us now, we should die every hour, every minute."

"You had so often wished to see her," said Lady Brenda, sympathetically.

"Indeed, that is true. I had wished it as I never wished anything in my life. You have seen me get my wish — you have seen my suffering. Do you think that such pain changes us? No, we can never change. What we have made ourselves we must remain, who knows? perhaps for ever. We suffer, and have no rest. All that the heart feels from boyhood to old age, we feel at every instant of this eternity. Do you wonder that when it is possible we rejoice at meeting the living, and speaking with them, and dreaming for one moment that we are alive again, and subject to change?"

"But there is hope still left to you," argued the lady.

"Hope — but such hope as you would not call hope at all. Do not speak to a dead man of hope, madam. It means the end. It is not hope, but doubt, for with the certainty of change, when time shall have worn itself out, there is the indescribable fear, the agony of uncertainty, the horror of what that change may be."

Lady Brenda shuddered and drew her shawl more closely around her. In the distance below she heard the sound of voices, Gwendoline's ringing laugh and Chard's deep tones as he called to the sailors. The boat had come back and the party were landing. The king held out his hand.

"I thank you for this pleasant hour, madam," he said, simply.

"Your majesty is not going?" asked Lady Brenda, almost ludicrously forgetful, for the moment, that her visitor was only a ghost. But she started as she took his hand which chilled her to the bone.

"Yes, I am going. But we shall meet again very soon," he answered, and in a moment he had left her.

## CHAPTER VIII.

"I HAVE made up my mind that I will never be surprised at anything again," said Lady Brenda, as the
party sat at their mid-day breakfast on the day after
the events last recorded. She had been telling the
rest about the king's visit.

"You are quite right," answered Augustus. "You
are quite right, my dearly beloved mother-in-law.
Surprise is nothing but a disturbance in the balance
of the faculties. Now, when a woman possesses faculties like yours it is a pity that they should not be
always balanced."

"Really, Augustus — "

"Quite so," continued Chard, imperturbably. "When
once you have discovered that we are likely to meet
dead men who talk very agreeably, almost every day,
it is as well to make the most of your opportunities.
The phenomenon will probably be explained some day;
meanwhile let us enjoy it as much as we can. It
would be very pleasant if these charming people could
dine with us, but I gather from various things that
they do not dine at all, nor even breakfast. Who is
going on the expedition this afternoon?"

"We all are," said the three ladies, with a una-
nimity as rarely found in the country when a walk

is proposed, as it is general in town when there is a ball.

They had determined to take a long walk among the mountains, and, as the day was comparatively cool, they started immediately after breakfast. Augustus led them up the rocky path, past their little stone hut which was the centre of his experiments, and along the steep side of the mountain over the sea. They were all four good walkers and fond of exercise.

"It would be very amusing if some of our friends would walk with us," remarked Diana, as she picked her way over the rocks.

"Delightful," said Gwendoline, steadying herself with her stick upon the summit of a small boulder, and looking at the view.

"Dear me!" exclaimed Lady Brenda, "who can that be? Do you see, Augustus? Such a very odd dress! Do they still wear three-cornered hats in this part of the world — and brown coats with brass buttons?"

"He is a very big man," said Augustus, eyeing the stranger, who was coming down the rocks and was not more than a hundred yards from them. "A very big man indeed. He must be some old peasant. We will talk to him."

They walked on and in a few seconds came up to the solitary pedestrian. Augustus spoke to him. He was of colossal size, with a huge head surmounted by an old full-bottomed wig and a three-cornered hat. He wore knee-breeches and stockings, with stout buckled shoes, and he carried in his hand a huge oak stick, which looked more like a club. Augustus addressed him in the dialect of the hills.

"Me fat'u piacè, m'andecat' a'ndusse wa p'annà a Pussità?"

"Sir," replied the stranger in English, in a loud, gruff voice, "from your appearance I take you to be an Englishman, like myself."

"I beg your pardon," said Augustus, very much surprised. "There are so few of our countrymen about here—"

"Your surprise is venial sir," returned the other, fixing his dark eyes on Chard's face. "I am not only an Englishman, but a dead Englishman; and, what is more, sir, I believe that a dead Englishman is better than a live Italian. I am Samuel Johnson."

"Dr. Johnson!" exclaimed the four living people in astonishment.

"Do not doctor me, sir," roared the great man in tremendous tones. "Do not doctor me, sir, for I am past doctoring!" He glared a moment at the party and then suddenly broke into a peal of laughter, in which the others soon joined.

"If I cannot frighten you," he continued, good-naturedly, "I can at least excite your merriment. But, sir, I have seen little boys in Scotland tremble at the sight of this stick."

"You have found it, then?" said Augustus. "I congratulate you."

"Yes sir, they stole it, the villains; I always said so."

In a few minutes they all proceeded on their walk. Augustus stated who he was and presented Dr. Johnson to his three companions. The doctor showed the greatest delight and explained that he had just met the party of dead men, who were passing the afternoon among the rocks. He was intimate with them, he said, and they had told him all about Chard and his experiments. Indeed the doctor had taken the road towards the Castello del Gaudio in hopes of meeting the inhabitants of the castle.

"I wonder," said Augustus, "that you should care to walk here — you who are so fond of trees."

"Since I have hung loose on the world," replied Johnson, "and have been at liberty to walk where I please, and as long as I please, I have grown tolerant of contrast. It is one thing to be obliged to traverse a country where there is no timber; it is another matter to be independent of those laws which, while we are alive, force us to spend some time in moving from place to place."

"Do you think," asked Lady Brenda, "that when one has as many beautiful things as one likes, one begins to like ugly things, just for a change?"

"No, madam," said Johnson. "I do not like ugly things, but I have learned that there are no ugly things in nature. In living persons the impression of the ugliness of external objects is purely relative; since we know that an African negro in the natural state sees more beauty in a black woman of his own race than in a white woman of ours, and that with ourselves the contrary is the case. But if the negro be taken to a country inhabited by white men and women, he soon comes to regard the white woman as the type of what a woman should be, and before long he will see beauty where he formerly supposed that there was nothing but ugliness."

"But of course white women are more beautiful than black!" exclaimed Lady Brenda.

"When you say that they are more beautiful, you imply that their beauty is contrasted with the less beauty of black women," continued Johnson. "For since you employ a comparative form in describing the one, it may reasonably be supposed that you find something in the other with which the first may be compared. Indeed, comparison is at the root of all intelligence, and, if other things be alike, the man who is able to compare any two things with greater accuracy than his neighbour, is the wiser of the two; for, if we suppose that two men are equally able to remember that which they have learned, it is clear that he who is able to discern the comparative value of the different things he knows, possesses of the two the greater facility for using his knowledge. It may be doubted whether Sir Isaac Newton possessed a more remarkable memory than Lord Chesterfield; but it cannot be questioned that, whereas, in the latter, the power of comparison merely produced a brilliant wit, in Newton the power was so great that it produced a very great man and a very great discoverer."

"Is it fair to compare a statesman with a scientist?" asked Diana, as the party paused in their walk.

"If statesmanship is a science, it is fair," answered the doctor, looking down at the young girl.

"Statesmanship must be the greatest of sciences," said Augustus. "There are a hundred scientists to-day alive, who are commonly called great. There are certainly not three statesmen alive to whom the epithet is applied now, or will be applied when they are dead."

"You are quite right, sir," answered Johnson.

"I suppose there is less room for them," remarked Gwendoline.

"I do not know," returned her husband. "There are hundreds of important places in which a man might distinguish himself, if we count together all the important governments in the world. If great statesmen were plenty, there would be no reason why a whole government should not consist of great men. Almost every university in the world pretends to boast of possessing one or two great men, and nobody seems able to prove that they are not really as great as is pretended."

"Scientists," said the doctor, "or men of science, as we called them in my day, are in a position which differs wholly from that of statesmen; for while the former are privileged to speak without acting, the latter are often compelled to act without explaining themselves in words. A man is not to be held responsible for his convictions, provided that he does not act upon them; but the actions of a statesman produce results of the sort which soon become manifest to all men and which influence the lives of mankind, so that mankind has the right to judge him. If all the theories of men of science were subjected to the test of experiment upon the *corpus vile* of whole nations, it may be doubted whether popular opinion would continue to be as tolerant of scientific opinion as it now is; for though one man might succeed in rearing men from a litter of monkeys, the next experimenter might very likely, by a small error, reduce men to the state of apes. One man rises up, and declares to the people that they must believe in him, but that, in order to believe in him, it is necessary that they should not believe in God. He exalts science to the position of the Deity, and tells people that they must worship it; but it is his own science which he exalts, and not that of his adversary, who has invented a different kind of idol. No, sir, science is a good thing so long as it is useful; but when, in its present state, it takes upon itself to tamper with so enormous and vital a matter as the belief of man in his Creator, it is pernicious, it is dangerous, and it will soon become destructive."

"You see, Augustus," said Lady Brenda, triumphantly, "I always told you that it was great rubbish."

"My dear mother-in-law," returned Chard, "you forget that I belong to the brotherhood of the Ignorantines. My principal conviction is that nobody knows anything.

"Sir," said Johnson, "you are not far wrong. One of the greatest mistakes of these days is the attempt to make people believe that they can know everything. Science cannot be made popular; for if it be within the reach of every one, and so simple that everybody can understand it, why then many persons could have discovered its secrets long ago; but if it be indeed a hard matter to understand, it must be reserved for those whose intellect is equal to so great an effort, and it is useless to make that popular which the people can never comprehend. If those men, who occupy themselves by attempting to substitute in others their own theories in the place of a wholesome religion, would confine their efforts to communicating such knowledge as they possess without endeavouring to destroy that belief which excites their unreasoning hatred, they might indeed deserve some credit; but their arguments are of so partial a nature, their language is so vehement and unrestrained, that we are forced to believe that they are animated rather by a desire to destroy religion than by a legitimate wish to extend the sphere of human knowledge and to do good to humanity by teaching that which is useful."

"Yes," said Augustus, "there is no reason why we should not learn the little that can be known, without upsetting religion. I think some modern scientists might read the life of Pascal with advantage, not to say that of Newton. I do not suppose that any of our living professors pretend to be as great as either of those two, who were extremely religious men."

"Pascal," replied the doctor, "was a tremendous young man. He discovered the weight of the atmosphere, he invented a calculating machine, he found the law of cycloids, he wrote like a father of the early Church, and he instituted the first omnibus that ever ran. A man cannot do more than that in thirty-nine years, but he did most of these things before he was five and twenty. As for Sir Isaac Newton he wrote a book of 'Arguments in Proof of a Deity' and a chronology of ancient history, both of which are much better than is commonly supposed."

"Dear me!" exclaimed Gwendoline, "I never knew that Pascal invented the omnibus. He must have had a great deal of common sense."

"Both common and uncommon, madam," answered Johnson, "and I venture to say that the common sense which can invent the omnibus is as valuable to mankind as the uncommon intelligence which is able to conceive that the atmosphere may have weight and that the cycloid curve may be reduced to a law."

"Yes," said Augustus, "but the weight of the atmosphere is more interesting than the invention of a public carriage. I should think that a man with a big intellect would prefer to study big things."

"No, sir," answered Johnson. "It is not more interesting, but it is more attractive. When a man

of science discovers a lacuna in his wisdom, he
makes haste to fill up the breach with a new theory,
in the framing of which he at once enjoys the pleasures of imagination and the satisfaction which is felt
in the exercise of ingenuity. His theory will stop
the hole in the wall until it is worn out, or until
some one finds a better theory to substitute in its
place; and those portions of his work which are the
result of knowledge acquired independently of the
imagination, even if not very perfect, will always
afford him some ground for congratulating himself
upon his own abilities as compared with those of
others. But the case of the man who occupies himself in endeavouring to better the condition of his
fellow-men by imparting to them some of the results
of his study, is very different. For, while the man of
speculative science acts upon ideas, theories, and the
like, the student of the applied sciences acts upon
things and in a high degree upon people. It is
clear that the immediate results produced by the
man who acts upon living men are, in the present,
incalculably more important than those brought about
by the student who speculates upon the origin of
the human race, or upon the ultimate nature of
human happiness; although it is true that where
speculation results in discoveries capable of being
widely and advantageously applied, the man of
science attains to an importance which cannot be
over-estimated. When Pascal discovered that the
atmosphere has weight, he laid the foundation for

the invention of the first steam-engine ; when Newton
established the nature of the laws of gravity, he gave
to science the means of weighing the earth, and on
his method of prime and ultimate ratios is founded
the most subtle, powerful and universally applicable
system of calculation now known.   But there are few
who combine common and uncommon sense in the
same degree as those two men; and we may safely
say that those persons who act upon men directly, as
statesmen, or upon things, as engineers, are the men
who, in the present, make their influence most widely
felt.   Any great railway of the world transports from
place to place in one month, affording thereby immense facilities to their lives, a greater number of
people than in the whole world have read, or perhaps
ever heard of, Mr. Darwin's book upon the origin
of man, or Professor Kant's work on the criticism
exercised by pure reason."

" The only measure of force, of which we know,
is the result produced," said Augustus.

" And will any one venture to compare the result
produced upon the lives, the wealth and the prosperity of mankind by so small a modification of an
existing machine as is comprised in the invention of
the marine compound engine of to-day, with the
result produced by Mr. Darwin's researches concerning the origin of man ?   The simple idea of using
the steam twice over in cylinders of different sizes
has revolutionised modern commerce, has been the
death-warrant of thousands of sailing vessels, and has

caused thousands of steamships to be built, employing many millions of men and upsetting all old-
fashioned notions of trade. But I will venture to
say that the theory which teaches people to believe
that they are descended from monkeys has neither
contributed to the happiness of mankind nor in any
way increased the prosperity of nations. If it possesses merits as a theory, which may or may not be
questioned, it can certainly never be said to have
any application bearing upon the lives of men; and
though it will survive as a remarkable monument of
the ingenuity, the imagination and the industry of a
learned man, it will neither inspire humanity at large
with elevating and strengthening thoughts, nor will
it help individuals in particular to better their condition or to surmount the ordinary difficulties of every-
day life."

"I should think not!" exclaimed Lady Brenda in
a tone of conviction. "But of course one has to pretend to believe what everybody else does — or at least
one must let other people believe what they please.
It makes life so much easier!"

"Madam," said Johnson, sternly, "it is always
easier to avoid a responsibility than to assume it."

"Oh dear! I did not mean to be so serious!" rejoined the lady. "But I really could not take upon
myself to persuade all the people I meet in society
that they are not descended from monkeys, when
they assure me that they are, you know."

"No, madam," answered the doctor, with a twinkle

in his eye. " So nice a matter should be referred to a court of claims, and the candidates for the honours of monkeydom should be judged upon their own merits."

" And if approved, be declared tenants in tail for ever," suggested Augustus.

" Sir," said Johnson, almost angrily, " puns are the last resource of exhausted wit, as swearing is the refuge of those whose vocabulary is too limited to furnish them with a means of expressing their anger or disappointment."

"I beg your pardon," returned Augustus, smiling. " Wit is much exhausted in our day."

" It must be, sir," answered the doctor, who did not seem quite pacified. But the three ladies laughed.

" Won't you let me make a pun?" asked Lady Brenda, beseechingly.

" No, madam. Not if I can help it," returned Johnson, smiling and resuming his good-humour. "I ask your pardon, sir," he continued, turning to Augustus. "I did not mean to imply that your wit was exhausted."

" It is, I assure you. So pray do not mention the matter," answered Chard, laughing. " The unconscious ratiocination of my feeble brain found expression in words."

" Some day," said the doctor, "I would like to discuss with you the nature of wit and humour. At present the digression would be too great, for we

were speaking of men of science, in whom wit is
rarely abundant and in whom humour is as conspicu-
ous by its absence as speech in a whale. But I
should except Pascal, who was a very witty man.
You would find great advantage in his acquaintance."

"Do you often see him?" asked Diana, eagerly.
She loved and admired the writer as distinguished
from the scientist.

"Sometimes," answered Johnson. "He is a most
unclubable man. He loves solitude and his own
thoughts, which, to tell the truth, are very good, so
that he is not altogether to be blamed."

They walked together along the ridge of the
mountain, stopping now and then to rest a little and
to look at the wonderful views which were unfolded
to their eyes almost at every step. The bare brown
rocks over which they climbed contrasted strongly
with the deep blue of the sea far below and with the
grand sweep of the Gulf of Salerno in the distance,
where the green and marshy plain beyond the white
city stretched back from the water towards the Calabrian hills. The sun was not hot at that high eleva-
tion and the sea breeze swept the rocks and blew cool
in the faces of the party. Suddenly the mountain
path came abruptly to an end as they reached the
foot of a high and inaccessible rock. It was evident
that they must go round it, and turning to the left
they ascended a little channel which led up through
the boulders. The sound of voices reached their
ears, and Gwendoline paused to listen.

"We shall find our friends here," said Dr. Johnson. "They must be just beyond that corner."

They hastened forward and soon they came upon the strange company, seated together in a half circle where there was an indentation in the hill. Cæsar was there, and Francis, Heine and Chopin and one other, whom they had not seen before. He was a man in white armour, complete save that he wore no helmet; a slender, graceful man seated in an easy attitude, his chin resting on his hand. His face was of calm, angelic beauty, pale and refined, but serene and strong. Short curls of chestnut hair clustered about his white brow and his deep-set blue eyes looked quietly at the advancing party.

"Who is the man in armour?" asked Gwendoline of Dr Johnson in a low voice as they approached.

"A very good man, madam," he answered. "That is no less a person, madam, than Pierre du Terrail, Seigneur de Bayard, known as the Chevalier Bayard, without fear and without reproach. A man, madam, of whom it is impossible to say whether he is most to be revered for his virtue, admired for his prowess, or imitated for his fidelity to his sovereign."

"Really!" exclaimed Gwendoline. But there was not time for more. The dead men rose to their feet together, and greetings were exchanged between them and their living acquaintances. King Francis presented Bayard to Lady Brenda, who in her turn presented Gwendoline, Diana and Augustus to the king.

"We feared you were not coming," said the latter, smiling pleasantly. "Indeed, we were planning the siege of your castle, and Bayard had volunteered to lead the forlorn hope."

"If we had taken him prisoner," said Augustus, "the ladies would not have let him go as Ludovico did, when he rushed into Milan alone."

"Indeed," said the chevalier, "I fear I should not have had the courage to offer a ransom."

"Let us go on," suggested Gwendoline. "I like to see the water — then we can all sit down and talk. "You are not tired?" she asked, looking inquiringly round the group.

"No," laughed Heine, "we are indestructible. We have not even the satisfaction of wearing out our shoes and of getting new ones. I will show you the way to a beautiful spot."

They all moved forward together, skirting the boulders for a couple of hundred yards. Then suddenly they came in sight of the sea, between the steep sides of the gorge. Heine and Johnson had gone in front and were already gazing at the view as the others came up.

## CHAPTER IX.

HEINE was standing against a huge boulder on the edge, looking down at the moving waters. Seated on the other side of the path, Dr. Johnson slowly turned his huge stick in his hands and bent his heavy brows as though in thought. The rest of the party stood together in the narrow way — Bayard and the king together, and Cæsar in the midst of the little group of living persons.

"Let us stay here," said Gwendoline. "It is a perfect place."

Indeed the spot was very beautiful. The afternoon sun now cast a deep shade from the overhanging cliffs upon the little plot of grass in which the daisies and the poppies growing thickly together made fantastic designs of colour. The wild cactus dropped its irregular necklace of fat green leaves and brilliant flowers from the rocks above, and on the very edge there grew a luxuriant mass of snowy white heather, almost unknown in those hills but sometimes found in singular abundance and beauty in remote and favoured spots. Through the opening where the little gorge abruptly ended the sea appeared far below in a blaze of sunlight and swept with fresh colour by the westerly breeze. The view of the water between the warm yellow rocks was like those strange Chinese jewels in which the feathers of the blue kingfisher are set in work of frosted gold.

All agreed to Gwendoline's proposition, and the living and the dead sat down together upon the grass, upon projecting stones and upon the dried trunk of a fallen pine-tree which lay along the side of the path as though purposely placed there to form a seat. For a few moments no one spoke. The living were absorbed in enjoyment of a rest after the ascent of the rugged path; the dead men, who felt no physical weariness, gazed mournfully on the distant sea and chased in sad restlessness the shadows of their great past which seemed to flit between them and the fair reality of living nature.

"I wonder," said Lady Brenda, who loved to throw out large questions for the sake of making people talk — "I wonder what, after all, we shall think we have most enjoyed in life?"

Cæsar smiled, and his expression was that of a man who is conscious of possessing the key to a difficult problem, a smile of calm certainty and of immovable conviction. Francis turned his head quickly to the speaker, and seemed about to speak some jest, but as suddenly, again, his face grew very grave, and a sort of rough despair gathered in the glance of his eyes and in the moulding of his full lips. Bayard's beautiful face never changed, as he quietly watched the king. Dr. Johnson began to shake his head and seemed to be muttering to himself, but his words were not audible ; his great hands grasped his oaken club nervously and he seemed much excited.

For a moment no one answered Lady Brenda's question.   Then Augustus Chard spoke out.

" Love and nature," he said, shortly.

" I do entirely agree with you," said Cæsar.

" I do," said the king, shortly.

" Sir," said Dr. Johnson, turning round upon his rock and addressing Augustus, " there is much to be said in support of your answer.   Nevertheless, however overwhelming the evidence may appear to be upon the one side, justice requires that we should not overlook the arguments in favour of the other."

" Let us argue the question," suggested Heine. " I will argue on both sides, since that is necessary to get at the truth."

" I never said it was necessary that one man should present both views of the question simultaneously, and then proceed to argue alternately in favour of the one and in favour of the other.   I said, sir, that each should support his own side, in order that we might judge of both, thus extracting the pure metal of truth from the mixed ore of individual impressions refined in the crucible of honest discussion."

" I beg your pardon," replied Heine.   " I only meant that I could without prejudice help both sides. I will not argue the fitness of your way of proceeding — "

" No, sir, you cannot," interrupted Johnson in loud tones.

" — which is only applicable when there are at least two people present," continued Heine, unmoved, " and which cannot be of the least service to a man who wishes to find the truth alone."

" Let us discuss the matter itself, instead of the way of discussing it," put in Lady Brenda.

" I say," said Augustus, formally re-stating his opinion, " that I believe what we shall in the end see we have most enjoyed can be expressed under the heads of love and nature — I mean the beauties of nature."

" It depends," remarked Cæsar, looking down as he sat, " whether man most enjoys those things in which he commands, or those in which he is commanded by forces superior to himself."

" You mean that they who enjoy love and nature more than anything else are dominated by love and nature ? " asked Augustus Chard.

" I think so. But love and nature are widely different. Love is a passion, but nature is an assemblage of objects in the contemplation of which we experience various sensations of comfort or discomfort, of pleasure or annoyance."

" Not so very different from love, after all," said Heine. " Woman is an assemblage of objects, such as eyes, nose, hair, lapdogs and gossip, in the contemplation of which we experience — "

" Woman, sir, has an immortal soul," said Johnson, sternly.

" Then that is the only difference," returned Heine.

"Nature, as far as we can judge, has no soul—a fact which accounts for her orderly regularity. If nature had a soul we should love her better than any woman—for she has the quality of faithfulness together with the absence of vanity."

"I think one should define love before arguing about it," said Diana, who loved poetry as much as argument, but wished to enjoy them separately.

"Love," said Dr. Johnson, "has fourteen meanings. The love of which we are speaking is the passion between the sexes."

"Precisely," said Francis. "That is a very good definition."

"I would make it wider," objected Bayard, speaking for the first time. "Love is the honourable and passionate attachment of man and woman."

"That," replied the doctor, "is the noble form of love. Love is the passion between the sexes; and though we may readily admit that in its highest condition it partakes of the angelic, it is not too much to say that as manifested in ignoble beings it savours of hellishness. But in regard to the objection of the Chevalier Bayard, since love in all cases springs from like or similar causes, and since it can never be agreeable to persons of refined intelligence to speak of that which by its nature lacks all refinement, let us set aside those baser manifestations of love whereby the sensibilities of our fair companions might be offended, and let us choose for the subject of our discussion only that pure and honourable pas-

sion, which, as we may not unreasonably believe it.
to proceed from God, we may without injustice or
exaggeration characterise as divine."

"By all means," assented Augustus. "And in
that case I should say that we ought to accept the
chevalier's definition. Love is the honourable and
passionate affection of man and woman for each
other. The definite article 'the' presumes that such
love is not one of many such affections, but the
only one. The word 'honourable' implies the quality of disinterestedness and consequently of unques-
tioning self-devotion, which is the soul of honour.
Lastly, the epithet passionate preserves to love its true
character as contrasted with the passionless affection
a man may feel for his friend."

"You put love beyond the reach of ordinary men,"
said Francis, dryly.

"No," replied Augustus. "There may be many degrees of love below the very highest ideal of what the
passion should be, and which are yet far from base."

"You do not distinguish between the ideal and
the real," objected Heine.

"I am sure, when one loves anybody in the best
way, one sees one's ideal realised, more or less," said
Gwendoline.

"That which is ideal cannot easily be realised,"
remarked Dr. Johnson.

"Exactly," said Gwendoline. "It is very seldom
realised. But when we are in earnest and in love
we realise it a little."

"Nevertheless," observed Cæsar, "the hope of realising the ideal is so strong that it practically dominates the whole human race."

"You admit that love is a dominant passion, then," said Lady Brenda.

"So dominant, madam," said Francis, "that there is hardly a human being in the world who has not been under its influence at one time or another. And when a man is under the influence of love he is not his own master."

"One never recovers from it. It is an illness which disfigures," remarked Heine. "Besides, when one is ill with it one does not mind being disfig- ured — when one is convalescent one thinks that the scars would disappear if one could only be ill again."

"That is true," laughed Francis. "You are very witty, Monsieur Heine."

"It is one of the disfigurements of the disease," answered the poet, with his strange, angular smile. "A dog that has not had the distemper is worthless, as your majesty may remember. I was a valuable dog, for I had it when I was young."

"You do not agree, then," said Diana, speaking to Heine, "that love in the end is one of the things we shall have most enjoyed?"

"To have loved is bad," he answered. "Not to have loved is worse."

"Sir," said Johnson, "of two evils a man ought to choose the less."

"Most people do," returned Heine.

"You, too, then, admit that love is a dominant passion," said Augustus.  "I believe Dr. Johnson admits it also."

"I do not admit it," replied the doctor.  "I know it already."

"It is the most noble of the passions," said Bayard. "A man should love his country with his whole mind, his king with his whole soul, his wife with his whole heart, and his God with heart and soul and mind."

"Sir," said Johnson, "that is a very good rule for a man's life; for, if he devote his intelligence to the welfare of his country, his fidelity, enthusiasm and courage to the service of his king, and his purest and warmest affection to the woman he has chosen to love, he shall certainly lead the life of an earnest Christian, in whom all intentions are based upon reasonable and pure precepts and in whose life good intentions find a fitting exposition in good deeds."

"That is what a man should be," answered Bayard, quietly.  "But I admit that of the men I have known, the greater number were far more influenced by their love for woman, than by patriotism, loyalty, or religious fervour.  Love is indeed the dominating passion of the world."

"Of passions, as we understand the word," said Augustus.  "I suppose no one will pretend that hate has more influence on the daily lives of men in general than love.  If jealousy be a real passion, it presupposes the existence of love and is one of its consequences. The passion of avarice certainly has great weight in the world, but no one has ever said — there is not even a proverb which says — that all men are avaricious. It is a rare thing to meet a miser. What other passions are there? There are vices indeed, but the reason we call them vices probably is that, as exceptions to the general rule, they offend our sense of social propriety. At all events the idea of vice is recent, since the words which express it are different in the different Aryan languages. Vice is not passion. The great passions in the true sense, are love, hate, jealousy, avarice, pride, ambition. The last two are not worth mentioning in speaking of the mass of humanity; for vanity is common enough, but pride, as a passion, is rare, while ambition is the rarest of all."

"It is also the most absorbing, and in its greatest development produces the greatest results," remarked Cæsar.

"No," said Johnson, "not the greatest results. It produces the most astonishing results. For, although, if we could remove ambition from the world, certain changes would immediately take place; yet the effect of extinguishing all love throughout the earth would be far more destructive. It is common to suppose that progress depends upon ambition, whereas there can be no doubt but that the daily wholesome progress of man proceeds from the mere desire to better his condition, and it will generally appear that those nations which are most advanced in the arts of civilisation are those in which the desire for physical comfort is the most felt. Ambition of which the object is mere physical comfort cannot properly be called ambition at all, any more than a reasonable desire for competence can be branded as a sin under the name of avarice, or — "

"Any more than the rosy, stupid, beer-sausage-Sunday-afternoon affection of the little burgher for his little wife can be dignified by the name of love," interrupted Heine with a smile.

" That which is good, sir," replied the doctor, " can be small without being contemptible; but that which is bad is contemptible when it is small and becomes monstrous when it grows great."

" I am glad I remained small," said Heine.

" I think," said Bayard, addressing him directly, "that on the contrary you are not bad, for you are too great to have any right to call yourself small, and we will all maintain that in your greatness there is nothing which shocks the senses of a gentleman."

" As usually happens when a man hears himself praised, I have nothing to say," replied Heine. But his face grew gentle and his smile less sarcastic.

" I think that you are right, in one way," said Cæsar, addressing Johnson. " But the results of ambition may be both astonishing and great at the same time. As regards the great mass of mankind I must admit that of all the passions love plays the most important part. I never was so deeply in love myself as to permit love to influence my plans."

" That was one secret of your success," said Francis.

" Perhaps," answered Cæsar, with a peculiar smile.
" If I had played a smaller part in the world, I believe that I should have regretted having loved so
lightly as I did.   But my life was an exceptional one,
and I know that, as far as my personal feelings were
concerned, it was more satisfactory than most men's
lives are."

" I fancy," observed Augustus, " that your ideality
was absorbed and fully occupied by the necessities of
your career, leaving nothing but bare reality in your
love."

" Since we have agreed that love is the dominant
passion of the world," said Bayard, " it would be
interesting to ascertain whether most people love the
ideal or the reality."·

" Very interesting indeed," assented Diana.   " I
fancy love is largely a question of the imagination.
Of course that makes no difference in the way it
dominates us ; the result is the same."

" I should not think it would be the same," remarked Francis.

" I suppose," said Augustus Chard, " that the ideal
is the result in each man's brain of all his intellectual
likings and physical tastes.   The real in each man's
mind is the result of all his intellectual and physical
perceptions.   The question ultimately depends upon
the balance between the likings and tastes on the one
hand, and the perceptions on the other.   In some men
the wish goes before the thought, and the thought

influences the perceptions. In less imaginative people
no vivid image is formed in the mind until it has been
once perceived by the senses. Cases are known of
men blind from their birth who dream of colours and
forms frequently and vividly; but many blind persons
do not dream that they see. I imagine that those
who do are more imaginative than those who do not,
and that if they suddenly obtained sight and were
able to compare the impressions received in their
dreams with the reality, those who dreamed of seeing
would without much difficulty recognise their ideal
in the real, attributing to the latter many of the
qualities  their imagination had previously defined,
but which would not be perceptible to persons who
were accustomed to the sight of the real from their
childhood.  The blind man who does not dream of
sight, on the contrary, would convince himself of the
nature of reality by slow experiments, not having any
very clearly • defined preconceived notions on the
subject.  By extension a man who has great imagination is likely to form a very clear picture of the
woman he would choose for his wife.  Unfortunately
his imperfect knowledge of the relations between the
intelligence, the character and the personal appearance in woman frequently leads him to fix his ideal
upon the wrong reality."

" Augustus!  What a lecture!" exclaimed Diana,
laughing.  "In other words, people who love ideals
are always disappointed."

" Naturally," said Heine.  " But in order not

to be disappointed a man must have no imagination."

"Men are not always disappointed," said Bayard. "The world is full of good women."

"On the other hand it is not full of good men," answered Heine.

"Man is a sad dog," said Dr. Johnson, who had been listening in silence for some time. "And woman is a dear creature," he added, in a tone of great conviction.

"Well?" asked Lady Brenda. "Have you decided about the ideal and those things yet?"

"Madam," said Francis, turning to her with a smile, "I do not understand a word they are saying. I probably have not much imagination. To me, a woman is a woman."

"'I call a cat a cat,' as Boileau put it," remarked Heine. "I would like to know how many men in a hundred are disappointed in the women•they marry."

"Just as many as have too much imagination," said Augustus.

"No," said Johnson, shaking his head violently and speaking suddenly in an excited tone. "No. Those who are disappointed are such as are possessed of imagination without judgment; but a man whose imagination does not outrun his judgment is seldom deceived in the realisation of his hopes. I suspect that the same thing is true in the art of poetry, of which Herr Heine is at once a master and a judge. For the qualities that constitute genius are invention,

imagination and judgment; invention, by which new
trains of events are formed, and new scenes of
imagery displayed; imagination, which strongly im-
presses on the writer's mind, and enables him to
convey to the reader the various forms of nature,
incidents of life and energies of passion; and judgment, which selects from life or nature what the
present purpose requires, and by separating the
essence of things from its concomitants, often makes
the representation more powerful than the reality.[1]
A man who possesses invention and imagination can
invent and imagine a thousand beauties, gifts of
mind and virtues of character; but unless he have
judgment which enables him to discern the bounds
of possibility and to detect the real nature of the
woman he has chosen as the representative of his
self-formed ideal, he runs great risk of being deceived.
As a general rule, however, it has pleased Providence
to endow man with much more judgment than imagination; and to this cause we may attribute the
small number of poets who have flourished in the
world, and the great number of happy marriages
among civilised mankind."

"It appears that I must have possessed imagination
after all," said Francis.

"If you will allow me to say it," said Cæsar in
his most suave tones, and turning his heavy black
eyes upon the king's face, "you had too much. Had
you possessed less imagination and more judgment,

[1] Johnson. — *Life of Pope.*

you might many times have destroyed the Emperor
Charles. To challenge him to fight a duel was a
gratuitous and very imaginative piece of civility; to
let him escape as you did more than once when you
could easily have forced an engagement on terms
advantageous to yourself, was unpardonable."

"I know it," said Francis, bitterly. "I was not
Cæsar."

"No, sir," said Johnson in loud, harsh tones.
"Nor were you happy in your marriages —"

"I adore learned men," whispered Francis to
Lady Brenda. He had at once recovered his good-
humour.

"A fact that proves what I was saying, that the
element of judgment is necessary in the selection of
a wife," continued the doctor.

"I think it is intuition which makes the right
people fall in love with each other," said Lady
Brenda.

"Intuition, madam," replied Johnson, "means the
mental view; as you use it you mean a very quick
and accurate mental view, followed immediately by
an unconscious but correct process of deduction.
The combination of the two, when they are nicely
adjusted, constitutes a kind of judgment which,
though it be not always so correct in its conclusions
as that exercised by ordinary logic, has nevertheless
the advantage of quickness combined with tolerable
precision. For, in matters of love, it is necessary to
be quick."

"Who sups with the devil must have a long spoon," said Francis, laughing.

"And he who hopes to entertain an angel must keep his house clean," returned the doctor.

"Do you believe that people always fall in love very quickly?" asked Lady Brenda.

"Frequently, though not always. Love dominates quite as much because its attacks are sudden and unexpected, as because most persons believe that to be in love is a desirable state."

"Love," said Cæsar, "is a great general and a great strategist, for he rarely fails to surprise the enemy if he can, but he never refuses an open engagement when necessary."

"I think," observed Augustus, "that we have proved love to be the chief ruling passion of the world, and Dr. Johnson has shown that, while all men must submit to it, the man who has the most judgment will find the submission most agreeable — not to say advantageous, because he will intuitively love the best woman of those likely to love him in return."

"I suppose that applies to all mankind," said Diana. "No one would love the wrong person if every one had enough judgment. What a dreary idea, that even love is a matter of calculation."

"The calculation is unconscious," objected Gwendoline. "It only means that when you know exactly what you want, you ought to be able to recognise it when you see it."

"Madam," said Johnson, "that plain statement is worth all of our conversation taken together. You exactly express my idea — "

"Then you ought to fall in love with me at once," retorted Gwendoline.

"O brave we!" shouted the doctor, wagging his head and clapping his enormous hands in delight, and then bursting into peals of laughter, in which the rest joined almost without knowing why.

"It does me good to see a dead man laugh like that," said Heine at last. "But out of all this logic what becomes of phenixes, rocs, poets and other mythological beasts who have no judgment at all and love so very truly that they are always crying and thinking how nice it must be to be married and live on the ground floor and eat potato soup and drink coffee and have pinks in the window like good, honest sensible little burghers?"

"Sir," said Johnson, "your similes are amazing. The phenix was a single bird, no mate existing of his species. The roc was as remarkable for its conjugal happiness and fidelity as for its monstrous strength. As for the poet, his imagination is so large and yet so refined, that he seldom has an opportunity of meeting such a woman as he imagines he might love. Most men love the real. A certain number love what they easily suppose to be real, are disappointed, and are unhappy with their wives. A very few love the ideal, and although in their own lives the vanity of their aspirations may expose them to the chagrin

of disappointment, yet it cannot be denied that by
their noble efforts to express the ideal of the good
and beautiful, they contribute to the sum of human
happiness by inspiring in their fellows a wholesome
and elevating admiration for goodness and beauty."

"The celebrated passions of the world have generally been those of poetic people," said Diana, "and
the most celebrated poems have either been inspired
by love, or treat of love."

"That is quite logical," said Heine. "For since
love dominates us all, it follows that, in its highest
form it must be the most interesting subject to everybody, and everybody will be anxious to read about it
in the books where it is best described. Everybody
likes to feel by proxy what it is to be the hero or
heroine of a thrilling love story, and there are not
many ordinary people who at one time or another
have not tried to invest their humdrum little affections with an air of romance. The schoolboy likes to
fancy himself scaling heights and creeping along
giddy cornices to the window of some lovely lady.
The grown man delights in asking himself whether
he would be willing to lose the world for a woman,
and generally decides that he would not — until he
has been a quarter of an hour in the moonlight with
the woman he loves ; after which the world may go
to any one who cares for it, and is willing to take the
responsibility."

"Man is like the needle of a compass," said Augustus, "and woman is the magnet. When she is away

his attention never swerves from his selfish interests, as the needle points to the north. But if woman comes near he whirls round like a feather in a storm."

"It is desirable that the woman should place herself in the same line as his interests," answered Heine.

"No one," said Cæsar, "has ever been able at one time to serve his passion and his interests. Clear your reason from what darkens it and you will be strong; if passion takes possession of your intelligence and dominates it, you will be weak."[1]

"Sir," said Johnson, who immediately recognised Cæsar's quotation from his own speech, "when you used those words you referred to the passion of anger and not to the passion of love."

"For that matter," replied Cæsar, suavely, "I used the word in both senses. You may remember that scarcely half an hour later a note was brought me from a lady, which the fathers supposed to be from one of the conspirators. I was exceedingly anxious about that note at the very time when I was speaking, and I daresay that if my mind had been less influenced by anxiety I should have spoken better. As it was, the incident had a bad effect and contributed to my failure on that occasion."

"That is true," admitted the doctor. "But I believe the note was not from your wife, sir, as it should have been, but from another lady."

"That is also true," replied Cæsar, with a light laugh.

[1] Cæsar's speech at the trial of Catiline, Dec. 5, 691 A.U.C.

"Then I may say that you were not under the influence of the best kind of passion," continued Johnson. "In general, I would not advise a man to engage in great affairs at the time when he is courting a pretty woman; but when he has married her and the anxiety concerning the result of his courtship has terminated in a natural and satisfactory manner, I say that the constant sympathy and affection of a refined and faithful woman do not hinder a man in the accomplishment of great enterprises, but, on the contrary, they produce serenity in his temper, they inspire courage in his heart and they add new confidence and vigour to his judgment."

"Yes—but is that passion?" asked Lady Brenda.

"It is love, madam, and love is a passion. When the flood-gates of a huge dock are opened for the first time the sea rushes in tumultuously, with great violence, so that it is dangerous to oppose it; but when the sea has filled the basin constructed for it, the tumult is soon succeeded by calm, great ships float safely in, and the very water which a short time before was a dangerous whirlpool, becomes instead a haven of safety, where the great operations of commerce can ever afterwards be conducted with security and profit."

"It seems to me," said Augustus, "that the only point which remains to be shown is that the recollections most men have of love are among the pleasantest which men have at all. That was my original proposition."

"It is useless to deny it," replied Dr. Johnson. "Men generally desire to experience love, and most men do in one degree or another. I believe that in the vast majority of cases the workingman, the gentleman, the soldier, and the scholar would all say that their affection for their wives has given them much lasting happiness; and those classes compose the greater part both of civilised society and of barbarous nations. For, although we regard the increasing harmony of life in the lower classes as an assurance that civilisation is advancing, we must not forget that many barbarians treat their wives with kindness and affection. Especially it is important to remember that in all ages men have fought in defence of their women, when they could not have been roused to fight for anything else, and it is reasonable to suppose that men love best that for which they will most readily give their blood. What men love best, must be what is most pleasant to them; and that which is most pleasant will also afford the most delightful recollections. Your proposition is proved, sir, and there is nothing more to be said about it."

And with that the doctor struck the end of his oak stick violently into the ground and looked from one to another as though to challenge contradiction.

"Can a recollection be sad and pleasant at the same time?" asked Heine, with a sigh, but as though not expecting an answer.

"I think so," said Bayard, who had been silent for a long time. "I am sure that one may rejoice and yet shed bitter tears over the same event. If I love a true and glorious lady, and if she die, my heart is full of a grand gladness because she is in heaven, but my eyes are filled with tears because she has passed away. My joy is for her, my weeping is for myself — both are earnest."

" You mean when she has loved you in return ? " asked Heine.

" It is the same," replied the chevalier. " If she died before she loved me, I would always believe that if she had lived she would have loved me in the end. We were willing to wait long for love when I was alive."

" Speak in your own name, my irreproachable captain ! " exclaimed Francis, gaily. " For my part I never could understand waiting."

" It has been said that your majesty inaugurated a new social era," answered Bayard, with a quiet smile.

" But," persisted Heine, "suppose that instead of dying you believed that she loved you, and that she then married some one else. Could your recollections of her be at once sad and pleasant ? "

" If she had deceived me, I would try not to remember her," replied Bayard. " If I had deceived myself, I still might be glad that she was happily married, for her sake, and yet be sorry for my own."

" But if she had deceived you, and you could not forget her ? " asked Heine.

" Then I would look for consolation elsewhere."

" With another woman ? "

"No. In a holy life," said Bayard, simply.

Heine sighed and turned away. Cæsar looked curiously at the man who had been the bravest of his day as well as the purest, and Francis wore a puzzled expression.

"You would do well, sir," said Johnson. "When a man has made a mistake and is unhappy, it is better that he should occupy himself in relieving the distress of others, than that he should manifest his own disappointment in a piece of verse."

"There would certainly be a decrease in the production of poetry in that case," said Heine, smiling in spite of his melancholy mood.

"If a man is really a poet," remarked Gwendoline, "neither happiness nor unhappiness will prevent him from doing beautiful things — only real poets are scarce, the sham poet flourishes like a green bay-tree."

"The difference is that the real poet is always a poet," said Augustus; "the sham bard is only poetic when the fit is upon him, and drivels vulgarly when he is in his normal frame of mind."

"The fit being frequently brought on by a paltry love affair," said Heine. "I do not call that sort of thing love at all. It does not even come under our discussion, for it dominates nobody, any more than a cold in the head does."

"How many times can a man be seriously in love?" asked Lady Brenda, glancing at Francis.

"Once," said Heine, "and that is too much."

"If I were alive, madam," said the king, "I would never be weary of loving."

"Man," said Johnson, "comes into the world with a certain capability for love. If the capability be great and is wholly employed in a strong affection for one woman, the result is a passion which may attain sublimity; but if, on the other hand, the whole force of love is squandered in contemptible driblets upon unworthy objects, the petty results cannot be dignified by the name of passion nor honoured by the name of love. It may indeed happen that one man may, at different periods of his life, love two women with great devotion, but I doubt whether he can love three, and I know that he cannot love twenty. The mere fact that to love twenty women in a lifetime, or even ten, strikes the meanest intelligence as a monstrous absurdity, sufficiently proves the existence of a limit. We cannot in all cases name the figure by which that limit is represented; but our common sense tells us that in the great majority of instances it lies between two and three, and with this approximation we must rest satisfied. The human mind is not capable of experiencing frequently very remarkable sensations without becoming so much accustomed to them as to regard them with indifference, for when they become frequent they must soon cease to excite remark. Love is to the human part of man what religion is to the soul; and as we conceive the Christian man who believes fervently in one God to be better than the heathen who

divides his belief among many idols and endeavours
to distribute his faith in a fair proportion to each, so
we shall not greatly err if we assume that a man is a
better lover when he loves one woman than when he
has loved several."

"The mistake I made was that I loved too few,"
said Francis, with a laugh. "Had I loved a dozen
more, love would have ceased to influence me or my
doings. Cæsar had the advantage of me there. He
wore out his affections when he was young and consequently found his intellect untrammelled when he
was in the prime of life."

"His majesty is very frank," said Cæsar to Gwendoline, with a quiet smile. But he took no further
notice of the thrust.

Indeed there was a singular harmony among the
dead men. They occasionally said things to each
other which among the living might be expected to
cause pain; but the sharpest thrust produced little or
no effect. When we know that words can never by
any possibility be translated into deeds, directly or
indirectly, we grow indifferent to sharp speeches and
soon learn that we are beyond their reach. The
vanity of Francis was not diminished by the accident
of death, and he loved to draw parallels between
himself and Cæsar; but the conqueror smiled always,
in his gentle and courteous way, willing that Francis should say what he pleased. A bitter jest might
be spoken sometimes, but the moment the words
were uttered the bitterness was gone from it. The

dead men knew that if they did not forget at once they would surely forget to-morrow, and in the gloomy prospect of eternal disagreement they had soon learned to forget at once. So true is it that man only harbours resentment so long as he dreams of revenge. Posthumous man is beyond the law of retaliation in kind ; it is no longer possible to injure him, and he no longer desires to inflict injury in return.

## CHAPTER X.

It was night and the party sat upon the terrace in the darkness; the light from within fell upon the white tiles in broad squares and a little of it was reflected upon the faces of the dead and of the living. Of the former, Cæsar and Heine had come together, and had brought with them a third man, on whom all eyes were now turned, as he sat in his straight-backed chair, talking in a gentle voice, and looking quietly from one to the other of his companions while he spoke. He was a thin man, rather dark than fair, with a broad white forehead and soft brown eyes that were full of light; delicate features, young but marked with lines and wrinkles that showed thought and suffering. He wore knee-breeches and shoes with plain buckles, a loose dark coat, with a broad white shirt collar, and a short wide cloak hung from his shoulders and was gathered round him on one side. His thin brown hair fell in natural locks upon his neck. The impression was that produced by a man whose head is too large for his body, whose mind has worn out his physical strength. He was the man of whom Dr. Johnson had spoken on the previous day — Blaise Pascal.

"It is not because I devoted the last fifteen years of my short life to religious meditation that I say religion is all-important," he was saying. "There is no lack of reasons by which the proposition can be proved."

"The advantages of it," said Heine, "are amply shown by the absence of religion in most men."

"Not most men," answered Cæsar. "Most men are religious by nature, until they become so bad that they give up religion rather than abandon their vices."

"Of course," said Lady Brenda. "Everybody believes in something."

"It is precisely because everybody believes in something that it is fair to assume that there is something in which everybody must believe," replied Pascal. "We dead men are past the necessity of making assumptions. But it seems that the living are as anxious to be original and as little capable of originality as they were more than two hundred years ago."

"Yes," said Heine. "The human mind, just at present, has turned itself inside out, like a bag. It will not hold any more than it did before, but it shows a different surface, and talks pompously of being very full, or even of being quite a new bag. But somebody will come along, one fine day, and turn it again."

"That is very certain," answered Cæsar. "Nothing repeats itself so surely as the human intellect. If similar chains of events recur in the world, it is not so much because the circumstances which produce them are the same, as because all humanity argues essentially in the same way about everything."

"About everything except religion," said Pascal. "Perhaps one ought to say, about everything tangible or manifest. The reasoning of Newton did not differ from the reasoning of Euclid on the same class of questions, any more than the later vagaries of Comté differed very much from those of Pythagoras; or the political economy of Stuart Mill from that of Confucius. One might multiply instances to any extent."

"Yes," said Augustus. "I have read that you yourself discovered the first thirty-two propositions of Euclid alone, without knowing that they existed already and without even knowing the names of the line, the circle or the angle. It has often amazed me, but it shows that the human mind in all ages argues essentially in the same way about tangible and manifest things."

"Yes," answered Pascal, quietly, "I never thought of my own case. But the interesting point to be discovered is not where human minds commonly agree, but where they have occasionally differed."

"I am not interesting at all," remarked Heine. "But I differed from everybody."

"I see you do," said Diana, laughing. "Even in regard to your being interesting."

"That is one of the points about which men take the longest time to agree," observed Pascal. "I mean in regard to the reputation of poets and writers."

"Because there are so many of them, that there are always plenty to lead an opposition," answered Heine, rather scornfully.

"No — I think not," objected Pascal. "I think it is because men do not argue alike in regard to the opinions of writers, because opinions and artistic conceptions expressed in words are not tangible nor manifest. There is not much difference of judgment about the very greatest sculptors or painters. There is a vast difference in regard to literature, and if possible a still greater variety of estimation in regard to religion."

"Primarily," said Cæsar, "most civilised men have generally agreed about the principal laws necessary to make civilised life possible, probably because the results of those laws are always manifest. But men have quarrelled from time immemorial about the origin of those laws themselves, generally attributing the conception of them to their national deities, which of course were essentially intangible. Religion, with us Romans, meant reverence for the gods long before it came to mean respect for the laws which we were taught in some measure to believe were framed by them."

"What is religion?" asked Gwendoline. "Does it not mean both?"

"In one sense, yes," answered Pascal, "but not in the more restricted modern use. The laws of God are essentially contained in the ten commandments, but a great part of these has been so incorporated with the laws of nations, that we do not generally connect the commandments, 'Thou shalt do no murder, thou shalt not steal' and many others, with any religious idea, because disobedience to those laws involves civil penalties. It was virtue to abstain from killing an enemy when one was not liable to be hanged for it, or punished in any way. At present it is not a virtue, but a necessity. But there is a class of divine laws which cannot reasonably be enforced by any government, which represent the contract between God and man and not between man and his neighbour. The Puritans attempted to enforce those precepts by means of civil penalties, and they failed egregiously."

"The times have changed," said Heine, "since a man was considered virtuous because he abstained from cutting other men's throats. I doubt whether people are better than they were, but they are certainly different. It is the story of the bag again. The virtue side is turned out, and the vice side is turned in."

"The whole mass of mankind is better, but the upper class is worse than it used to be," said Cæsar, musing. "The morality of the working classes has improved, by the abolition of slavery and the spreading of a religion of which morality itself is the basis. When any great population believes in something good, the result must be improvement of some kind. With us the great body of working men consisted of slaves. Their ideas, their habits and their morality

were base, and they could not help it. A man who
can own no property, who cannot call his children
his own, and who is precluded from engaging in any
kind of competition, must sooner or later become
degraded, and it is not just to expect much from
him."

"But until man is utterly demoralised he will
always fight against such a position," answered Heine.
"The whole question turned upon that during the
French Revolution. Saint-Simonism was only an attempt to teach every man how to own property —"

"By destroying competition," interrupted Cæsar,
"and in the end by destroying the rights and claims
of paternity. That left a man no incentive to work
but the certainty of having just as much property as
every other member of the community."

"But the competition was with the rest of the
world, outside the community," objected Heine.

"Yes," replied Cæsar, "and if it had not failed
for other reasons, its success would have destroyed
it. I grant that it might have spread more widely.
What then? When it had absorbed the greater part
of the nation, the competition with the rest would
have ended, and internal competition would have
begun. Some parts of the community would have
grown richer than some other parts, and the equal
distribution of goods would have ceased. Factions
would have gathered in centres, and centres would
have allied themselves to form parties. The moment
there are parties in a nation, there ensues the

government of the weaker by the stronger, and the
Saint-Simonist notions of equality forbade such a
government.    All such theories and systems are
absurd because they are founded upon the supposition
of the impossible — namely, the absolute similarity of
all men, which I think has nothing to do with their
equality."

"Men may be free and equal," said Pascal, "but
they can never be brothers.  Liberty and equality
are facts, fraternity is a sentiment.  Experience has
proved that.   You may put men into certain conditions which may be permanent.  You cannot put
into the men themselves sentiments which can be
lasting.  The French Revolution was partly reasonable, partly sentimental.  The sentiment has vanished,
and with it the way of addressing men as 'citizen'
and calling them 'thou.'  The practical results have
.remained, with various modifications, and have been
felt from one end of the world to the other."

"I have noticed the  same  thing  in regard to
Christianity," remarked Heine, with an angular,
ironical smile.   "Everybody says it has improved
the morality of the world, but nobody says 'See how
these Christians love one another,' as Tertullian said
in his day, with some reason."

"Yes," said Pascal, "but I am bound to confess
that he wrote those words during a great persecution
of the Christians, and that, after all, he broke with
the Episcopal Church and died a sectarian.    It
appears that Christians were not, after all, so unani-

mous in treating each other as brothers in those days, as one might suppose.  But the religious sentiment is the only one which all men may experience in a somewhat similar degree, because it is based on fact, supported by experience and presents the advantage of apparent probability even to the most sceptical intellect."

"I always admired your theory of the probability of heaven," observed Augustus.

"It was not precisely a theory of probability," answered Pascal.  "It was rather a demonstration of the advantage of taking it for granted.  I put the question in the light of a wager.  If there were a God, a heaven and a future existence, I represented that a man had everything to gain by living a good life, since the blessings to be obtained hereafter would be immeasurably great as well as eternal; and I argued that even if the wager were lost, and existence ended with death, a man who had lived in the hope of heaven would have lost nothing by his goodness."

"Undoubtedly," said Cæsar.  "The question of religion was always of paramount importance, because it is the question of morality.  I myself was obliged to make a profound study of religion, when I was endeavouring to be elected Pontifex Maximus. I am glad the works I wrote on the subject have perished, for I was conscious of sacrificing my convictions to the prejudices of the college of pontiffs, and even of the whole people.  With the people, religion was a polytheism, an image-worship and a worship of genii. With me it was a mysticism very like what was afterwards called Neo-Platonism. We were very uncertain of everything in those days, but most of us were quite sure that there was something in which we ought to believe. At this interval of time it seems hard to understand how utterly in the dark we were. The only very definite thing which attracted every one to speculate about it was the certainty of the immortality of the soul, in one shape or another. Most people held Plato's theory which, after all, was the best."

"No nation of whom we know anything ever questioned the immortality of the soul," said Pascal. "The consequence is that when any one denies it, he is simply told that he must prove its non-existence."

"It is impossible to demonstrate a universal negative," answered Augustus.

"No," returned Pascal. "But that is not the case here. It would be enough to assume that the soul may exist, and then to demonstrate that if it exists an absurdity must follow as an unavoidable consequence."

"I do not understand," said Gwendoline. "What do you mean by an absurdity?"

"A generous uncle," suggested Heine, with a laugh.

"Not exactly that," continued Pascal, unmoved. "An absurdity in logic, is when it is shown that if something be assumed, something else is at the same time true and untrue ; or in geometry, for instance, to assume an angle, and then to deduce that in the figure, if the angle is what it is supposed to be, then one line is at the same time longer and shorter than another line, which is impossible."

"But then it could not be proved," objected Gwendoline.

"It can be proved; but the fact that a thing manifestly untrue can be proved by means of an assumption, is enough to prove that the assumption itself is untrue.   Apply this method to the non-existence of the soul.   Assume that the soul exists and survives the death of the body.   Then make all the deductions you can.   When you can show me that if the soul exists, all men must inevitably be born with one leg, or must necessarily walk upon their heads, or are all murderers or all suicides, then I will grant you that the soul does not exist; because you will have shown me that if it existed, men would be different from what they are.   But no such absurdity can be demonstrated.   Assuming the existence of the soul, it is impossible to draw any deduction from the fact which is not in accordance with the evidence of our senses.   A vast amount of ingenuity has been expended in the attempt, but it has signally failed. It is clearly impossible to disprove the fact.   Therefore when a man stands up and says there is no soul, and fails to prove what he says, he utters as foolish a negation as though he had said that space contained no stars beyond the range of the most powerful telescope."

"Evidently," assented Augustus. "The modern argument is that it is not necessary to assume the existence of a soul, to account for man's actions, nor to believe in God in order to account for man's origin. Having stated this, scientists proceed to show to the best of their ability that life in the first instance resulted from the inevitable changes in the state of the matter upon the earth's surface, and that an unbroken series of developments has produced the human animal from protoplasm. It is impossible to study the matter without perceiving that the series is in fact very far from complete, and that scientists are only too ready to pass lightly over the important *lacunæ* in the history of evolution, in order to give undue weight to those facts which seem to support their hypothesis."

"Just as a clever lawyer makes up a plausible narrative out of circumstantial evidence," remarked Diana, thoughtfully.

"Yes," answered Pascal, "and just as in law people are beginning to question how far merely circumstantial evidence can be trusted, so people are beginning to question the right of science to set up, as facts, theories which are only supported by a number of circumstances which give to the whole an air of probability. How many men have been convicted and put to death upon evidence which seemed absolutely conclusive, and have yet been found innocent when it was too late! How many scientific systems have been accepted and believed by civilised mankind for generations, and then suddenly upset and forgotten for ever! If durability be a proof of truth, then Christianity has a stronger basis than any scientific theory with which we are acquainted."

"When I was young," said Cæsar, "the acknowledged road to popularity and notice was to bring accusations against prominent persons, and if possible to prove them. The surest course in order to get notoriety was to attack something or somebody of importance. The moderns know that and practise it. Nine-tenths of modern scientists are much more anxious to destroy than to build up, because science is slow and affords little material for building, whereas it is easy to find fault with the moral architecture of human ideas. The principle upon which the Athenians put Socrates to death was very reasonable. They held that scientists had a right to be inquirers, but were not entitled to attack received beliefs of the religious kind, because to undermine belief was really to weaken the state. We may condemn Socrates's judges, because they profoundly misunderstood him. But we cannot deny that if the charges against him had been fully proved, the Athenians would have been justified in silencing him. Socrates was not a martyr to his own system of morality; he was the victim of an ignorant court, or of a popular prejudice. He was not condemned for what he did say, but for what ignorant or malicious persons swore that he said, as many a less remarkable man has been condemned before and since. The principle that men should not undermine the public morality is not bad because it has been often twisted to satisfy the hatred and prejudice of the ruling class, any more than our old law of *perduellio* was unjust because Labienus and I made use of it to work up a case against Caius Rabirius. He was condemned, but of course I never meant that he should die, and the accusation did him no harm whatever, while the success of the suit did me a deal of good. That was the way we handled the laws in my time, to our own advantage. But the laws themselves were good and founded on important truths. Similarly it follows that the criticism exercised by pure reason is not a bad thing in itself because modern scientists distort it in order to get notoriety by attacking so important a matter as religion, instead of being satisfied to employ it legitimately in their own sphere of inquiry."

"That is the great division," said Pascal. "My father, who was a wise and accomplished man, taught me that objects of faith are not objects of speculation, and I never saw any reason for thinking otherwise. I turned all my inquiries upon things in nature. I never applied myself to the curiosities of theology. It is not the part of science to dabble in transcendentalism. Scientists only speculate upon religion to destroy it. Fanatic believers build up theories about it and distort it out of all sense and proportion, like Swedenborg with his ideas about celestial marriage and the like. So soon as religion is made an object of curiosity, the vanity of the human mind appears in its fullest and most ludicrous proportions. Could anything be more outrageous in premisses, or more pernicious in results than the religions invented by man? Look at the Mormons, the Skopts, the Shakers, the howling dervishes, the Theosophists and the Fakirs. If anything should appeal to the common sense of mankind it is the divine moderation of Christianity at the present day, after nineteen centuries of existence. Who was the fanatic? Christ, who taught men in simple language to lead a pure life, or Giordano Bruno, who called Christ a charlatan, and boasted that he himself would perform greater miracles? The Archbishop of Paris, murdered by communists, or Jean Richepin who writes a poem called 'Blasphemy,' for which that word is too dignified and clean a title? Who are mad? The English country clergyman and the hard-worked London curate, giving their lives to help their fellow-creatures, or our so-called scientists, boasting themselves to be somebody and employing their choicest sneers in defaming a religion which they admit with truth that they cannot understand?"

"I think you are right in that," answered Cæsar. "I lived before Christianity, and I have had a good opportunity of judging, from the point of view of a heathen and of a Christian. Religion has always been necessary to government. Otherwise, before

Christianity, it was a matter of opinion, often a matter of taste. As for me, I always had a leaning towards monotheism and especially towards the Jews. The latter were deeply attached to me, and after my funeral they spent many nights before the rostra, where my body had been burned, keeping up fires and uttering lamentations. Yes—religion was necessary to government, both in its essence and in its forms, because there is no government without a morality of some sort. Christianity is acknowledged to be the best moral system, and is therefore the best basis for governing men. Indeed no ruler has ever tried to govern without it, since it has become universal. An attempt was made under the French Revolution, but Bonaparte soon put a stop to that. He was not an irreligious man. One of his earliest steps as First Consul was to cause the words 'God protect France' to be engraved upon the edges of the coins he struck. At Saint Helena he had a chapel in his house and attended the services every day. That may have been due to a change in his personal feelings; but as far as government was concerned, he showed the importance he attached to religion by the way he insisted on being crowned by the Pope. The Romans were naturally reluctant to give up their traditions in favour of a simple faith which inculcated a severe morality, but they could not resist the new influence for long. It was felt the sooner because it offered such a startling contrast to the immorality of some of my successors."

"The morality and the importance of Christianity are beyond question," said Augustus. "But different ages have thought differently about the practice of it."

"It seems to me," remarked Heine, who had said very little during the discussion, "that like everything transcendental which is so generally accepted as to affect the lives of men, Christianity has two aspects, the divine and the human. The human aspect is the practice and the result of the practice. The practice of anything at any particular period must depend upon the state of civilisation and thought at the time. In these days men will not go barefoot to Jerusalem for a penance. Most people would think it outrageous to give a tenth of their incomes to the poor, after giving five or six tenths to the government under which they live. Still less will you find men who will give all they have and go in rags in order to relieve the distress of others. Our friend Pascal, here, who was neither priest, nor monk nor hermit, gave up his house to a sick family of beggars when he was dying himself — "

"Why do you speak of that?" interrupted Pascal, deprecatingly.

"If you will mention an instance which will do as well, I will not speak of you," returned Heine, with a smile. "I only say this to show what people formerly did. The force of contrast was what produced such surprising results. The great lord in former times was like a lion among rats, a creature superior

in every way to the common herd.  If he chanced to
be a saintly man, the impression made on him by the
poverty he saw, as compared with his own wealth,
might well turn him to wild extremes.  He became
a fanatic.  He longed for nothing so much as to sit
in rags on his own doorstep, devouring mouldy crusts
with a herd of other beggars.  It either did not strike
him that he could have done more good by devoting
his income for many years to the poor, as Pascal did,
instead of sinking his whole capital in one charity;
or else property was too unstable a thing to be disposed of in such a way.  But it was the contrast
which attracted the man.  He believed that poverty
and humility were the same.  He thought that a
patched coat was the outward sign of a whole soul.
He convinced himself that hunger was a means of
salvation, and that the suffering of being dirty was
pleasant to God.  He advised his fellows to follow
his example, and proposed to emancipate the soul by
starving the body.  When men suffer like that, they
are in earnest.  John Bunyan was in earnest when
he renounced the pleasures of bell-ringing and tipcat,
and he proved it afterwards.  Saint Simon Stylites
was thoroughly in earnest when he established himself on the top of his column, and so was poor Louise
de la Vallière, when she abstained from drinking any
kind of liquid, for a whole year, in the Carmelite
Convent.  It does not follow that everybody must
renounce tipcat, live on a pillar and abjure liquids in
order to be saved."

" Really — I hope not!" exclaimed Lady Brenda.

" Certainly not," continued Heine, " and that shows that the practice of Christianity differs in different ages and with different individuals. Asceticism and mortification of the flesh may do good in some cases, but if the population of the world consisted of one thousand million John Bunyans and one thousand million Saint Catherines of Siena, there would be a serious hitch in the progress of civilisation. Now, mankind are not meant to stand still."

" No," said Pascal. " Every man should do in his own sphere what he can for the general good. I was not an ascetic, except by necessity, through my illness. I would have thought it very wrong to starve myself, because I think it is impossible to suffer voluntarily any pain without feeling a moral satisfaction in the mortification of the body, and that satisfaction is vanity and destroys the good done. I ate and drank exactly what was prescribed for me, but I tried to take no pleasure in the eating and drinking. It seemed to me unworthy of the soul to perceive such base things. But my constitution was feeble and my appetites insignificant. There was little credit in what I did."

" Do you suppose that a man like King Francis could live like that?" asked Lady Brenda.

" Certainly not, madam," answered Heine. " Even Bayard could not. Strong men, who fought as people fought in those days, needed to eat and drink well, and I should be sorry to think that they never en-

joyed their dinners.  But Bayard was moderate where
Francis was sensual.  A hungry coal-heaver who eats
a two-pound loaf at a sitting is moderate, while a lazy
fine gentleman who takes an extra ounce or two of a
*pâté de gibier*, or an extra glass of dry champagne,
merely because he likes those things, is immoderate.
Fortunately for the morals of humanity, in respect of
eating and drinking, the hungry coal-heavers are in
the majority."

" The foundation of morality does not lie alone
in the question of eating and drinking," said Pascal,
with a smile.  " It is a deeper matter.  Morality is
a code of laws so framed that, by practising them,
every man may exert himself to the utmost in his
own sphere, without injury to himself or disturbance
from his neighbours.  Morality is the human side
of Christianity, as the belief in the redemption of
mankind is the divine side.  Those who oppose
Christianity assert that the practice of morality can
be successfully pursued without entertaining any belief in God, and some even pretend that the Christian
system of ethics can itself be improved.  But it cannot.  It provides for every circumstance of human
life with equity and justice and teaches men to be
honest, industrious and moderate.  No system of
ethics ever proposed more, and no system ever accomplished so much.  And as for the divine part
of Christianity, I say that no incentive to morality
can be offered by those who deny the future life one-
tenth as strong as the hope of heaven.  There is a

balance of forces in Christianity, as a system, which stamps it as being of divine origin. No human mind could have conceived it, whole and complete, exerting a tremendous influence in a few years, dominating the civilised world after a few centuries. Cæsar was the greatest man that ever lived, and the results of the changes he made and the force of the ideas which he inaugurated, have produced more lasting effects upon the world than have been brought about by any individual in ancient or modern history. He is here, with us to-night. Ask him if the sum of his influence can be compared with the sum of the influence of Christianity."

"I was only a man," said Cæsar, simply.

There was a short silence. The stars were shining brightly and the gentle ripple of the sea upon the beach came up to the ears of those who sat on the terrace. The night was very soft and sweet and the light breeze stirred the broad leaves and blossoms of the young orange-trees that grew in their great earthen pots along the balustrade. At last Heine spoke.

"I can find another reason why religion is good," he said, "but I do not feel sure that it applies any more to Christianity than to other systems. It is good, because it has been the foundation of all the best poetry in the world. If man has any good feelings he tries to express them in verse; so that the excellence of verse is a sort of religious barometer."

"That is a very good argument," said Diana. "I

have always thought that the best poetry was written when there was the most religious feeling abroad."

"I think that is questionable," objected Augustus. "The best poetry of the Romans was not written under the influence of religious ideas."

"Because it was purely imitative," answered Cæsar. "But the models we took were. Without Homer there would have been no Virgil — and but for Virgil there might have been no Dante, though Dante was not an imitator."

"The finest poem in the world is the Book of Job," said Heine. "The next best poem is the *Iliad*, the next the *Divine Comedy*, the next *Paradise Lost*, the last great poem the world has seen is probably *Faust*, though it is not properly a poem, but a tragedy."

"But *Faust* was not written under religious influence," remarked Gwendoline.

"Pardon me, madam," replied Heine, "I think it was. I think *Faust* is an inquiry into the means of salvation. Goethe did not take Faust through a series of horrible temptations and finally represent him as saving his soul by good works, without a religious intention."

"Perhaps not," acquiesced Gwendoline. "But what becomes of Shakespeare?"

"He was a great poet, who never wrote but one poem, and that was not worthy of him. He was a dramatist. That is a different matter. Æschylus, Sophocles and Euripides were dramatists; so were

Racine and Corneille, so was Schiller. Dramatic poets are descended from epic poets, who were originally inspired to write by subjects more or less supernatural. There is a difference between the Tragic muse, the Epic muse and the muse of the Sublime Hymn."

"Of whom the last was the first, the greatest and the most religious," said Cæsar. "Even with us, who were imitators, religious tradition lay at the root of almost all poetry."

"Why are modern hymns so horribly bad?" asked Lady Brenda.

"Because Milton, who was the only modern capable of writing sublime hymns, only wrote one — the 'Ode on the Nativity,'" answered Heine. "Modern hymns are rough specimens of poetry, when they are poetry at all, and are not written by poets as a rule. Some of them are stirring enough, some are pathetic, a great many are sentimental and all are religious. But they are poor literature. People do not avoid reading them because they are religious but because they are badly written."

"Then why do not great poets write hymns?" inquired Gwendoline. "I should think it would be very easy for you, for instance."

"Not so easy as you imagine, madam," answered Heine, with a smile. "To write a hymn one must be a great, great poet, which I do not pretend to be; one must be directly inspired by the strongest religious emotions, such as I never felt; and one must have the power to be grand in simple language, which power no one has possessed since Milton. But though nobody writes hymns in our day, religion has such a part in poetry that I doubt whether any one who knew absolutely nothing about Christianity could understand five stanzas of any good modern poet. Christianity pervades everything we think, write and do. We cannot get rid of the consciousness of it. Men may blaspheme and abuse it, but they are only losing their temper because they cannot break Christianity down, as a child screams and beats with its little fists on the heavy door it cannot open. Atheists would be less violent in their language if they were really persuaded that there was no God. Religion is there in spite of them. Other men may be indifferent, selfish and occupied with their own affairs; but they are perfectly conscious that they mean to be tolerably religious when they have time, and they feel an uncomfortable sense of uneasiness when they have done something which is not contrary to law but contrary to religious morality. It is laughable to see a man of that sort trying to beat the devil round the bush, while perfectly conscious that the devil is there, and how he will make haste to do the bad thing he wants to do while he has succeeded for five minutes in muzzling his conscience, lest the uneasy sense of doing wrong should mar his enjoyment in it. A man in that condition always reminds me of a dog, meditating the theft of a piece of meat. He hesitates, wags his tail in anticipation, then looks away with a sheepish expression, wags his tail again, springs on the morsel, gulps it down and then skulks off with his tail between his legs in the profound consciousness of sin."

" Yes," said Cæsar, with a soft laugh. " Men have always been like that, but they are more so now than they used to be, because Christianity has popularised the notions of right and wrong and extended them to many points which they did not formerly cover. The question, when a man wanted to do something for his own advantage, used to be ' Can it be done safely?' The question now is, ' What will the world think of it?' "

" Rather contemptible," remarked Augustus.

" No, I think not," objected Cæsar. " It shows that morality has improved, when a man hesitates to do a bad deed on account of what the world will say. It shows that he wishes to appear moral, because most people are moral, and he desires not to be thought different from other men. It does not prove him any better, but it shows that the general standard is higher; it is a good evidence that whereas formerly might was right, at the present day what is called right is right according to a universal and established opinion. In other words men are restrained from doing wrong by a principle and not by the violent opposition of anybody who is strong enough to resist their outrageous deeds."

" And the change can only be attributed to the influence of Christianity," said Pascal, who had been listening in silence for some time. "I do not see that it can be referred to anything else, because nothing else has been felt through all civilised nations at once. Races differ fundamentally in character. Governments are not in any two modern nations conducted on the same principles. But the broad questions and rules of right and wrong are established everywhere alike upon the Christian system, and cannot be said to have been derived from any other source. It is useless to tell people that they may arrive at the conclusions of Christianity without accepting Christianity itself, by analysing the elements of happiness according to the laws of reasonable inquiry. Perhaps they can, but if they do, they have only proved how good a thing Christianity is. If you compare the number of men who might be induced to lead good lives from purely logical motives with those who have led good lives by believing in their religion, the number of the first will appear insignificantly small. To sustain this valuable morality, therefore, you must do one of two things. Either you must maintain the religion that inculcates morality as a consequence of belief, and which has done it successfully; or you must show that every ploughboy, who has been taught at Sunday school to distinguish between right and wrong, is enough of a philosopher to grasp a highly philosophical topic, to follow it through its inevitable logical stages, to arrive at its conclusions and to practise the laws he has thus elaborated, because they satisfy his reason, and not because they appeal to his conscience. I will not use any strong epithets to designate the judgment of those who believe the ploughboy capable of all this. It is enough to say that ploughboys are not able to think deeply enough to do what would be expected of them. But should your reformer persist in destroying religion, in the hope that the ploughboy may be made a philosopher in the course of a few generations of education, your reformer, aforesaid, will find himself obliged to employ a stronger force than existing civil law to coerce the ploughboy, during the interval between the loss of conscience and the acquisition of the philosophical capacity."

"That is true," answered Cæsar. "I see many proofs of it in the present day. These perpetual riots of the anarchists in all parts of the world are the work of men who have lost their belief in religion and their sense of right and wrong, but who have acquired no philosophical intelligence in the place of what they have lost. The result, as you say, is the necessity of coercion, ending in the hanging of numbers of these fellows. It is characteristic of these men that they do not say what they want. On the contrary they say they want 'nothing,' as they express it. Their object is to tear down, not to build up. This wanting 'nothing' is the result of their thinking 'nothing,' during the suspension of their intellectual faculties which have lost belief and gained nothing instead."

"And what would you do to stop all this?" asked Lady Brenda.

"I would maintain religion and the law," said Cæsar. "It is not my opinion that the existing morality of nations can be so easily destroyed; but it is certain that it should not be molested. The only objects of government are the maintenance of safety against dangers from without and of order within the state. Governments which fail in either of those points must inevitably fall. Therefore any government which permits anarchic principles or a condition of morality which will lead to the propagation of such principles, is doomed."

"Yes," answered Heine, "and it is doomed to a very odd kind of civil war — a war in which the question will be, ' Do you believe in God?' Not unlike the French Revolution, except that it would be worse. I daresay the unbelievers might get the better of it for a time."

"In the Latin nations — nowhere else," said Cæsar. "Popular fury of that sort soon dies out, because it never really spreads to the masses of the people. It is a kind of insanity to which the great centres are subject. Bands of furious men spring up, curse God and die, and the next generation sows its wheat upon their graves, and quietly puts up the crosses they tore down. Southern people are more liable to such fits."

"It is dreadful to think what such a civil war must be," exclaimed Diana. "We cannot realise the French Revolution, nor anything like it."

"If there is to be such a war in any nation," said Pascal, "modern scientists as a body will be held responsible for it, rightly or wrongly, just as Jean Jacques Rousseau, Voltaire and their various supporters have been said to have caused the French Revolution. But I do not think that such a catastrophe is to be expected. The French Revolution was really caused in a great measure by the fearful oppression of the nobles. Now the cry is the oppression of capital. That means that the immediate object of the anarchists is to divide the existing wealth of the capitalists, and the object is insignificant as compared with the question of emancipation from the old seigneurial rights. You may destroy capital, but it will accumulate again in an incredibly short space of time. The utter futility of the idea stamps it as that of most ignorant men, who, as Cæsar said, think 'nothing' and wish to produce nothing by tearing everything to pieces and gorging themselves with the fragments. But it is quite true that if there are enough of these fellows in the world to make a revolution, the result will be a civil war in which the question asked will be, 'Do you believe in God, or do you not?' And those who do and those who do not will make up the two armies in the field."

## CHAPTER XI.

" Oh, do let us be less serious to-day ! " exclaimed
Lady Brenda, on the following afternoon, as the
whole company found themselves together on the
sea-shore in a deep and shady cove of the rocks.

" *Paullo minora canamus !* " said Dr. Johnson,
thrusting his oaken club into the sand and sitting
down upon a smooth boulder.

" Is it possible to be funny, to order, whenever
one likes ? " asked Gwendoline.

" Rarely," answered her husband.  " The majority
of people are most amusing when they least wish to
be, and most dull when they give themselves the
greatest trouble to amuse."

" What do you mean by being funny ? " asked
Diana, turning to Gwendoline.

" Making people laugh, to be sure."

" Making intelligent people laugh," suggested
Heine, by way of improvement upon the definition.
" It is easy to make fools laugh.  That is the reason so
many people believe themselves to be witty.  The
question amounts to asking whether it is possible to
manufacture wit and humour, of a good quality.'

" Anything that makes one laugh is good," said
Gwendoline.

"You remind me of an American I once knew, my dear," answered her husband. "He used to say that there was no bad whiskey; but he admitted that some kinds of whiskey might be better than others."

"Sir," said Johnson, "we are not all omnivorous, nor omnibiberous either. Sir, your friend was a guzzler."

"He was," assented Augustus. "A man who drinks everything he can lay his hands on is a drunkard, and a man who laughs at everything he hears is a fool. But my wife says that anything which will make a man laugh is good. Now men are not all alike. One of my sailors would laugh if one of his companions got wet. But it must be a good joke indeed which would make you smile."

"How do you define wit?" asked Lady Brenda, who had a happy faculty for putting very difficult questions.

"In the sense in which we are speaking of it," answered Dr. Johnson, "wit means the effect of wit, for the word wit means originally the faculties of the intellect; but what we mean is the result produced by the efforts of a lively fancy. The principal means of exciting laughter in others is to present to their eyes or minds a brief and forcible contrast. Madam, I have seen the vulgar at a penny show laughing very heartily at the sight of a very tall man standing beside a very little man. The tall man alone is an object of astonishment, and the

dwarf alone will elicit remark owing to the exiguity
of his body; but the two must be placed side by side
in order to excite laughter by the contrast of their
proportions. I will go further, and say that the dwarf
may be laughed at by men of ordinary size, because
he is contrasted with them to their own advantage;
but ordinary men do not laugh on seeing a man bigger
than themselves, unless he be a badly-made man,
because they feel an involuntary respect for his
apparent physical superiority. Generally, when we
are amused by the contrast between two things, it is
because the magnitude of the one causes the meanness
of the other to appear contemptible."

"Yes," said Pascal, musing. "I think that one of
the surest methods of ascertaining the truth of a comparison is by reversing the terms of it. When it is
untrue, the effect is so startling that it produces
laughter. Call Molière the Aristophanes of his age
if you please. It is a great compliment to Molière.
But when you say that Aristophanes was the Molière
of his age, the comparison strikes me as ridiculous,
and I laugh. But you need not go far to find com-
parisons much more absurd and untrue than that, and
far more laughable if reversed. It is the contrast displayed which makes us laugh."

"Dr. Johnson did that very effectively," remarked
Augustus. "He said of Lord Chesterfield, that he
had thought him a lord among wits, but that he found
he was only a wit among lords."

"That was not wit, sir," answered Johnson, "it
was truth."

" Cannot the truth be witty? "

" Yes, sir. When it surprises. The discovery that
poor Chatterton was a literary forger was surprising
but not laughable, because his position was not great
enough to admit of a great contrast when he was un-
masked, and because the work he did was his own.
But we cannot help laughing at the theories of the
ancients about nature, now that we are acquainted
with a few of her laws. What scholar has not laughed
at the idea of Kosmas, the Alexandrian, that the sun
retired behind a mountain to spend the night? And
that the earth, the ocean and the fabulous mountain
were all included and enclosed in a luminous oblong
box of the exact shape of the tabernacle of Moses?
The contrast is very great and it is in our favour, so
that we laugh. Even Aristotle might have laughed
at Kosmas, and with justice."

" But there must be something inherent in the contrast, besides the truth or falsity of it, which makes it
laughable," said Heine. " It was easy for me to call
the young Hanoverian nobles, asses. That would not
have been funny. But when I said they were
asses who talked of nothing but horses, everybody
laughed."

" Because the first statement is only a brutal comparison," answered Pascal. " By adding the second
half of the phrase you introduce a second piece of
abuse which implies a contrast, associated with the
first by the connection between the ass and the horse
in our minds. Wit of that kind is produced by clev-

erly taking advantage of your opportunities in order to illustrate some preconceived opinion. Mere brutality can never be amusing to intelligent minds."

"Very little," returned Heine, "and then only when it is grossly disproportioned to its object, and perfectly harmless. Now I remember in England hearing a navvy say 'damn my eyes if I don't have a pint with you.' I laughed — but I did not laugh the next time I heard it. I grew sick of the exaggeration."

"I remember a story of that kind," said Augustus. "It was told me by an officer who commanded a corps in the American Civil War. He was in his tent one morning, when a shell fell somewhere in the camp and exploded. His quartermaster, who had never seen fire, rushed into the tent in the greatest excitement. 'General,' he shouted, 'hell's busted and there's a mule killed!' The story struck me as very funny; probably on account of the tremendous contrast between the picture evoked by the idea of hell bursting, and the insignificant consequence of such an explosion."

"I think that is more humorous than witty," remarked Gwendoline.

"It is not true wit," assented her husband, "because there was no witty intention. The quartermaster did not mean to be funny, but we laugh at the liveliness of his imagination. It is very much the same with Irish humour. It is often unintentional. Since I am telling stories I will tell you an Irish one of that kind.

An Irish cook one day informed her mistress that she was about to be married. 'And who is he?' inquired the lady. — 'And I'm sure you'll be remembering the burial in the spring,' answered Biddy. 'And it's the husband of the corpse, m'm, and you'll be sure that was the very toime he honoured me by saying that I was the light of the funeral.' Bridget did not mean to be funny — it was pure accident. That is unintentional humour. The Irish love of putting things agreeably, too, is often very amusing. An Irishman rings at the door of a house on a snowy day and asks the housemaid to lend him a shovel to clear the pavement before the next door. She gives him what he wants — a plain shovel, just like any other. 'And is it your spade, miss?' he asks. — 'Yes,' says she. — 'Well, miss,' he answers, 'I'm tremendiously obleeged to ye, and mirover I'm bound to say that you have a very pretty taste in spades.' He only meant to be complimentary. He was funny by accident."

"It is easy to understand why we laugh," remarked Pascal. "It is another matter to analyse the nature of what makes us laugh. I believe that a man who understands that, can construct witty phrases and stories at will. In the first place it is certain that wit depends chiefly upon some striking contrast and then upon the way the contrast is expressed. Then comes the question of bringing the contrast into the right part of the sentence, which is a matter of style. Wit then depends upon imagination, command of language and good taste, and those who have possessed all three in the highest degree have usually been the wittiest men.  Probably Shakespeare had all three more than any other man who ever lived, and he is probably the wittiest writer who has ever been known."

"Altogether," said Heine.  "No one man ever wrote so many witty things, and I think that your definition of the requirements of wit is a good one.  Command of language and good taste may with study and judgment make an essayist, an historian, or a philosopher, fit to rank high in literature apart from their mere acquirements.  A poet must have a good imagination, of the sensitive, delicate kind.  But it is the man of redundant, overflowing, well-fed, sanguine imagination who is witty, and who, if he possess a command of language, can produce the works of a Rabelais, and if he have good taste besides can write the plays that Shakespeare wrote."

"The witty man," observed Johnson, "must command an immense variety of images, in order that he may select grave ones or laughable ones according to the dictates of his taste.  Discrimination, sir, is a great element in wit.  Thomas Paine was right when he said that 'one step above the sublime makes the ridiculous, and one step above the ridiculous makes the sublime again.'  It is very true."

"I always thought Napoleon said that," remarked Lady Brenda.

"He may have said it, madam, but I do not believe he invented it.  Paine wrote the book in which that sentence is contained in the year 1793, when Napoleon was nobody and Robespierre was not yet president. Paine, madam, was a bad man with too much common sense."

"'In digging up your bones, Tom Paine, Will Cobbett has done well: You visit him on earth again, He'll visit you in hell,'" quoted Augustus. "Byron was of your mind, sir," he added.

"Yes, sir," answered Johnson, with a deep laugh, "and I have no doubt he has by this time had ocular demonstration of the truth of his prophecy."

"Why do you say that?" asked Heine.

"Well, perhaps I should not have said it. I will take it back, if you please, but I should not have liked Byron, if we had lived at the same time. He was born four years after I died, but I watched some parts of his career with interest. But to the point, sir, let us to the point. Let us consider the beginnings of humour and wit, so far as we are acquainted with them; and when we have traced the history of human merriment from its origin to its state in these present days, let us see if we cannot draw from our studies some deduction which may illuminate the subject of our discourse after exercising the faculties of our reason."

"I am afraid that will take a long time," suggested Gwendoline.

"Madam," returned the sage, "time may be made for the living, but it is certainly not made for the dead. Madam, I could tuck in my legs and talk for a thousand years."

"The subject would be exhausted by that time," remarked Cæsar. "But there is much sense in your suggestion. A great deal of modern humour is descended from our times. The Italian Pulcinella and Stenterello with their comic masks are the great grandchildren of the masked comedies of Plautus. All that is buffoonery. There is very little real wit in it. We had witty men, and literary wits made a good living. But even their productions were very personal. I was often annoyed by them myself, and my successors found them an intolerable pest."

"They were good at epigrams in those days," remarked Heine.

"Unpleasantly so," answered Cæsar, with an odd smile. "But their epigrams were constructed very much on the same principle as the modern jest. State a fact seriously in one sentence. In the first half of the second sentence make an apparently grave deduction. Then in the last half drop suddenly into some absurd bathos, or spring into some wild and fanciful exaggeration, or merely state a simple fact, known to be true, which makes all the first member of the statement appear in a ridiculous light. Take a little epigram of Martial upon Bassus. 'Bassus,' you are told, 'has bought a travelling cloak for ten thousand sestertia, and has made money by the transaction.'—'What,' you ask, 'do you call that cheap?'—'Of course—he will never pay for it,' answers your friend. The joke has probably been repeated several millions of times since then. 'They told me he was a fool, and I bought him,' complains another; 'give me back my money — he is wise.' That expresses very wittily what a man feels when he discovers that he has employed a man to serve him who turns out cleverer than himself."

"The sensations of the Directory with regard to Bonaparte," suggested Heine. "That is a good rule for making a joke. Let me see whether one could be made off hand on that principle. Take two things which are strongly contrasted, but have a hidden resemblance. For instance, ordinary men, and professors of universities. State in one sentence a fact, seriously. 'Professors resemble men.' Make a deduction. 'Professors resemble men, who are two-legged animals without feathers.' That is the definition of Plato, I believe, before Diogenes improved upon it. That is the first half. I suppose that in the second member it is necessary to hit upon the main difference between professors and two-legged animals, without feathers. The main difference is that professors act as though they were not featherless animals, but feathered white birds, web-footed, prone to waddle in the mud and cackle loudly when it rains. To be short, you may say 'Professors try to resemble men, who are two-legged animals without feathers, by tearing out their quills for pens to write down their cacklings.' You may turn it and polish it. You may say, 'If men are two-legged featherless animals, a professor need only make quill pens of his feathers and write himself down a man.' That is an instance of a joke constructed on a fixed principle. You can vary it still more, changing the basis by one degree. Since professors call themselves men, you may say: 'Professors are two-legged featherless animals. A goose need only make quills of his feathers and sign himself Professor Doctor Gans.' But in this particular case it is unnecessary to state in concise terms a fact so universally known."

"Why do you hate all professors so much?" asked Gwendoline.

"Because they made my life a burden to me when I was taking my degree," answered Heine, with a laugh. "A professor in his glory, bullying a miserable student in his ignorance, is a sight to rejoice the most indifferent and disillusioned fiend. He is one-eyed, but he is king among the blind; he is only one step higher than the village schoolmaster beating A, B, C, into the village fool. He produces nothing that endures, as other men do, but he deafens quiet, well-behaved people with his diabolical cackling. He is endless as his own discourse. He dies daily, like Saint Paul, at four o'clock, but he rises at lecture time like a phenix from his ashes, or like a jack-in-the-box from his wire spring, screaming the most sour and distressing rubbish at people who do not want to hear him. He is the terror of the young, the bugbear of grown men, and even old age is embittered by the memory of him. He is overbearing with his inferiors, a bore to his equals, a gadfly to his superiors. He believes in nothing, he respects noth-

ing, and if he knows anything he has only learnt it
in order to scoff at the ignorance of somebody else.
Wherever two or three of his kind are gathered together there is bitterness, strife, and all uncharitableness; there young men go down to their graves,
consumptive with the effort to learn, or go to the
good, old-fashioned devil rather than abide in the
clutches of the modern fiend, there — "

"Really," exclaimed Lady Brenda, " you are very
bitter, you know!"

"No, sir," cried Dr. Johnson, "professors are not
all alike. There are good men among them who do
not despise the intelligent intercourse of their equals,
any more than they trample upon their inferiors in
learning or wear out the patience of those who stand
above them in the scale of knowledge. A man who
knows something is not necessarily a detestable fellow, a wrangler, a breeder of strife and a scoffer. The
perseverance by which a man has acquired wisdom
does often lead him to suppose himself endowed with
some other and more brilliant qualities in a like degree; but where those higher gifts are really found,
the faculty of exercising them is not often absent.
A man who is endowed only with strength and deter-
mination may envy his companion who possesses besides these a quick wit and a ready tongue; and
where there is envy of a superior there is very likely
to be hatred of an equal and overbearing insolence to
inferiors. But there are men, and many men, sir,
who, although they have not attained to any high

pinnacle of excellence, have acquired knowledge
which they are able to impart to others, and which
may benefit their pupils to whom it is imparted; and
who, because they have learned much without much
difficulty, do not conceive themselves vastly superior
to those who have learned less, any more than they
consider themselves unable to overtake those who
have surpassed them, by making a reasonable effort.
Teachers, tutors and all instructors are generally ill-
tempered in a like ratio with the labour they have
expended in acquiring their knowledge, for it is not
by the knowledge itself, but by the labour it has cost
to get it that men compare themselves with others.
Historians, sir, whose work is very laborious and un-
imaginative, are often insufferably arrogant, and not
unfrequently make their books unpalatable, by inter-
larding them with remarks depreciating other men
who have chosen the same field of inquiry. Scholars,
who live among the great works of imagination produced in the past are often very cheerful men, witty
in themselves and ready to see wit in others."

"They are witty because they grow imaginative,"
said Pascal, "and imagination is the chief source of
wit, as fact is the chief source of satire."

"Is that true?" asked Diana. "I should think
satire were merely a form of wit."

"Satire," answered Pascal, "is the art of detecting
the absence of wit in others, so that one may seem
witty by comparison. It is impossible to be satirical
unless you have facts to deal with, and facts concern-

ing persons.  The most terrible satire upon a liar is
the publication of the truth, but unless some one has
lied the truth does not seem witty.  It is impossible
to be satirical in a work of pure fiction, unless the
fiction be made the direct means for exposing some
existing error or vice.  The statement of the truth
leaves the liar the alternatives of passing for a scoundrel or for a madman, but it ruins at a blow all the
credit of his life and his claim to have any credit in
future.  Satire is not intended to evoke mirth, but
disgust, its object is not to make a man ridiculous for
a day, but to destroy belief in him for ever after.
That is the reason why, when satire fails, it makes
the satirist seem a fool.  It is so serious a matter
that it involves a question of life or death."

"And what about parody?" asked Augustus.  "It
is a kind of satire."

"A very low kind," replied Pascal.  "Parody of
a poem or of a piece of prose, means an imitation of
the measure, or of the rise and fall of the sentences,
often of the individual phrases, in which meaningless
words or contemptible sentiments are substituted for
the words and sentiments of the original.  Parody
may sometimes attract attention and applause, but
only when the work parodied is already beneath
contempt."

"Homer," said Johnson, "composed the *Iliad*, but
Pigres wrote the *Batrachomyomachia*.  It may reasonably be supposed that unless the original had been
so great, the parody would never have been heard of.

But it required an ingenious fancy to interline the hexameters of Homer with pentameters of Pigres's own construction."

"Parody is to satire," remarked Heine, "as a harmless little house cat is to a young tiger. They are both pretty pets in their way, but you must handle them differently — in the catching."

"Satire is certainly the dangerous one of the two," answered Pascal. "Where there is real ground for a satire it is not so very hard to produce, either. Much may be done by holding the object of one's attack to the absolute meaning of his words. It is very hard to satirise men who deal in very simple, plain language, where each word has but one possible meaning, and by its position stands in a clear and unmistakable relation to the other words. When men write like that it is not even easy to parody their works, because they do not strike anybody as ridiculous. It is not even easy to imitate their style. It is not every man who can write like Cæsar in describing the greatest events. Can you imagine a parody upon Cæsar's *Commentaries?* There is no hold for ridicule in them. But though Cæsar was never parodied he was satirised more than once, and he admits that the satires were good enough to hurt him."

"Truly they were," said Cæsar. "As for my style, I thank you for what you say. I tried to reduce every expression to its simplest form — as you did yourself. The chief element of success in everything is simplicity of thought. The moment you admit complication you destroy force. It is well to remember details, if you can; but it is better to forget them than to let them turn your mind for one moment from your main object. The great man is he who can choose men, for the greatest of men cannot do everything at once. It is ruin to attempt it. A ruler must depend upon his ministers for the details in carrying out his plans, though he may depend upon himself for the plans themselves. In the same way, in writing, a man should be clear and strong in his language, if he has anything to say; if he has not, he may divert himself as much as he likes with the elaboration of an artificial style. If he cannot make an impression on his times he may at least hope to amuse his fellow-creatures."

"That is the rub," said Heine. "To amuse and to be great at the same time. To be Cæsar, Rabelais, Shakespeare and oneself — one's one detestable, delectable, contemptible, adorable self at the same moment! That would be a life worth living. Could we not conspire to possess the body of some quiet little gentleman of leisure for a year or two and see what he would do?"

"He would go mad, sir," said Dr. Johnson.

"If he did he would only be a poet — one might do worse," answered Heine. "One might be a sane banker. What an awful fate, judging from my uncle!"

"Envy, malice, and all uncharitableness!" muttered Dr. Johnson, rolling his head and poking his stick into the sand.

"Ah, it is easy for you to say that," exclaimed the poet. "You never had an uncle, and if you had had one he might never have been a banker — and though you are called Samuel, your uncle's name might not have been Solomon!"

"Sir," cried the sage, "if your uncle had been Solomon himself, he could not have treated you more wisely. If he had given you money, sir, you would have done nothing that we should care to speak of. There are no more powerful incentives to labour than an empty stomach, a patched coat and cold fingers. You did not indeed suffer those ills in the flesh, but the prospect of being exposed to them stimulated your imagination to produce works of lasting beauty. Bless your Uncle Solomon, sir, for cutting you short. He killed the canker that eats genius."

"I would have been willing to make nearer acquaintance with the parasite before he was killed," answered Heine. "But we were talking of being great and amusing. Uncle Solomon was neither, though he was rich. Brevity is the soul of wit, says Polonius — I could almost believe my uncle had been witty, his communications were so very brief. But why is brevity the soul of wit? Is it? Was Polonius talking nonsense, as he often did — or was he right for once?"

"Anything which is to make a very strong impression at once, should be sudden, I suppose," remarked

Augustus. " The din in a great factory is as deafening as a peal of thunder, but it does not produce
the same effect upon the senses. A tallow candle
will go through a deal door if it goes fast enough,
but a hundredth part of the slow pressure that is
needed to force a piece of iron through the plank
would squash the candle into a wafer of grease."

"The resemblance certainly extends to wit in
speech," said Cæsar. · "One word spoken at the right
moment, if it is the right word, will sway a crowd more
than an hour of dull talking to the same effect. The
human mind is very limited and consequently very
liable to be surprised. If you surprise it agreeably,
you may do anything with it. If you surprise it disagreeably, it may do anything with you."

"Like a woman," suggested Heine. "Only women
are more often the source of surprise than the
persons surprised. Woman, like wit, is full of
delightful and surprising contrasts. Some women
are like good wit, for one is never tired of them.
Others are like bad jokes which will not bear repeti-
tion. Like wit, a woman's sudden appearance in a
man's life produces a tremendous effect, but if he
has grown up with her from a child the effect of her
presence is much less. There is pleasant wit, bitter
wit, every-day wit, and best-company-manners wit;
there are pleasant women, bitter women, women who
are agreeable every day and women who are only
tolerable in a ball-room. Some wit pleases everybody, and some wit only pleases its author; there are

women whom everybody likes and women whom nobody likes but themselves. It seems to me that there is no end to the resemblance."

"No, sir," said Johnson, "there is no end to it, because it is founded on a false principle. Every word you say of wit I will say with equal truth of a pudding. Are not puddings frequently sources of agreeable surprise? Is not a pudding full of the delightful and surprising contrasts produced by the variety of ingredients from which it is made? Are not some women like good puddings, of which one is never tired, while others are like puddings over-sweet and cloying to the taste, so that one cannot eat of them twice? To a man who has never eaten a fine pudding, would not the first mouthful produce a tremendous effect, whereas a man who has eaten puddings from his boyhood regards the tempting dish with a complacency amounting almost to in-difference? Are there not pleasant puddings, bad and bitter puddings, every-day batter puddings, and noble plum puddings for fine company, not to men-tion the weekly pudding at the 'Cheshire Cheese' in Fleet Street? The latter, too, would make a man ill if he were to eat of it every day. Do not some puddings please everybody while some only suit the taste of the cook who makes them? Sir, upon this principle life is a pudding, woman is a pudding, man is a pudding, and indeed everything is pudding, and nothing but pudding. Sir, to compare things which affect our minds with things which affect our bodies, is futile and ineffectual, except for purposes of poetry; for since everything with which we are brought in contact through the senses is either agreeable, indifferent or repulsive to us, things of all kinds may be compared with ideas, which, to the mind, are also inevitably either repulsive, indifferent or agreeable."

"But why do you say it is admissible in verse?" asked Diana. "I should think that nothing ought to be admitted in poetry which is not logical and reasonable."

"In a piece of poetry," answered Johnson, "the object aimed at is to awake sentiments by means of lively images. Any image will serve the poet which calls up in the reader the feeling which the writer intends to evoke. Heine may compare wit to women in a poem, if he is inclined to do so, and I have no doubt he could produce very pleasant images; but in examining the nature of wit itself, I maintain that such images are out of place. For if, as I have sufficiently shown, anything which affects our senses may be compared to wit, it is clear that the selection of the particular comparison is merely a matter of taste; since the resemblance in all cases is limited to the similarity of the sensations evoked, and in no way extends to any similarity in the things themselves. It is one thing to awaken a sentiment by comparing man's life to a flowing river; it would be quite another to attempt to explain the nature of life itself by studying the nature of the stream."

"Evidently," said Heine. " I was not philosophis-
ing — I was only thinking. Happily that does not
mean the same thing in these days. As for the
nature of wit, I believe that it cannot be defined.
You may define a joke and make one according to
the nature of your definition. But wit itself escapes
definition. You can only classify jests by your taste,
and say this is wit, that is humour and that other is
buffoonery. You can only say that the more wit
makes you think, the better it is, and the further
removed from farce."

"That is true," observed Cæsar, " and it adds
another condition to the definition of wit. It ensures
it from grossness by providing that it must appeal to
the higher parts of the intelligence. Very fine wit
does not always provoke laughter and, generally, when
wit degenerates into buffoonery, laughter becomes a
mere physical paroxysm. Then it is easy to prolong
it, because it has become morbid and no longer is
the expression of a mental state, but of a state of
the body. Very fine wit never causes a paroxysm.
A man under the influence of any bodily disturbance,
even when that has proceeded from a state of the
mind, is not capable of the free exercise of his intelligence which is necessary to appreciate wit, or to
produce it. Whenever he is so disturbed his mental
sight is dimmed and his humour is grosser. A man
who cannot help laughing is no better than a woman
who is hysterical and must cry and sob, whether she
have any cause or not."

"Rather less wearing on the nerves," remarked Gwendoline.

"The finest wit," said Pascal, "is elicited by controversy. The finest humour is the result of a jovial constitution, seconded by a mind very keen in small things."

"I detest rules," answered Heine. "A man may be witty, humorous, pathetic, melancholy, heroic and ridiculous in one day."

"Yes," replied Augustus, "but he may be humorous, pathetic and the rest without ever being witty, in our sense of the word. To trace the origin of wit and humour to the character and constitution of man is altogether impossible. We may understand something about the nature of earth and water, but we can never be certain of the conditions which produced them. But is it true that the best wit results from controversy?"

"It must be true," said Cæsar, "because it is only in controversy that the mind is fully exercised, imagination, force of logic and power of language all playing great parts together, and all stimulated in the effort to make the enemy seem contemptible. Perhaps no one but a man who has fought with words really understands the power and the use of wit, as well as its construction."

"Yes," answered Heine. "Pascal himself has shown that. He is the father of French style and one of the oracles of French wit, and to attain that position he only wrote eighteen letters in a great con-

troversy.  Dr. Johnson himself was never so witty
as when he was arguing something with somebody.
Resistance evokes wit, as well as action.  There is
no more certain method of making a pig run in one
direction than to pull his tail the other way.  That
is a pig's idea of wit, I suppose.  Abuse a great man,
and he will often say a good thing.  Agree with him,
and he will take you for a fool and talk blatant rubbish to satiety.  It is incredible how much may be
got out of a man of the most ordinary intelligence,
merely by denying everything he says.  Tell a
labourer that the sun does not go round the earth,
and he will laugh at you.  Tell a schoolmaster that
the earth does not go round the sun, and he will be
positively amusing at your expense.  The British
workman when contradicted knocks down his adversary with his fist, if he does not chance to have a
crowbar in his hand.  The fine gentleman of the
nineteenth century contents himself in such a case
with making depreciatory remarks about the colour
of his enemy's hair.  Professor Diæthylmethylologi-
cus of the University of Nudelsuppenwurstburg, if
you contradict him, will hold you up to the scorn of
all ages and especially of the whole principality of
Schwartenmagen-Limburger-Stinkenstein."

"You seem to say," observed Augustus, "that real
wit must necessarily be directed against some person
or something.  If that is true it is at once distinguished from humour."

"Yes," said Pascal, "that is certainly true, and

mere humour may become wit by the way in which
it is used. A humorous saying gains keenness and
force by being directed against a real person or thing,
with genuine or apparent truth. Humour invents
the absurd and laughs at it. Wit sees the absurd in
the flesh and holds it up to ridicule. There is a
vast difference between the two. The one laughs at
itself, the other bites its enemy and laughs at his
discomfiture."

" Really," answered Lady Brenda, " I do not think
that wit is always bitter, by any means. People may
be very witty about things that hurt nobody."

" Yes. But their wit is directed against the thing,
and you know that it is impossible to be witty about
inanimate things in nature. Therefore when you
exercise your wit upon a thing made by a man, such
as a book, a coat or a piece of music, you are attacking the maker of the thing through his work. The
more the person to whom you are speaking is in
sympathy with you, the better he will appreciate
your wit; the more he likes the thing or the person
you attack, the less he will like what you say. You
may, if you please, set up an object to be knocked
down. You may write a play, full of wit. But you
can only do it by making one character witty at the
expense of another. When a man is witty at his
own expense, he is only humorous, because he is not
in earnest. One might find instances of both in one
phrase."

" Yes, sir," said Johnson, " Polonius says to Ham-

let: 'I will most humbly take my leave of you.'
Hamlet answers: 'You cannot, sir, take from me
anything that I will more willingly part withal.'
That is a thrust at Polonius.   Hamlet adds: 'Except
my life, except my life, except my life.'   That is a
thrust at himself.   But it is not humorous, though it
be witty, since he who says it is in earnest.   A man
may be witty who attacks himself with the same
energy that he would employ against another; but
one who lightly holds himself up to ridicule is merely
indulging his taste for humour.   Sir, I agree with you
that wit only exhibits itself in attack or in the answer
to an attack, that is to say, either in attack or in
controversy."

"Most men prefer the former," remarked Heine.
"Most men think it very pleasant to shut the door
closely and whisper to their loving wives that other
men are idiots.   When the wife is loving she per-
ceives the joke; when she is not, she consoles herself
with the reflection that her husband is himself idiotic
and every fresh proof of the fact is a new delight to
her."

"What a dreadful idea!" exclaimed Gwendoline,
looking at Augustus and laughing.   "Is the converse
true, I wonder?"

"No, madam," answered Heine, with a smile.   "No
man can possibly believe a woman foolish who has
shown enough intelligence to marry him."

"Sir," said Johnson, "this is paradox.   One may
be complimentary without being paradoxical, as one

may be strong without being violent. A man, sir, should never believe a woman to be foolish, until he knows himself to be wise, any more than he should call his enemy weak before he has vanquished him, or his friend unfaithful until he has himself made exhibition of his own fidelity. Sir, I will apply to women what our host's friend said of whiskey; there are no bad women, nor foolish women, either, though some women are better and wiser than others."

" You are asserting a negative," retorted Heine.

" No, sir," roared the doctor, " I am asserting positively that all women are more or less good. Badness is the negative of goodness, and no one can assert that it is universal. The only business of wit is to point out the cases where there is badness, as the only purpose of the barometer is to warn men of foul weather. Nobody, sir, need be warned of the approach of fine weather, and no man need be cautioned that his neighbour is a good man. In the African desert there is no use for barometers and in heaven there will be no wit; for where all is good it will be as unnecessary to speak of evil, as it is senseless to carry an umbrella amidst the sands of Sahara, where it never rains."

" You have at least shown a new and surprising relation between wit and the barometer," answered Heine. " After all, it carries out the theory that wit is only found in attack or in controversy, since it is clear that where attack and controversy are impossible, wit must be out of the question. In a place where there are to be no professors, no fools, no bad poets and very few good ones, it is not easy to say what is to become of wit, satire, sarcasm, irony and Heinrich Heine. In future I shall regard the falling of the barometer as a piece of most exquisite wit, equal at least to Voltaire's attacks on Frederick of Prussia and on Jean Jacques Rousseau."

"But if it is true that wit is only used in attacking something or somebody," said Diana, "wit can never be harmless — that is, it is always used with the intention of hurting a good or bad person or thing."

"Yes," answered Pascal, "it is never meant merely to excite laughter, except when the whole attack or quarrel is pure fiction, as in a romance or a piece for the stage, and then the author purposely sets up somebody or something for a butt. Apart from fiction, true wit must always be used as a weapon, and the pleasurable sensation caused by it in the mind is only excited in those who are on the side of the assailant; on the other side nothing is experienced but pain or indignation. Humour, on the other hand, has no intention of giving pain either to just or unjust persons, and its sole end is to cause laughter. Humour begins with the comic mask and ends with the harmless jest. Wit begins when pain is felt by some one, or would be felt if that some one heard it."

"Humour is a parade, wit is warfare," said Cæsar. "Fine humour often shows the power for keen wit, but never uses it. The sham fight holds the dangerous place between the two, as when friends argue a question for their pleasure. How often does Plato tell us that some one interposed in the discussions he reports, in order to prevent high words and anger! But the parties never showed any inclination to quarrel, until from being humorous they grew witty first, and then abusive; as when Dionysodorus proved to Socrates that words could never have any sense, and Ctesippus fell out with him and his companion Euthydemus and told them they were talking nonsense, which was very true, so that Socrates had to interfere to keep the peace. Sham fights may easily end in real battles, unless there is a supreme commander to whom all questions are referred."

" That is the reason why they have a Speaker in the House of Commons," remarked Augustus. " In countries where the Speaker is not respected the members quarrel violently and try to be as witty as they can, until they are ready to proceed from words to deeds."

" Words are so much cheaper and more easily handled," said Heine. " We have invented a formula for making jests on men of any size. It would be another matter to invent a rule whereby a little man might always be able to break a big man's neck."

" That is the general's business," answered Cæsar, " and that is a soldier's idea of wit. To lie in wait in secret places, to anticipate exactly the movements of the enemy, to be always striking and never struck, to move quickly and unexpectedly, to be always ready

and never surprised — that is warfare, and in controversy it is wit. The one may be reduced to a rule
like the other, and success of the one like that of the
other depends upon fertility of imagination, upon the
nature of one's tools, and upon practical skill in making the tools perform what has been imagined."

"That is better than comparing wit to woman, as
I did," said Heine. "Dr. Johnson cannot put pudding in the place of warfare in Cæsar's simile."

"No, sir," answered Johnson. "Wit and warfare
may be employed in the attainment of any object,
bad or good; but pudding is an object desirable for
its own sake, like woman; and, as the Greeks
attacked Troy in order to recover the person of
Helen, and sent many heroes' souls down to Hades in
the prosecution of a fair and justifiable siege, so also,
with an ingenuity and courage worthy of a greater
cause, hungry schoolboys in all ages have employed
the most subtle cajoleries of diplomacy and the bold-
est arts of predatory warfare in the effort to obtain
for themselves a larger share of pudding than that
allotted to them by the economy of a parsimonious
cook or by the reasonable prudence of a careful
mother."

## CHAPTER XII.

" IT seems to me," said Lady Brenda, " that if all this is true, men have no right to try and be witty for wit's sake."

" I suppose not," assented Augustus. " Since wit is a weapon, it cannot be an aim, but it can be used in attaining an object, provided a man has the power to be witty. It is like the differential calculus, the steam-engine or revolver — a mere instrument to an end."

" Men who try to be always witty," said Heine, " generally get the reputation of being spiteful. So do men who cannot help being witty, just as a strong man who is always knocking down other men is called quarrelsome. Strength and wit can only be objects of cultivation for the sake of the results they produce. Before being witty, or exerting one's strength, one ought to consider what one wants to obtain."

" People say that no one really wants anything but happiness in the world," remarked Diana.

" Of course," answered Heine. " And if every one knew exactly what would make him happy, a great deal of struggling and fighting and vulgar noise would be spared. The mistake most men commit is in forming a wrong idea of happiness and then in spending the rest of their lives in trying to get into their hands the means for attaining the end they have imagined. What is happiness?"

"A state," said Cæsar, "in which all the noblest passions of man exist, continue, and are constantly satisfied, without being weakened by satiety, and where the ignoble passions do not exist. That would be human happiness. But it is unattainable."

"We do not even know which are our noblest passions," laughed Heine. "The nobler they become the fewer people possess them. Probably there exist very noble passions which nobody possesses, and of which we have no idea."

"Then, sir, they do not concern us," said Johnson. "But I do not think there are any noble passions of which we have no idea."

"I will give you an example," answered Heine. "Do you think ambition a noble passion or not?"

"Ambition to shine by conferring great benefits upon the human race is a noble passion," replied Dr. Johnson.

"Well then, do you think that in a village community of Italian labourers, for instance, you are likely to find one man who conceives of an ambition to shine by conferring great benefits upon the human race? Do you not think that a community might be found where there should be no such man?"

"It might be found, sir," assented Johnson. "It is conceivable that it might be found."

"Then the conception of noble passion depends upon enlightenment," pursued Heine. "The more enlightened people are, the better will be their chance of forming noble conceptions."

"Undoubtedly," replied the sage.

"Have men reached the highest possible state of enlightenment?" asked the poet. "Do you believe that the most intelligent and cultured man now living knows as much as can ever ultimately be known by one man?"

"No, sir, men will know more some day."

"Then is it conceivable that if men some day know more than they know now, they may some day form a higher idea of nobility of conduct than they now possess? Or is it not conceivable?"

"It is conceivable," answered Dr. Johnson. "It is even probable."

"Then our present idea of happiness is relative, and must be so," concluded Heine. "No one will venture to deny Cæsar's definition, I presume. A state where all our noblest feelings shall have full play and be constantly satisfied without ever being wearied, and where ignoble feelings shall not exist at all, must be a state of perfect happiness. But since we do not know everything, we do not know what we may some day feel. Consequently when we speak of our noblest feelings we do not know what our noblest feelings may ultimately turn out to be. Therefore we can only guess at what perfect happiness might be, by what men feel at present."

"Evidently," said Cæsar. "There are very noble feelings in men to-day which were wholly unknown in my time. The Romans of my day could not have imagined a man sacrificing his life in order to convert the Japanese to Christianity. They would have been amazed at the courage of the man and would have called him a madman. Now, his courage excites the same astonishment as ever, but the man is called a martyr. The list of noble feelings is longer now than it was then."

"But it would be impossible, in a state of perfect happiness, to be constantly satisfying the noble desire to be a martyr," remarked Gwendoline.

"The desire to be a martyr only proceeds from a strong religious feeling, which is the really noble feeling at the bottom of the action," answered Cæsar. "That feeling may be supposed to remain and to be fully satisfied without satiety, when the necessity for converting barbarians has quite ceased. There have always been men willing and anxious to sacrifice their lives for glory — that was a noble feeling, in its way. Men have now been found who will do the same thing for religion, for a purely transcendental set of ideas. It is not impossible that men may be found hereafter who shall be animated by great and noble aims of which we know nothing. A man is happy who thinks he is happy, because his desires are satisfied. But no two men ever seem able to be happy in precisely the same way. The way to be happy is to find out what is best in ourselves, and to try and satisfy the longings of the best part of us."

"That sounds very simple," remarked Lady Brenda.

"Yes," said Heine. "But there is a bitter irony in the word 'best.'"

"For Heaven's sake," cried Lady Brenda, "do not let us relapse into definitions and meanings of words! My brain reels."

"In the case of goodness, definition fails," answered the poet. "Indeed, it is quite useless. To know what goodness is we need only imagine the opposite of what we are; just as what we want is always the opposite of what we have."

"I prefer to think that I have something good in me," said Augustus. "I do not expect any one else to agree with me, of course. The only way to judge of a man is to find out what has been the happiest hour in his life, and then to judge of the circumstances which made up his momentary happiness. What was your happiest moment like, Herr Heine?"

"The happiest moments of my life?" repeated Heine. "I think they were spent in a sail-boat, tacking about the little island of Nordeney. I used to watch the clouds, and listen to the sea-tales of the sailors, and make verses about the ocean. My noblest aim was to lie on my back and think how I would surprise the Germans with descriptions of the sea."

"There was nothing very bad about that," answered

Augustus. "A man who could delight in such inno-cent things for a long time could not be a bad man."

"Badness shows itself much more in unhappiness," said Heine. "It is absurdly easy to be good when one is happy, as a man feels sympathy with the cook when the dinner is particularly to his taste. But the language a man uses when the dinner is bad shows his real nature. I used a great deal of surprisingly bad language in my time."

"You are the *procurator diaboli* against yourself," laughed Augustus. "No man is bound to prevent his own canonisation."

"What is that?" inquired Lady Brenda.

"When a person has been dead some time," said Dr. Johnson, "and is considered to have led so virtuous a life as to deserve the title of saint, an ecclesiastical trial takes place before the honour is conferred. Then a cunning lawyer is chosen, who is called the devil's advocate, whose business it is to show good cause why the deceased person should not be canonised. If he can show such cause, the proposal is rejected; but if not, the devil loses the suit and the saintship of the dead person is pro-claimed. When the devil proves his case, madam, there is no appeal, and the matter ends."

"I will not play the devil any longer in that case," observed Heine.

"Sir," said Johnson, "no man was ever canonised for making puns."

"No," retorted the poet. "But patience displayed

in listening to those made by others might deserve saintship."

"Sir, it is a form of martyrdom to which no saint was ever condemned, nor sinner neither. An English clergyman once said that the most dreadful death he could imagine would be to be preached to death by wild curates. To be punned to death, sir, would be equally horrible, though perhaps less exciting. Puns are like the prematurely withered leaves of a fine tree which, being separated from the branches by a breath, fall ineffectually rustling to the ground, a presage of approaching winter or a warning that the tree itself is about to perish and decay. The green leaves above rustled pleasantly yesterday, there is music in them to-day, and to-morrow the summer breeze will make them laugh together; but the withered leaf rustles but once, and poorly then, when it falls to the ground dead, like a pun, never to chime softly again with its fellows in the belfries of the woods. A punster, sir, should have a good memory, like a liar, or he will repeat himself; and a large wit, or he will pare it o' both sides and leave none i' the middle like King Lear."

"I think you are rather severe," observed Augustus. "I believe you more than once made puns yourself."

"Yes, sir, but they escaped from me by accident, as wise words sometimes fall from the lips of fools."

"And pray, what was the happiest moment of your life?" inquired Heine, who did not seem in the least annoyed by Johnson's attack.

"The day I was married, sir," returned the sage, without a moment's hesitation. "And the saddest day of my life was that on which my wife died. Success and failure are insignificant compared with the life and death of the one we love best."

"But may not the whole sum of a life's success, taken together, be more important than the sum of a life's affections?" asked Diana.

"To others, not to oneself," said Heine, sadly.

"Wait till you are married," laughed Augustus, looking at his sister.

"A man's success may depend to a great extent upon his affections," answered Johnson, quietly. "But it can never be foreseen whether the satisfaction of the affections will increase a man's activity, by implanting in him the desire to be successful in order to please the woman he loves, or whether, in the luxurious indolence of a happy and prosperous home, those qualities may not grow effeminate and unserviceable, which might have produced greatness under the pressure of a sterner necessity."

"Few poor men who have married rich wives have ever accomplished much afterwards," said Augustus. "The position is contemptible, in most cases, and a man ends by despising himself."

"Instead of despising himself from the beginning, as most men have good cause to do," remarked Heine, rather bitterly. "But I suppose that when one is in pursuit of happiness, one objects to sneering at oneself."

Just then King Francis appeared upon the narrow path that led down to the little beach, and striding forward paused, saluted the ladies with a courteous gesture and sat down beside Cæsar.

"Why should a man ever sneer at himself?" asked the king, with a smile on his bold face. "A man who despises himself will always be despised by others."

"Yes," said Cæsar. "Self-contempt is the result of all this morbid modern philosophy."

"It must be," answered the king. "In my time no one despised himself unless he ran away. Any man who would stand and fight was respected, and knew it. Life was simple then, and often pleasant. But the king risked it alike with the common spear-man. War was a grand thing then. There was something in our existence that was like that of the Greek heroes. We fought hand to hand, we broke lances in single combat, we rode to battle instead of going into the enemy's country in railway carriages. We plundered and pillaged the towns that opposed us, and when we came home victorious, we feasted and hunted and enjoyed life the more for having exposed it lightly. Those were royal times, when the king was king and the churl was churl, and nobody questioned the fact. One day was as happy as another, and yet no two days were ever the same."

"Your warfare was not warfare, it was chivalry," said Cæsar. "I should not even call your happiness happiness at all."

"And why?" asked Francis in deep tones.

"Because I cannot understand it. It was happiness to you to skirmish away your life, and to feast riotously between the skirmishes, but it would not have been happiness to me. I never was happy unless I felt that I had done something which must endure, whether men wished it to endure or not. I never was satisfied unless I had directed circumstances and events into a new groove from which they could not escape. You did that to some extent by developing your absolute authority and laying the foundation of an absolute monarchy. But you do not refer to that as having contributed to your happiness. What, in your whole life, do you remember with the greatest pleasure?"

"Many things," replied the king. "I hardly know. One was the victory of Marignano, where I beat the Swiss and made Bayard give me knighthood on the field of battle. Another was when I tripped Henry of England and threw him in our wrestling match on the field of the cloth of gold. Then, when I pardoned the people of Rochelle, after frightening them soundly for their behaviour — that was a happy day. I had many happy days, and I was a happy man during most of my life. Happiness means getting what one wants, and I generally did that. I wanted to be the first knight of France, and I fancied that I was. I never could understand Charles Quint, who lived on broth mixed with milk and vinegar, drank iced beer and plotted destruction over his prayers, like a cat that pretends to be asleep

until the sparrow hops within reach. I was very
happy when I used to visit Lionardo in the short
time he was with me before he died; for I loved
art, and beautiful things, and people who could
make them."

"It was fortunate that you were a king," said
Heine. "In any other condition of life you would
have had difficulty in satisfying your tastes — not
to say your aims, if one may speak of satisfying
aims — "

" The aim is satisfied when the mark has been hit,"
remarked Dr. Johnson.

" I remember that you once illustrated your meaning upon a publisher," replied Heine, with a laugh.
" I suppose that if one has any aims one ought to
make an effort to attain them. The way to be happy
is not to have any wishes which cannot be satisfied —
the simplest plan is to have no wishes at all. Man
is only happy when he thinks he is happy, because
happiness is a purely personal sentiment, resulting
from a purely personal impression of satisfaction.
The more ideas a man has, the less chance he has
of being happy, because ideas mean wishes which
must be fulfilled to obtain peace of mind. Poets,
who have more ideas than other men, are proverbially
unhappy. Oysters, on the contrary, are thought to be
very happy indeed — every one says ' as happy as an
oyster.' Unfortunately we cannot all be oysters, nor
conquerors, nor even poets."

" Fortunately, I should say," said the king. " Fort-

unately, that sort of equality is a myth. Everybody
has an equal right to try and be happy, I suppose,
but there is a deal of difference in regard to the
capacity for happiness."

"It is a strange thing," remarked Cæsar, "that
there should always be a class of men in the world
who think and maintain that the body of the world
is sick.   They call themselves philosophers, and they
propose an immediate cure for creation by applying
themselves to the world as a plaster, a universal
panacea.   In three thousand years philosophers have
not learned to understand that nobody cares what
they think nor will ever try their remedies.   Men are
not philosophers, though oysters may be.   No one
will ever govern man by a set of theories — the thing
is not possible.   You cannot civilise man by the head,
because all the ratiocination of man's intellect inevitably leads to conclusions closely connected with
individual advantage.   The beginning of all great
modern changes for the better is to be found in
sentiments, but the origin of most changes for the
worse in the lives of nations has lain in the miscal-
culation of the national interest."

"That is a delightful theory !" exclaimed Heine.

"It is not a theory, it is a fact," answered Cæsar.
"The Puritans who practically founded the American Republic were inspired by sentiment and not by
interest.   The people who nearly overthrew that same
Republic a few years ago were largely inspired by
interest.   The French Revolution began in a senti-

ment which soon became a means of satisfying a desire for vengeance; its most powerful effects were felt under the rule of one man, so long as he himself was inspired by a desire to make his country great, and the crash came when that man's personal ambition began to outweigh his patriotism. England reached the zenith of her power about thirty years ago, after having adopted a number of highly sentimental measures, such as the union of Ireland, the emancipation of Catholics, and free trade. But the sentiment of those things has worn itself out and the place where it was is now the battle-field of party interests. The result is that England is rapidly losing influence and importance in Europe. You can make people enthusiastic, you can make them move, for the sake of a sentiment, but not for the sake of a theory. Men feel first, and then invent theories to explain their feelings. It is a fatal error to confuse people who feel nothing by teaching them theories about what ought to be felt."

"It is a mistake to suppose that every one who has five senses has sense," said Heine. "If everybody were alike one might make theories, but it is unsatisfactory to attempt to theorise about a thousand million individuals, each of whom is quite different from all the rest. Nobody has ever got any further than making theories about himself. The' little burgher has the best of it after all. To live cleanly, so as to preserve the affection of his family and the friendship of his neighbours; to live moderately, so as to increase his property by saving money, and to maintain enough religion to inculcate those principles in his children — the burgher has no other aims, and I do not see why any one should want a more comfortable, moral, utterly dull and well-fed philosophy. There is very little else that is of any real importance to mankind, in spite of philosophers — because mankind itself is not quite as important as it likes to fancy itself. But in these puny days it is most abominably unfashionable to be simple, or to talk of anything but the solemnity of the aims of man. There is a complication nowadays in the little aims of this little world which is enough to make one's hair stand up on end. The little man of to-day is easily bored — even if compared with the man of the last century, and everybody knows that only bores are ever bored. The little burgher is right. Nothing really succeeds but property and keeping quiet — nothing — not even Mr. Herbert Spencer or the French Commune."

"If every man," remarked Johnson, "had a wife and a little property and the quality of holding his tongue, the world would be a very peaceable place. But, sir, those things are not easily got, and those who do not get them are very likely to turn anarchists, for the sake of stealing what belongs to others."

"What is Mr. Herbert Spencer?" asked King Francis.

"The American woman of the future," answered Heine, without hesitation.

"Imperfectly disguised as the Englishman of to-day," added Augustus.

"What an extraordinary pair of definitions!" exclaimed Lady Brenda.

"Do you think so?" asked Heine. "Mr. Spencer's books seem to me to be all about what we should do if we knew everything. Evidently American women are the only human beings who stand any chance of illustrating his theories."

"There were no American women in my day," remarked the king, "but I have seen something of them since, without being able to understand them. They are not very like women. I mean that their idea of what a woman should be differs from mine."

"Sir," said Johnson, "I suppose so."

King Francis swung his plumed cap in his hand and looked towards the sage with a light laugh.

"Yes," he answered. "The aims of woman do not seem to coincide with the aims of man so often as they formerly did. I cannot imagine what women want with aims."

"Generally, a husband," returned Heine. "It is in New England, where there are the fewest husbands to be had, that women have the most aims. In Tartary, where they do not attempt to rear the superfluous females, the women have enough to do in keeping house, or keeping tent, for their husbands. Aims, as you call them, are the result of idleness. If every man were obliged to work as hard as he could for his daily bread, there would be no time for scheming and no aims for anybody — we should have perpetual peace and no nonsense with it, no high-sounding talk about

the solemnity of creation, no professional pomposity.
We should have nothing to think of but bread and
the price of bread. That is real advancement. That
is modern socialism. That is the ideal republic.
That is freedom — not only from tyrants but from
lecturers. Do away with everything, and especially
with education. When a man and a woman must
labour all day for bread at a trade, and may never
have more than their daily allowance of bread, no
matter how they labour, what possible good can education do them? Let us turn socialists and destroy
at a blow those differences which mankind has taken
scores of centuries to create. If a baby is born with an
exceptionally intellectual skull, knock it on the head.
It is for the public good that there should be no differences. It is for the freedom of humanity to kill
everything above the average. If any man stand
more than five feet four inches in his stockings, cut
him down to the average of humanity. Excellence
is damnation, for it means superiority, and the superiority of one man suffices to demonstrate the degraded
idiotcy of millions who, but for him, might justly call
themselves wise."

"I thought you began by abusing aims and am-
bitions," said Gwendoline. "I should think that
nothing else could save you from the idiots you last
mentioned."

"Ah, madam," replied Heine, "to end an argument on the same side upon which one stood at its
beginning would show a lamentable lack of imagina-

tion! Forgive my turning about — there is such a
difference between a poet's ambition and the theo-
retical desire for evolved goodness which Mr. Herbert
Spencer preaches. There is such a vast difference
between Freedom in rhyme and Freedom upon
stamped paper! One reason why I hate all this
modern philosophy is because it never takes into
account the fact that a man may change his mind,
that he may like buttered bread to-day and dry bread
to-morrow, rest one week and hard work the next.
Is man a machine that he should live not only by
law, but by inflexible rule? Is he a wheel, that he
must for ever turn upon one axle? A steam-engine
of which the philosophers are to handle the throttle-
valve and the reversing lever and adjust the expan-
sion gear to the measure of their steam supply?
What is man, in the name of common sense? Is he
a thinking creature, capable of thinking for himself?
Or is he a learned ass to be taught to perform tricks
in the circus of philosophy before a critical public of
graduates in the science of teaching asses? Is man
not only to eat, drink, work, and rest by method,
but also to love by rule, to be ambitious by rule, to
sacrifice his neighbour to himself when the rule tells
him he is more valuable to the community than his
neighbour, to weep by rule a nicely calculated number of tears, and to adjust his laughter to the subject
which excites it, by the infallible method of prime
and ultimate ratios? Is there to be no choice left,
no free will, no imagination, no poetry, and no prose

but the tiresome account book wherein is reckoned up the happiness of the greatest number? Are civilised men to slave at a daily task in Europe, binding themselves by an oath never to want more than their equal portion, in order that an idiotic African or a pot-bellied Hindu vegetarian may have a like portion with themselves — to wit, sixteen ounces of bread and a glass of water, more or less? Go to! These dreams of equality are rubbish! The frog who tries to puff himself up to the size of the ox must burst, and the ox who tries to reduce himself by privation to the size of the frog will starve. There are big animals and little animals, big brains and little brains, big thoughts and little thoughts. The only freedom worth the name is that which gives each man a fair chance to find his level and leaves the rest to himself, which allows one man to pursue happiness and another man to pursue greatness, and which admits that what would make one man happy would make another unspeakably miserable. Show me the philosopher who has changed the destinies of mankind by his theories, and I will talk seriously with you. Prove to me that any one of the great men of the earth, beginning with Cæsar — or with Menes, the Thinite, if you please — governed according to the precepts of any philosophy, and I will admit then that philosophy has played a part in the world."

"It seems to me," said Diana, "that freedom comes under the class of things, or ideas, or prin-

ciples, with which philosophy has dealt. Many
nations have fought for that, and have governed
themselves solely with the intention of remaining
free."

"Freedom never was made the subject of philosophical speculation, until men had lost it," returned
Heine. "When a boy has plenty of jam he does not
invent plans for stealing more."

"Exactly," argued Diana. "Philosophy professes
to teach men how to obtain what is good for them,
when they do not possess all that they have a right
to possess — and it teaches men to be contented
when they cannot get what they hanker after."

"If you mean to impose that definition on the
world," replied Heine, "you must set up a High
Pontiff among philosophers to decide what is legitimate philosophy and what is not. In other words
you must persuade all men to accept the judgment of
one man, which means that all men must be subjected to a supreme tyrant, that is to say, liberty is to
be destroyed. That is the result of the philosophy of
freedom. Either it will end by destroying freedom,
because it will force everybody under the rule of a
tyrant, or it will set up half a dozen different kinds
of freedom which will fight each other to death,
which is contrary to the definition of freedom. That
is a pretty dilemma."

"Sir," said Johnson, "I do not believe that there
is any dilemma which can defy common sense. According to Varro, the son of Antipater broke the

head of the philosophic dilemma with a mattock, with the 'quick argument by the single horn' — in other words by a forcible application of common sense. Freedom, sir, is the contrary of enforced servitude."

## CHAPTER XIII.

DIANA had wandered from the house alone one
morning and as she picked her way among the rocks,
she paused now and then to pluck the wildflowers
that grew in every cranny and carpeted every little
plot of grass among the boulders.  She was thinking
of all she had heard during the past days and trying
to reconcile the many varying opinions expressed by
the strange party.  She wished that she could go
back into the closed centuries and see the lives of
these dead men as they had been, and she sighed as
she realised how far she was from understanding the
real existence and conditions of existence of humanity
in past ages.

"After all," she said aloud to herself, "we are not
sure of ever understanding any history but that of
our own particular lives.  We dislike people who talk
about themselves, and when they do not we are angry·
with them for not telling us what we want so much
to know.  Vanity of vanities!"

"And yet," said a quiet voice beside her, "next
to ourselves, nothing interests us so much as other
people."

Diana turned and recognised the beautiful features
and the lofty figure of Lionardo.

"I thought I was alone!" she exclaimed in some surprise. "I am so glad it is you," she added, quickly.

"Not more glad than I am," answered the old man, courteously. "You were thinking aloud — I took the liberty of joining in the conversation of your thoughts. You were saying, or thinking, that people are interesting. Indeed there is very little else in the world which has any great interest for those who live in it, or for those who have lived in it."

"I am glad to hear you say so," replied Diana. "I have sometimes thought that it is bad for the mind to occupy it too much with people. Inanimate things seem safer; they do not change so fast. When we know anything about them, we feel quite sure of what we know. It is not the same with people."

"People progress. Things either remain as they are or decay," said Lionardo, looking thoughtfully at the young girl. "It is clear that although in the last thousand years mankind has improved, nature has tended to degenerate wherever she has not continued to be as she was. The sea knocks away the cliffs and slowly eats the land, the sun melts the glaciers, man makes holes in the mountains and the moon moves more rapidly round the earth, the earth revolves more slowly upon her axis. In rather less than twenty millions of years the moon will probably go round the earth once a day and will remain apparently stationary in the heavens."

"That is a long way off," laughed Diana. "It will not come in my time."

"No. Your time, as you call it, is the time while you are alive. After that, time will belong to the next generation — not to you. The reason why time is so tremendously important to you is because the time of your life is all the time there is, so far as you are concerned. As you help to make it, so your time will appear to the view of those who follow you."

"Past time always seems more interesting than the present," said Diana, looking into the painter's deep eyes as though she were trying to conjure up the life that had once surrounded his. "I have often wished that I might have lived when you did."

"It was an age of individuals. This is the age of the millions."

"And what will the next age be?" asked the young girl.

"The age of collapse and of barbarian domination, I suppose," answered Lionardo.

"Of the three, yours, the age of individuals, is the most interesting."

"It seems so to you. People who live in luxurious leisure, using their intelligence in refined study, easily fancy that in an age of individuals talent played a greater part than it does now, and that they themselves would have been important figures in their times. But the people who lead the millions, in the age of the million, think their own century the most interesting. They think that in my time, for instance, they could have led everybody just as certainly and with half the trouble, so that they get more credit now than they would have got then."

"Do you think they really could?" asked Diana. "Do you think that Prince Bismarck would have succeeded in unifying Italy under one rule, as Cesare Borgia tried to do?"

"It is quite certain that Cesare Borgia would have failed to unify Germany in the nineteenth century in Prince Bismarck's place," answered the artist, with a smile. "Cesare's mode of operating was different. He was Machiavelli's ideal — cunning, cultivated, witty, unscrupulous. Bismarck is the incarnation of consistency animated by gunpowder. He has confounded the diplomatists of Europe for five and twenty years by telling them the truth. He goes upon the principle that honesty is the best policy for people who are able to hit very hard. Cesare Borgia considered that lying was the appropriate dress of strength and that secret murder was the only expression of force. He did not see, when he had subdued a great part of northern Italy to his own rule, that his position depended upon his father's life and influence. When his father Alexander the Sixth, died, Cesare naturally fell."

"I have heard it said that he might have maintained his conquests if he had not been ill from poison just at the critical moment," said Diana.

"I do not believe it. People are always finding

excuses for fascinating men who fail after making
a great deal of noise.   After all, why did you bring
up Cesare Borgia as an example?   He was hand-
some, clever and a scoundrel, but he never came near
greatness."

"He is a specimen of the times, that is all.   I
would like to have seen him — I would like to hear
him talk with Bayard, for instance.   It would be
such a delightful contrast.   Besides, he was a typical
Italian."

"Ah, my dear young lady," replied the artist,
"you are unfair to us.   I cannot let you say that
Cesare Borgia was a type of our nation.   We are
better than that; on the faith of an artist, we are not
all murderers and poisoners and traitors.   There
have been good men amongst us."

"Savonarola," suggested Diana.

"Savonarola — well — Savonarola," repeated the
old man in doubtful tones, spreading out his hand
with the palm downwards and alternately raising the
thumb and the little finger, as though balancing the
good and evil genii of the Dominican monk.

"You seem to hesitate," remarked the young girl.

"Savonarola — he was not a bad man — no — but he
was a detestable fellow.   He fell a victim to a piece
of his own very gratuitous political scheming."

"What an extraordinary view!   I always heard
that he was burnt by Alexander as a heretic."

"So he was," replied Lionardo, thoughtfully.

"Well, then — I do not understand," said Diana.

"I will give you the history of Savonarola in three words — Enthusiasm, Fanaticism, Failure. He began to preach in 1489, under Pope Innocent the Eighth, and he inveighed against Lorenzo de' Medici on the ground that he had usurped the sovereignty of Florence. He forgot that Lorenzo inherited the supremacy from his father Pietro, whose father, again, Cosmo de' Medici, had already been practically the ruler of Florence. He forgot, too, that Lorenzo himself had narrowly escaped being murdered with his brother by the agents of Sixtus the Fourth, the Pazzi, the so-called friends of liberty. Savonarola took upon himself to refuse absolution to Lorenzo when on his deathbed, on the sole ground that the latter would not renounce and abdicate the power he had inherited. That was in 1492. In 1494 Savonarola excited the Florentines against Pietro, Lorenzo's son, when he returned from his attempt to treat with Charles the Eighth of France, and succeeded in driving him out, thus thrusting his fellow-citizens into the arms of the French king, who forthwith entered Florence as a foreign conqueror; and the Florentines had great difficulty in getting rid of him. From that time Savonarola continued to preach an alliance with Charles the Eighth, which practically meant a submission to him. Meanwhile Alexander the Sixth, Rodrigo Borgia, scandalised the world by his conduct and Savonarola openly denounced the Pope. He forgot, however, that Alexander the Sixth, with all his vices, had been one of the founders of the league which had driven the French out of Italy. Alexander resented Savonarola's propaganda of the French alliance and, seeking occasion against him, declared the monk a heretic for assuming to be endowed with supernatural gifts and for his attacks on the government of the Church. Savonarola refused the ordeal by fire himself, and his friend and fellow-monk, Domenico Buonvicino, refused it at the last moment, when the pile was erected. Every one declared Savonarola an impostor, and he was delivered over to the Pope. Under torture, he weakly confessed all manner of misdeeds which he had not committed, and he, with his two friends Buonvicino and Marraffi were strangled and their bodies were burnt in the Piazza della Signoria. That is the history of Girolamo Savonarola. I do not see that there is material for making a martyr of him since his death — there was certainly not the stuff of a hero in him when he was alive."

"That is a very prejudiced account of him," remarked Diana.

"I could say far worse things of him. He was an iconoclast, a destroyer of everything that was beautiful, a Vandal! If he had lived to carry out his schemes he would have left not one work of art in Florence. He detested Lorenzo for his love of the antique and would have got rid of all the Medici for ever, if he could. Pray, what would Florence have been without the Medici?"

"Nevertheless," objected Diana, who would not

relinquish her point, "people have been found to defend him as a hero and a martyr even in our day."

"As they defend Giordano Bruno," retorted the artist. "But Sismondi, the most important of modern Italian historians, and who was profoundly prejudiced against the popes, did not defend him in his actions, though he admired him for his original qualities. Sismondi accuses him of taking his own impulses for prophetic revelations, by which he directed the politics of his disciples, and states without comment the fact that the monk pushed the Florentines into an alliance with Charles the Eighth, the enemy of Italian liberty. Sismondi, who hated the popes, and especially detested Alexander the Sixth, could not refrain from stating that Savonarola was burnt alive, contrary to the evidence of all the best authorities, but he does not conceal the fact that Savonarola pretended, like Mahomet, to be receiving constant and direct revelations from God. Machiavelli speaks of him as veering from point to point, to paint and colour his fraud and cunning. That is natural enough, since Machiavelli was deeply attached to Lorenzo de' Medici. Your English historian Roscoe who may be supposed to represent the judgment of Protestants upon the Dominican monk, speaks of him with unmeasured scorn. He says that Savonarola entitled himself to the homage of the people of Florence by foretelling their destruction and that he contributed essentially to the accomplishment of his own predictions; and he further adds that he entertained the most vindictive animosity against his patron, Lorenzo de' Medici. I do not see what other evidence you can want. The fact that he was enthusiastic when he began his career does not excuse him for having been vindictive at a later period, nor for having acted the impostor in pretending to receive divine revelations of which the object was the ruin of Florence. Believe me, my dear young lady, all this sympathy for Girolamo Savonarola is sentimental. It is of a piece with the modern fashion of extolling the virtues of Lucrezia Borgia and of making out that Nero was a gentle, sensitive, and misunderstood artist of genius. I can defend Alexander the Sixth and Cesare Borgia as eloquently as you can defend Savonarola or Giordano Bruno, upon different grounds."

"Upon what grounds?" asked Diana. "I do not see how you can compare two profligate tyrants with two men who were certainly moral in their private lives, if they were nothing else."

"Moral!" exclaimed Lionardo. "Savonarola — yes — he was moral enough, he meant to be a good man. But Giordano Bruno! One portion of his writings is not fit for man or beast, much less for woman![1] When he was not spiteful he was filthy, and when he was neither, he was blasphemous, though he was frequently all three together."

"Of course I have never read his works," answered

[1] It is to be presumed that Giordano Bruno's English defenders have either never seen his complete works, or have not understood the low Neapolitan dialect in which he often wrote.

Diana, quietly, " but I believe he was something of a philosopher, not to say a scientist."

"I will do him the credit to say that he defended the system of Copernicus," assented the artist, with a smile, " and he quarrelled with all known and unknown philosophies. But the system of Copernicus does not in itself constitute a morality, and it was on the ground of his morality that you proposed to defend him. I did not say he was a fool. I said he was a bad man. He was not so bad as Cesare Borgia, but he was very far from being so important a personage."

" The greatness of the Borgias was not of the kind to be envied. I cannot see why you cling to them."

" You yourself said you would like to see Cesare," answered Lionardo. " Believe me, if you could see half a dozen of those men together, and talk with them, you would not think our age so delightful as it looks through the stained glass of three centuries. We artists enjoyed our lives more than other men, I suppose, because the reigning princes always had need of us, whoever they chanced to be. In my day I served the Florentine Republic, Ludovico Sforza of Milan, Cesare Borgia, Louis the Twelfth of France, Leo the Tenth and Francis the First. I painted for Florence, I made canals for Ludovico Moro, I fortified towns for the Duke Valentino,[1] I made more

[1] Many critics found fault with Mr. W. W. Astor for calling Cesare Borgia by this name. Machiavelli in the last paragraph of the third chapter of the *Principe*, says: " I had an interview about

canals for Louis and I painted pictures for the rest.
No one ever molested me, and I had a very happy
life. But look at the governments I served. Florence was the battle-ground of the Medici and the
popes, Ludovico Sforza died in a dungeon, Cesare
Borgia was killed in a skirmish after having been
exiled for many years, and even Leo the Tenth is
now generally believed to have been poisoned. Their
lives were not easy and their deaths were less so, but
we artists were rarely molested. We enjoyed a special immunity because we were always wanted."

"Artists are not often molested in our day, and
as far as numbers go they have the better of you,"
replied Diana. "But apart from that, there was an
individuality in your age which we do not understand. Single characters stand out, like Cesare Borgia, Ludovico Sforza or any of those men — but we
form no distinct idea of their surroundings. I wonder
why that is so. When I think of Cæsar, I think of
him in connection with the other men of his time, as
coming soon after Marius and Sulla, as the rival of
Pompey, as the uncle of Octavius —"

"Cæsar was a greater man than our personages
of the fifteenth and sixteenth centuries. You know
more about him."

"That is not the reason. I sometimes think I
would rather know more about your times than about
ancient history. I have a much clearer idea of the

this at Nantes with the Card. d'Amboise when VALENTINO, *as the
son of Pope Alexander was commonly called*, occupied Romagna."

surroundings of Alcibiades than of the daily life of
Cesare Borgia."

"I think," answered Lionardo, "that the complication of small events in our day was too great to be
remembered distinctly. There were too many ro-
.mantic characters, involved in desperately romantic
circumstances, producing on the whole very little
effect upon the world. One remembers the individual without connecting him with the event. A
fictitious interest is often attached to romantic personages which does not seem justified by their deeds.
Hence it is not easy to compose a history of one of
them which shall not disappoint the reader."

"You artists, at least, are known by what you
accomplished," said Diana, looking at the old man's
expressive face.

"And perhaps some of those princes deserve only
to be remembered for having paid the price of our
works," returned the painter. "We were often
obliged to sing our own praises in order to obtain
orders from them. I remember writing a letter to
Ludovico, which I should be ashamed to write in
your times, but it was necessary then. I professed
myself able to build public and private edifices as
well as any one alive, to construct canals against any
known engineer, to produce statues of bronze or marble or clay, and to paint, all as well as any living
artist. It is true that Michelangeolo was a boy at the
time. Titian was a baby then, and Raphael and An-
drea del Sarto were both born in the year I wrote

the letter. Nevertheless I have often thought with wonder of my own assumption in enumerating my talents. On the other hand, if I had shown any modesty or diffidence I should never have attracted Ludovico's attention. This was the way in which our individuality asserted itself. Men knew that their success depended on their ability to force themselves upon the attention of the great, unless they were great by birth, in which case they were obliged to rule as much by inspiring terror as by exhibiting clemency. The artist of course knew that if he failed to fulfil his promises, it was in the prince's power to ruin him, and the prince himself, having power to destroy the artist, readily put faith in the professions of a man who showed himself ready to run so great a risk. The result of all this was the contrast of individualities which has surprised posterity. Where great forces are called into play, the will and intelligence of the leader are easily confounded with the executive power he directs, owing to the magnitude of the result. To take an instance from more recent times, such as the failure of Bonaparte's expedition to Russia; I fancy that you think quite as much of Marshal Ney and of the 'Grande Armée,' as of the emperor himself, when you recall your general memories of the campaign. Most people do. But when you think of Cesare Borgia and his attempt to conquer the north of Italy, you think of the man alone and your mind probably provides you with no picture of his soldiers, his lieutenants, or his counsellors. He is, to you, a detached monster of wickedness, little better than Eccelino Romano, the tyrant of the Trevisan March, though a little more clear to the historical vision. The atrocious deeds of Cesare and Eccelino are not rendered insignificant by enormous military operations, decisive victories or defeats entailing the ruin of an empire. The background is but a panorama of petty warfare in the darkest episodes of which the princes themselves are the chief actors. Their individuality stands out like a black figure in the foreground of a grey picture. To understand those men thoroughly you must study their surroundings, you must fill in the middle distance and the background until you feel that the whole composition is harmonious. You must learn how the various classes of men lived in those days, and especially what the various classes thought of the princes who governed them. The light of history falls unequally on the armies of the past, as they stand drawn up in their dead ranks. The figures that chance to be illuminated look much as they did in life, but the effect they produce is exaggerated by the darkness which surrounds them."

" For the sake of posterity," said Diana, " painters should paint nothing but scenes from their own times. It might be less interesting to themselves, but it would be vastly more valuable to the people who live after them. Each succeeding generation paints subjects from the preceding times. Even in our day it is fashionable to paint pictures of persons in

the dress of the beginning of the century. For a
long time, anything later than shorts and silk stockings was considered impossible on canvas. Artists
have now attacked the incroyable period. It is reserved for the genre painters of the next century to
represent men in trousers and evening coats and
women in costumes invented by Doucet or Redfern.
I believe there are a few original geniuses who have
tried even that. After all, why is it not better to
preserve accurately for posterity what we can see,
than to revive more or less inaccurately that which
belonged to the past? Why should what we meet
every day in real life look ridiculous in a gilt frame,
unless it chances to be in the portrait of some living
person? Why cannot history be painted as well as
written? Raphael and Pinturicchio have left a series
of frescoes in the library of the Cathedral of Siena,
which give one a complete idea of the life of Pius
Second. Why could they not have done the same
for Alexander Sixth who lived in their own time? I
would have artists perpetuate the events of their day,
and I would have governments bear the expense of
such pictures as being valuable historical documents."

"It would be good for history and bad for art,"
answered Lionardo, thoughtfully. "A series of coloured photographs would answer the purpose without degrading art. But I doubt whether anything
of the kind, if you had it, would recall our age to
you as it was. A gallery of portraits of people
assembled upon an important occasion and dressed

in their best clothes would not suffice to create in your mind an impression of the way in which those people lived. Nor is it the object of art to perpetuate common and often repulsive details. Art, without a little inspiration, can be nothing but a laborious substitute for photography, whereas it should be the object of photography to perform at a cheap rate the drudgery which true art must always despise, or to reproduce at an insignificant price the works of good artists for the delectation of those persons who are unable to see the originals. Painters must paint portraits of all sorts of people, since the appreciation of beauty is greatest where there exists at the same time the most profound knowledge of the commonplace. Beauty being exceptional, the understanding of it requires a detailed acquaintance with what is not beautiful, since it is by constantly eliminating the imperfect that the highest perfection is attained. Much that is thought to be beautiful really borders upon the unnatural, and it needs both study and experience to decide at what point the exaggeration of one or more good features begins to produce the strange feeling of dissatisfaction that arises from the discord of proportion which is nicknamed ' the grotesque.' Therefore I say that painters must paint portraits of all kinds of people in order to be able to imagine and paint faces of ideal beauty."

"I fancy it is generally believed that the way to create beautiful works is to study only the beautiful," said Diana. "But your theory seems true."

"It is because men have been confined so long by the schools to the study of the beautiful, that they have suddenly thrown themselves into the opposite extreme. From having been taught to believe that only one class of subjects ought to be represented, they have fallen into the error of supposing that nothing is so hideous as to be unworthy of the artist's pencil."

"You used to paint very ugly things yourself," remarked Diana.

"For study," answered the artist. "I was fond of physiognomy, as every painter should be. I loved to study the origin of expression in the face. When a beautiful woman laughs lightly the same muscles are in motion which produce a horrid grin in the face of a drunken boor. As far as the lines go, supreme beauty and repulsive ugliness are only a quarter of an inch apart."

"Nothing quite symmetrical is entirely displeasing to the eye," said the young girl. "The most horrible masks and gargoyle water-spouts are used as architectural ornaments and are not disagreeable, so long as their features have some symmetry."

"Symmetry is a vertical notion," replied Lionardo, "and corresponds to the horizontal notion we call proportion."

"I do not understand," said Diana.

"Our idea of symmetry only extends to the right hand and the left hand of a central vertical line," answered the artist. "It does not extend above or

below a horizontal line. In the latter direction we
have only a desire for proportion. A church door,
for instance, having two pillars on the one side and
three on the other, would shock us by its lack of
symmetry; but a temple in two stories may have
seven pillars below and six or five above — we do not
demand symmetry in that direction, though we require
proportion. A building broader above than below
would strike us as an architectural monstrosity on
account of the evident lack of stability in the. equi-
librium. But a pyramid is pleasing to the eye. A
pyramid in any other position than standing on its
base would be offensive to our instincts. It is the
same with the human face and the human body. We
require that there should be an eye on each side of
the nose and an ear on each side of the head, but we
do not feel that, to be pleasing to the sight, the human
face should begin again, in the reversed order, from
the line of the hair upward, so that there should be a
second forehead, a second pair of eyes, a second nose,
mouth and chin, all upside down. The symmetry to
right and left, however, is indispensable; if you preserve it you may invent any monster to be carved in
wood, stone or metal. The result may be terrible,
grotesque, or beautiful, it will never produce the sensation evoked by incongruity — it will never be half
so frightful as the effigy of a monster with one eye on
one side and a smooth surface in its place on the
other. You may obliterate both the eyes without
producing the startling effect caused by effacing only

one of them. The absence of nose or mouth in a drawing only makes the face look unfinished — the lack of an eye inspires horror. If you preserve symmetry, you may paint grinning peasants to any extent of variety, and the painting of them will be useful as a study. Even commonplace heads are good to paint, as I said before, because you learn to eliminate gradually all that is not beautiful."

" Do you mean that artists ought to begin by studying the ugly ? " inquired Diana.

" They should not begin by drawing only academical noses and architectural eyebrows, as they generally do. They ought to draw alternately beautiful and ugly faces, and above all they should draw from the first faces having a great variety of expression. Over-study of the academic often produces a distaste for the beautiful."

" As a child ends by hating the Collects and Gospels which he has been forced to learn by heart on Sunday," suggested the young girl. " I suppose that the same truth extends to other things. People who make a hard and fast rule for themselves are sometimes more inclined to go suddenly to an opposite extreme than people who go along without any particular principle. When Karl Sand had murdered Kotzebue he fell on his knees before the crowd in the street outside the house and solemnly thanked God for his victory, while stabbing himself in the breast to escape justice. He lived long enough to be beheaded, after all. What an outrageous set of contradictions ! And yet he was theoretically no more illogical than the painter who paints anatomical monstrosities because he is sick of the staid style of the academy."

" Savonarola came very near being an instance of the same thing," answered the old artist. " As for my good friend King Francis, when he was tired of imitating Bayard, he imitated Cesare Borgia. He was nearly as successful with the one as with the other."

" Francis the First was one of the most inconsistent men who ever lived. I do not like him."

" And yet he meant to be a good man. He fancied himself always what he really was on very rare occasions. But he was inconsistent, except in his desire to found an absolute monarchy."

" I suppose it is something to a king's credit if he is consistent in one thing," said Diana. " One must not expect too much."

" I have sometimes thought that with all their faults the Italians of our age were more consistent than the foreign princes who attacked them," replied Lionardo. " The most apparently inconsistent of all was Gian Galeazzo Visconti, who lived before I did, but of whom people still talked when I was alive. And yet his inconsistency was only apparent, it was not real. He so concealed his own intentions that people were not able to reconcile together the results he produced. But it was clear in the end that every action of his life had tended to his own aggrandisement. When he locked himself up in his castle and pretended that he was afraid of being assassinated if he stirred abroad, no one suspected that it was a mere comedy calculated to increase the confidence of his brother Barnabò, whom he murdered at their next meeting. There was certainly an evil consistency at the bottom of his most contradictory actions. But Francis was really inconsistent. He was theatrical. He was easily moved to produce striking effects, and very hard to move to anything which did not amuse him. He won the battle of Marignano against the Swiss by his own heroic personal courage, and he lost the battle of Pavia by an unlucky display of vanity — by taking the advice of Bonnivet against that of every one else; and giving battle from a disadvantageous position. He loved glory when it was to be had by physical courage — he did not care for it when its price was the sacrifice of his own inclinations. He broke a very solemn promise made to the emperor when he was a prisoner, and he broke it for his own advantage. Then, when he had the emperor in his hands, he treated him with the utmost magnanimity, entertained him splendidly, and sent him on his way in peace."

"That was to his credit, at all events," said Diana. "A smaller man would perhaps have kept his promise in the first instance, but would have locked up Charles in the Bastille when he had a chance."

"And what would a modern sovereign do under the circumstances?" asked the painter.

"I suppose that if he were defeated as Francis was

at Pavia, his people would dethrone him and make a revolution. That was what happened to Napoleon Third."

" Would the same thing happen if a king of England were caught and made prisoner by his enemies in these times?"

" I do not know," answered Diana. " The English would fight for their king, I imagine, and perhaps they would dethrone him after they had got him back."

" That sounds inconsistent."

"No. They would be too patriotic to allow their king to remain a prisoner. That would touch their national pride. But as far as their relations with their sovereign were concerned, they would be independent enough to dethrone him if they were not satisfied with his kingship. Patriotism is not loyalty."

While they were talking the sun went down, and all the sky grew soft and purple above them.

" Another day is gone," said Diana almost sadly. " Let us go home. You will come with me, will you not?"

" I will come with you a part of the way," answered the artist. " But I will come again this evening with the others of our friends. Why are you sad?"

" The sunset is like the autumn," sighed the young girl. " The saddest time of the day, and the saddest time of all the year. It must be like dying. The light will go out some day, and leave us in a world we do not know, through which we cannot find our way."

"Were there no other spring, nor any other rising of the sun, death would be dreadful indeed. But you are young to think of such things."

"Yes," answered Diana, smiling a little. "Besides, if we were logical we should look at things differently. We ought to consider the condemned criminal, who is told that he is to die on a certain day of the month at a certain hour, as the happiest of mortals. He, at least, knows exactly how long he has to live, whereas I may go on for sixty years, or die to-night. What a lottery!"

"Ah, my dear lady, we must not be discontented with the beginning. There is peace yet to come. All life is but a step towards peace. Sometimes when men live to be very old, peace begins for them before they have crossed the threshold. To others it comes later, but to all good men and women it comes at last."

"How strange those moralities sound — when you utter them! What are you? I see you and talk with you. I have touched your hand and heard your voice. I know you as I know the others — what are you?"

"We do not know what we are," answered the venerable artist very gravely. "We know only that we are still ourselves, and shall be for ever. And somewhere, too, are all the million, million selves that have played parts in this little corner of the universe since the beginning. That is all we know. Good-bye — we shall meet again this evening."

"Good-bye," said Diana, taking his cold hand fearlessly in hers, and gazing for a few seconds into his deep, liquid eyes.

Lionardo left her, and she hastened homeward through the deepening twilight. What he had said had produced a profound impression upon her, the stronger for its extreme simplicity. She wondered whether it were true, and whether, even when her last sun had set and her last breath had trembled upon the air of a mortal world, she should still not know the great secret. In youth death often seems very near because we fear it, in old age it is nearer still, because men desire peace when they are weary, and have little joy of life when the strength is gone from them.

## CHAPTER XIV.

THAT evening at dinner there was less conversation than usual. The strange life which the party at the Castello del Gaudio had been leading for some time was beginning to produce its inevitable effect. They all grew silent and were often preoccupied with one common thought, wondering constantly what was to happen next. Every one wore a look in which ·a question was expressed and an uncertainty, for they had been trespassing in dreamland, or shadow-land, whichever is the name given to that misty country, by the shades that dwell there.

"Why should it not last for ever?" exclaimed Diana, suddenly.

"Oh! I should go mad, if it did!" said Lady Brenda. "Not but that it has been most delightful of course. But it is so weird, and altogether — I cannot explain it at all."

"No," answered Augustus. "I believe you cannot, nor I either, nor any of us. But I am not sure that I would like it to go on for ever. This sort of life makes one unfit for anything but loafing. Slang? Yes, you must forgive me. Only dead men are quite above slang."

"I think," said Gwendoline, "that people will find

us dreadfully changed when we go home. But I would not give up all we have had here for anything in the world."

No one spoke again for some minutes, for Gwendoline had expressed what was passing in the minds of the others. They would not willingly have forfeited such memories.

" It may change our way of thinking," said Augustus, at last. " But I am not sure that we should any of us care to think differently about most things."

" We should not be ourselves if we did," answered Gwendoline. " I know we should not be happier. 'Ourselves' means what we think we are."

" Together with what other people think of us," added Diana.

" When I say ' myself,' I mean what I am," put in Lady Brenda. " What other people think about me does not change me."

" I do not know," said Augustus. " But even if it does not, do you know what you are?"

" I suppose I could describe myself, if I tried — and if nobody were there to hear the description," answered his mother-in-law.

" That would only be telling what you think of yourself. You might be mistaken. It is commonly said that we should know the truth if we could see ourselves as others see us."

" I do not believe that is true. Other people will generally over-estimate or undervalue us. No one can know what I am, but I myself."

"But even you yourself do not quite know," objected Diana.

"Then nobody knows. What difference does it make?" retorted Lady Brenda, laughing. "And if nobody knows how can any one know that I am changed after talking to a dozen or so of intelligent ghosts for a month, more or less?"

"It has been more like a dream than a reality," said Diana, with a little sigh. "Sometimes dreams do affect our lives, for a little while. I think it is strange that we should feel as we do about these spirits, or manifestations, or whatever they are. We all feel their unreality when they are gone, and yet they are so much like living people that they do not startle us when they appear."

"It is certainly very odd," Gwendoline remarked. "And I wonder how they all chance to be together. Do you remember our first dinner here? We each named some one whom we would like to see, and most of them have come. Perhaps it is only a creation of our brains."

"I was going to propose a moonlight sail this evening," said Augustus. "What do you all think of it? We can sail round the Galli, or the isles of the Sirens — whichever they are — and if all these ghosts have been the creation of our brains, why then — "

"We might see the Sirens themselves!" exclaimed Gwendoline.

"I wish we could hear them," answered Diana.

"If we do — really, we shall have to send for keepers and turn your castle into a lunatic asylum!" said Lady Brenda.

"I have had everything got ready for this evening," replied Augustus. "We have only to go on board. The sea is like glass and this queer breeze from the rocks will carry us as far as we like to go — all night if we please. The natives call it the *puizza*. The other night a boat was nearly capsized by it, though the water was like oil."

The party left the room and soon afterwards reassembled on the terrace whence a flight of steps led to the descent to the beach. They all stood together for a moment and looked out at the quiet sea. The moon was not yet full, but the light was strong and clear, already high and casting few shadows.

As they went down to the shore, walking carefully over the rough path, they began to feel the cool air that pours over the edge of the land in a continuous stream from sunset to sunrise, rushing over the water, swiftly at first and then more slowly, till it floats out silently into the night, tempering the heated surface of the calm southern sea with a restful freshness. The yacht lay less than fifty yards from the beach, mainsail and topsail hoisted, only waiting for her passengers, ready to slip her moorings from the buoy and glide away through the silent moonlight. She was a large and beautiful cutter, winner of many a race, and famous for her doings on rougher seas than the Gulf of Salerno or the Bay of Naples. A neat gig, manned by four men, was waiting by a projecting rock that served as a landing, and in a few minutes the whole party was on board. Augustus took the helm himself and the three ladies established themselves upon chairs near him. The men went forward and in a few minutes the yacht was moving swiftly along, westward, towards the Campanella and Capri.

Presently there were other forms upon the white deck. One by one, the strange companions who had become so familiar to the inhabitants of the Castello del Gaudio, became visible, standing and sitting in various attitudes, all grouped about the four living people at the stern of the yacht.

"This is the river Styx, and I am Charon!" exclaimed Augustus. "Whither shall I ferry you? Are the Isles of the Blessed near?"

Then Augustus and his three companions heard a sound that was not the rushing of the night wind through the rigging, nor the swirl of the deep dark water under the raking stern. It was a deep, mysterious breath, more felt than heard, full of human sadness, but without the reality a sigh takes from human suffering. It came from the breasts of those shadowy beings who had learned the great secret, but could not impart it to the living with whom they lingered. There was an infinite pathos in the expression of it that deeply moved those who heard it. It floated away into the night and was lost in the breeze, like a last farewell, that echoes and is gone, while the responsive heart-strings still quiver and repeat the bitter music roused by that dear voice.

"The Isles of the Blessed!" said Heine, at last. "No, they are not near. Your ship cannot sail to them."

"I wish we could all sail there together," said Diana. "It would be so simple."

"Who knows?" returned the poet, who was standing beside her. "Only what we know is simple."

"And we know nothing," answered the young girl, sadly. "I do not know certainly that you are not one of my dreams. When I touch your hand and find it cold, I may be asleep on the terrace at the castle and my fingers may have fallen upon the marble balustrade, or against a glass of cold water."

"Of course. And for all I know, I may be alive still, dreaming that I am dead."

"That is impossible," replied Diana, quickly, "for I have read of your death."

"You may have read it in your dream, or I may be dreaming that you have dreamt it. But it has been a very long dream!"

"Sir," said Dr. Johnson, "I will not permit you to consider me a mere morsel of your dreams. The unconscious ratiocination of your brain cannot have the power to call into existence the personality, and the sequences of memory and thought, by which I know myself to be an individual being. If it could, sir, I should talk like you."

"But I know something of your works and I could very well imagine how you would talk. Nothing proves to me that you are not my dream. Nothing can prove to our living friends here that we are not their dreams, especially if we should chance to send them to sleep, so that on waking they should find us gone."

" Ay, the waking, sir, the waking!" repeated Johnson, shaking his head violently from side to side.

Again that melancholy sigh trembled on the air and then died away in the sound of the breeze.

" Why are you all so sad to-night?" asked Lady Brenda, who hated anything approaching to melancholy.

" Indeed, madam, we have reason for sadness," answered Francis, at last. " When you speak of such things, I wish I were Bayard. Unfortunately —" he stopped short.

"You never could have been," said the lady, with a smile. "Perhaps you would not if you could, or it may be that you could not, if you had had the will."

" I do not know why your majesty should wish to exchange with me." It was Bayard who spoke.

" A man would sacrifice much to leave behind him such a name as yours," said Augustus, " a man without fear and without reproach."

" Reproach had a different meaning in my time," replied the knight, calmly. " I was no saint. I should

perhaps scarcely pass muster in your modern society.
I went through life with one idea, or motto."

"What was that?" asked Gwendoline, quickly.

"Always do what you are afraid of doing — it is a
good motto, I think."

"Yes — provided it is not a wrong thing."

"The thing one fears to do is seldom bad," answered Bayard. "Fear is the devil's barrier between
man and good deeds."

"What a part in your life of to-day is played by
those ideas of right and wrong!" exclaimed Cæsar,
suddenly joining in the conversation. "When I
lived, the question was, whether an act was legal or
illegal. No man's conscience asked more than that."

"What did Horace mean, then, by his *integer
vitæ?*" asked Augustus.

"An honest man," replied Cæsar. "That is, a man
who lived according to the laws. He adds *sceleris-
que purus*, innocent of crime. The conjunction of
epithets explains everything. If one of your contemporaries spoke of you as 'an honest man,' he
would hardly think it necessary to add that you were
'innocent of crime.' The one term is now supposed
to contain the other."

"But you had also the religious idea. *Fas* and
*nefas* expressed it, as an equivalent to our right and
wrong."

"Our religion, or our fifty religions, had very little
hold upon anybody in the higher classes. *Fas* came
to mean, generally, what you would call unwritten

law ; that is, it meant the verdict of educated public opinion, and included every kind of superstition as well as every idea of social propriety. But what does it matter how we thought? Thoughts may go on and change, but the end of life is the end of action, and inaction is torment."

The calm intonations of his voice trembled a little, as he spoke the last words, and he turned his face away from the moonlight.

"And must inaction last for ever?" asked Gwendoline, softly.

"For ever, perhaps. Perhaps only until to-morrow's dawn. Who knows? Not we, who walk between three worlds, shadows, and less than shadows, memories, and yet more than memories. Nor can you know, you, who live, and can still find something to do that has not yet been done."

"But where are the rest?" asked Diana, after a pause. "Where are the shadows of old time, and the shadows of yesterday? Where is Achilles? Where are the Sirens? Where is the king who died last year, the beggar who died last night?"

"With yesterday, as we are — you only are with to-day, and the world may never see to-morrow."

"But that yesterday — what is it? where is it?"

"It is not. It has no reality, though it was once real. It is a memory with those who knew it. For those who knew it not, it is nothing, no more than the shadow of a cloud that lingered a moment on the hillside to-day."

"As for the Sirens, their music is as sweet as ever," said Chopin, gazing through the dreamy moonlight at the islets, now far astern of the yacht but still clearly visible.

"If we could only hear them!" sighed Gwendoline. Then she laughed at the idea.

"Why not?  It is just such a night as they love."

"If anything could make the night more beautiful, it would be music," said Lady Brenda.  "But I am afraid you are quite, quite mad, Gwendoline.  Of course the Sirens never really existed."

"Then why did people write so much about them?"

"Madam," said Dr. Johnson, "that which is beautiful has a permanent existence, but those things which are in contradiction to the nature of beauty, are destined to perish and decay.  Those who seek to resuscitate, by the active exertion of their imaginations, the noble and elevating thoughts of forgotten ages, will certainly obtain success in a measure proportional to their ability and industry; but such persons as lack the originality necessary to conceive great works, the application which is indispensable for their execution, and the faith in beauty, through which alone the poetic inspiration can be conveyed, are by nature unable either to revivificate the glories of the past, or to contribute anything new to that assemblage of eminently excellent things with which mankind are already acquainted."

"But where there is the faith alone, there is always

the capacity for enjoying the beautiful," suggested Gwendoline.

"Ah, my dear lady, you have it there!" answered the doctor. "The faith is the thing."

"Then we might hear the Sirens after all. If they were bad and cruel their songs were divine. We might hear the song, even if we could not see the women."

"I will go about when we are abreast of the cape, my dear," said Augustus. "This breeze will end there, and in coming back we will run under the islands."

"Oh, do!" cried the two younger ladies in a breath.

"It would be worth while to hear the Sirens and live to tell of it," said Heine. "How often I longed to listen to the pixies and water-sprites! I was always sure that they lived somewhere in the green depths."

"But of course it is quite impossible," said Lady Brenda, who was still incredulous.

"Nothing is impossible," answered the earnest voice of Pascal. He was sitting at a distance from the rest, apparently lost in a reverie, a look of wonderful peace upon his face.

"Really," returned Lady Brenda, "I always thought everybody knew that a great many things are altogether out of the question."

"Unusual things seem impossible until they happen," answered the man of learning. "What could

seem more impossible to a human mind than the
creation of this world?  What more impossible than
its destruction?"

"That is true.   But we have grown used to the
world as we see it and know it.  There are changes
imaginable in the world which look far less probable
than the final catastrophe—the last day, as people
call it."

"There are things beyond this earth which none
of you can even imagine, and yet they have a very
real existence."

"The creations of the mind are as real as the
manifestations of matter," said Lionardo.

"Yes," assented Lady Brenda, "because they can
be printed in books, printed on canvas, or carved in
stone.  Then they become real things."

"Pardon me.  That is not what makes them real.
Many great books were handed down for centuries
before even writing was invented, and they had a
tremendous influence over the human race."

"But words are almost things, after all, and if one
learns them by heart they are just like books."

"What are words?" asked the artist.  "They are
symbols of thoughts.  Letters only represent words
by convention, and are symbols of symbols.  The
reality lies in the ideas which all these symbols call
up to countless generations of men who hear the
words or see the letters.  The idea is then the
reality, and the material part of a picture or a book
is the vehicle, not affecting the idea but communi-

cating it more or less correctly and completely to men."

"But if a picture is not a thing — I grant you the matter of the book — where does the painter's merit lie ? "

" In knowing how to convey to you what he sees, just as the poet's skill consists in making his thoughts pass through your brain. The poet's ideas live longer because the symbols which convey them can be reproduced and are used by everybody. The artist's symbols are his own, and no one else can use them in the same way to express the same idea."

"We were talking about the Sirens," remarked Heine, suddenly. "If we could only find their 'symbols,' as you call them — "

"Music is not a symbol. It is an ever-living reality," said Chopin. "It is a reality that makes itself felt without being always defined."

"Your music is your thought," replied Lionardo. "You gave it shape by your skill, and thus transmitted it to others. Therefore it is the symbol of your ideas."

" The expression, not the symbol. There is a vast difference between the two."

" The symbol is the means of expressing," argued the artist. " A sequence of symbols constitutes a whole expression."

" Not in music. The written notes are the symbols. The strain of living music is the expression. Otherwise you would have a right to say that I derive as much pleasure from looking over a page of music, because I know how it would sound, as I get from actually hearing the same music performed."

"That is true," said Lionardo, thoughtfully. "Is music after all the greatest of the arts? Perhaps it is."

"No," answered Chopin. "As great as the rest, but not greater. But it is more real, because in music the expression is inseparable from the idea. You cannot imagine a prose translation of music. And yet there are prose translations of poems, which are still capable of moving the heart; and there are copies and drawings of pictures and statues, which still give some part of the pleasure a man would feel in seeing the original. You either hear music, or you do not hear it. There is no compromise for the uninitiated, like a translation, nor any substitute for those who cannot enjoy it directly, such as copies or drawings."

"Music is like action," said Cæsar. "What is the description of a great deed, compared with the deed itself? What is an action that is only thought of and never performed? Nothing, unless it furnish a little matter for speculation, and inquiry into its possibility."

"And love," suggested the king, "what is it, until a man feels it? It is like music that has never been sung."

"Music is love, and hate, and peace, and war, and

all great passions and great deeds," replied Chopin.
" It is the only art which can express everything that
is infinitely noble and grand, and yet which need
never define anything."

" Sir," said Johnson, " music suggests that which
cannot be expressed, nor defined either, by any art
with which man is now acquainted. Nevertheless,
it is instructive to observe, that those pleasing aspirations, which harmony is so eminently capable of
inspiring in the human heart, are only awakened in
certain hearers whose organisation is especially fitted
to receive a musical impression. To my mind, sir,
music is not even a cheerful noise ; but I once heard
certain solemn music played on French horns at
Rochester, and the impression made upon me was of
a melancholy kind."

" If you were affected by the sound of a French
horn," remarked Heine, " it is impossible to say what
you might feel if you heard a Siren."

" We shall see, sir," replied the doctor, curtly.

" I hope so,' said Gwendoline. " Do you not
think we could go about now?" she asked, turning
to Augustus.

" Yes," he answered. " It will be safer, too.
There is something brewing down there in the south-
east."

He whistled to the men forward to mind the jibs,
and he put the helm down. A man came aft immediately to manage the sheet, as the cutter's head
came up to the wind. Augustus expected to see him

start with astonishment at the sight of the strange guests. Then, glancing round, he saw that they had disappeared.

"Let her go a little free of the wind," said Heine's voice, as the breeze caught the sail and the vessel went over on to the port tack. The sailor instinctively obeyed the order, allowing a few feet more of the sheet to run through the blocks, but he turned his head sharply round, and stared at Augustus.

"Excuse me, sir, but did you give that order, sir?" he asked, in queer tones.

"No — well — it's all right, Jameson. You can make fast. And keep your eye on that stuff down there," added Augustus, pointing to the clouds that were piling up over the Calabrian hills.

"Ay, ay, sir," answered the man, somewhat reassured. He went forward again, and as he disappeared the figures of the dead men became once more clearly visible in the moonlight.

"You nearly frightened the fellow out of his wits," said Augustus, with a laugh. "I thought that when you had disappeared you were gone altogether, and could not have made yourselves heard."

"We are never gone," replied the poet. "But the power of your currents is diminishing. You yourself will soon no longer see us, nor hear us. I wonder that my voice could still reach that man who is not in the same chain as you."

"Are you really going? So soon?" asked Diana in sorrowful surprise.

"Very soon — too soon," answered Heine, sadly.

Again that deep and melancholy sigh swelled, hovered on the breeze and floated away over the rippling water, as though it were itself a spirit burdened with grief, that sought rest and found not where to lay its head.

For a long time there was silence. As the yacht ran farther from the land the night wind lost its strength, and the vessel moved slowly in her course. Almost unconsciously Augustus steered for the three sister islets. The moon's rays caught the uneven surfaces of the rocks and made them stand out of the white distance. Though the cutter seemed to be hardly moving, the islands came nearer and nearer, and gradually grew more distinct. At last the sails hung idly down, flat and unstirred by any breath. The shore was now not a hundred yards distant and the yacht had scarcely any way on her. At less than twenty yards from the beach she stopped, and lay motionless in the perfect calm.

The shore was low and flat, covered with dark wet sand in which the moonlight found tiny points of reflection, that glistened like diamonds. In the background, and at both ends, the rocks rose up in weird, irregular shapes, full of deep black shadows. A little way down the beach a row of jagged timbers stuck out of the sand, and were all that remained of some poor fishing vessel wrecked long ago.

But as the eyes of all on board gazed at the quiet scene, three moving figures grew up out of the misty moonlight. Three white women sat grouped together on a projecting boulder, three women wonderfully fair, and each so like the other, that their faces were as one face seen from three different aspects. Their hair, golden, even in the moonlight, seemed wet with the sea water, and their lips were red with life. As they looked out to seaward their deep eyes gleamed like a constellation of soft southern stars. One of them held in her hands a coral pipe with two stems, the other a tiny lyre made from a conch shell; the third clasped her ivory fingers together and sat between the others, her lips just parted as though her song were trembling to come forth.

"The Sirens," said Gwendoline under her breath. But no one else spoke, and all was still.

And so, as the white-winged vessel lay motionless in the enchanted moonlight, those three pale faces were turned upwards, and from the mysterious lips there issued a wild and changing harmony, and words of a half-forgotten speech, which by some strange magic were yet wholly understood by those who heard : —

> The moonlight bathes the sea
> And the ripples wash the sand,
> The song of our hearts goes free
> Down the shelving silver strand.
> Neither goddesses are we, nor women,
> Nor angels nor spirits of death;
> We are maidens of evil omen
> And we breathe the sea spray for our breath.
>
> The gods love us not in heaven,
> The souls of drowned men in hell

Curse us, from morn till even,
For the songs we sing so well.
We are neither alive nor dead,
We know not of death nor of life
But the life of man is our bread
And the tears of widowed wife.

When the Mother of all, before the light,
Laboured to bring forth gods to Chaos,
Wrapped in the pall of ancient night —
No mother had we in her bosom to lay us,
To dandle and fondle, caress us and nurse us,
For we sprang out of moonlight and soft sea mist
And we sing that the sailors may love us, and curse us,
And die in the song of the lips they have kissed.

In the thick darkness the ages moaned
When the Mother travailed, the shapeless god,
The awful father, Chaos, groaned
Shaking the vaults of space as he trod.
Then the Mother laid hold on the pillars of night
And bowed herself and shrieked aloud,
Till the firmament rocked beneath her might
And split, and was rent into streamers of cloud;
The broad black waste of space was torn,
The arch of heaven was burst to the day,
The sun leapt up, and the gods were born,
And Chaos the father passed away.

But gods and men have bodies and souls,
And they live and they know that their lives are sweet,
While the dear sun shines and the blue tide rolls
While the heart is full and the pulses beat.
The beasts of the forests, the flocks on the mountain,
The bright-winged birds and the fish in the deep,

All drink of the water of life's clear fountain —
All die at the last and are lost in sleep.

We are bodiless, spiritless, mingled together
Of the rays of the moon that deceive men to sin,
Of the spray of the sea and the salt sea weather,
Of mists out of depths that suck men in.
Our hands are transparent as white alabaster,
Our fingers are skilled to the holes of the pipe,
Our song swells sweet, as the oars dip faster
And the long ash bends in the sailor's gripe.

While the strange voices from the shore were singing their unearthly song, the great clouds in the southeast had grown blacker and more angry. A small portion of the mass, detached and driven by some upper current of wind, far to westward, obscured the moon. A cool stream of moist air rushed over the water, low and swift, not reaching the yacht, where she lay in the lee of the rocks, but crisping the water at the end of the little island and making the ripples ring against the jagged stones. Suddenly a bright flash of lightning illuminated the distant cloud-bank and a far-off peal of thunder rolled out through the night and reverberated along the shores of the great gulf. Louder and clearer, faster and wilder, the song of the Sirens swelled in the gloom : —

In the crags of the south the dark cloud-heaps are piling up
    mountains,
The storm slaves of Æolus howl to be loosed from their caves,

The dark depths of the waters well up from their fathomless
    fountains,
From the brooding breast of the sea, and the womb of the waves.

There is sullen wrath in the voices that distantly rumble,
In the dark, the white plumes gleam and flash, as the sea-
    horses plunge
Through the masterful waves and the billows, that heavily
    tumble
Where the storm-riders charge into battle, meet, buffet and
    lunge.

The sharp screech of the swift-streaming storm cleaves the
    deep sounds asunder,
And the blade of the lightning stabs the deep sea with a dash,
Then the wail of the wounded waves is drowned in the thunder
That bursts out and rumbles and roars down the track of the
    flash.

The wild tide, massed in mountains of back-driven waters
    defiant,
Rears, towers and totters, then falls all its terrible height,
Roaring forward and pounding the shore like a great, maddened
    giant
Tossed out of the caldron of storms to devour the night.

In the crashing and flashing of thunder and blazing lightning
The whirlpools are rattling the ships like dice in a bowl,
The taut weather shrouds are all parting, the wet rigging
    tightening
Snaps like grass at the blocks and drags down by the board at
    each roll.

In the match between gods and sea-giants for souls of sailors
The stiff triple-reefed sail bursts the bolt-ropes and sprains the
    slant yard,

While the slave in his chains, doomed to drown at his oar with
    his jailors,
Bows his back and pulls desperate strokes in the dark, straining
    hard.

For the sea is Death's garden and he sows dead men in the
    loam,
When the breast of the waters is ploughed like a field by the
    gale,
When the ocean is turned up and rent in long furrows of foam
By the coulter and share of the wind and the harrow of hail.

The distant thunder gradually subsided, as it so
often does in those southern seas, borne away in a
new direction by the changing currents of the wind.
The streamer of cloud, that had hidden the moon for
a few moments, now disappeared and showed her far
down upon the western horizon. Her beams fell full
upon the white, supernatural beauty of the sisters'
faces. Suddenly their song changed, and twining
their smooth arms about one another's necks they
moved slowly forward till they stood on the edge
of the sand, so that the gently rippling water washed
their gleaming feet. And thus they sang: —

    Hail, summer's moon, pale with soft deathly love!
    The silent stars, thy messengers and slaves,
    Thy faithful linkmen in the roads above,
    Show thee the paths that lead o'er dead men's graves —
    O'er the great grave of all, through which they drove
    Their raking craft, mid storms and lashing waves,
    Hither, whence dying gales on languid wing
    Waft seaward through the night the song we sing.

Come, weary mariners! Come, tired souls,
Faint with the watch and labour of the sea,
With tugging at the oar where mad surf rolls,
With staring for the light upon the lee,
Worn out with waking when the watch-bell tolls —
Here is the land you seek! Rest and be free!
Slack sheet and halyard, furl and stow your sails,
Smooth gleams the harbour and the storm wind fails.

Long have you toiled upon the hard oak seat,
Your limbs are stiff and aching with the blast,
Your hands are cramped with grasping the wet sheet,
Your eyes are dim with watching from the mast
For some faint light amidst the driving sleet!
Now sinks the storm, now is the tempest past.
Run the long ship securely on the sand,
Stretch your strong limbs and leap upon the land!

The moon is low, the heavy hours that toiled
So slow about the dial of the night,
When wave yawned back from wave, and hissed and boiled
Bathe now their crystal coronets in light.
Poseidon's trooping monsters now have coiled
Their slimy length to sleep, far out of sight.
To distant depths subsides the storm-god's roar
And tuneful ripples tinkle on the shore.

Think not, as o'er the swinging ash you bend,
These rocks too rough, or this wet strand too cold!
Dread not the reef, as with long sweep you send
Your ship abeach! Nor keel, nor laden hold
Shall grate upon one sea-shell that offend
The smooth long planks, the deep sweet sand shall fold
Your tired bark as in a sea-bird's nest,
And on our velvet shore your limbs shall rest.

Fear not the shadows flitting in the gloom!
Think not that some forlorn, unhappy ghost,
Of mariner unburied, from his doom
Has risen to haunt the crannies of our coast;
Nor that from unknown depths of ocean's tomb
Dead men come back, a ghastly, dripping host!
Those are not faces, those dim forms are wreathed
In ivory moonlight through the sea-mist breathed.

Nay shrink not! These are not white bleaching bones
Of drowned men — that is not a sailor's skull!
The moonbeams paint strange pictures on the stones —
That jagged thing is not a rotting hull!
Lend not your ears to melancholy tones
Blown out of low-mouthed caves when tempests lull!
Our song is soft, our voices swell, our lips
Shall teach you sweet things, ere the young moon dips.

Look on us maids, for we are young — and fair!
Nor misty as we seem; a woman's arm
Is warm and smooth, and pillowed in her hair
A sailor's weary head may rest from harm.
What? Are ye men, and do you then not dare
To yield your bodies to a woman's charm?
Ah, mariners! we love you — let these tears
Warm your chilled hands and melt away your fears!

Waste not your looks on shadows, in our faces
Read the sweet signs and oaths of woman's love!
Read, that these hearts are yours, these sea-born graces,
These lips of ours, that kissed the gods above —
This golden hair, tangled in misty laces
Fine as the Lydian web Arachne wove —
All yours, love's kisses and entrancing powers!
Yours, and in being yours, we make you ours!

The gods, exiled beyond this sweet earth's life,
Envied the love withheld from cold immortals,
And longed for love and hope, and human strife,
Till, gazing down from heaven's golden portals,
They burned to clasp a breathing, living wife.
So love we you, ye brave and strong-limbed mortals
Half goddesses, our hearts can never tire —
All earthly, womanly with love's soft fire!

It is not true that we were born of spray,
Mingled with moonlight glancing on the water!
Where silent Pindus rears up to the day
His tree-crowned head, Melpomene, dark daughter
Of deathless Memory, paused in her way,
Ere Heracles, half mad with rage and slaughter,
Had fought with Achelous in that glade
Whence the great river plunges through the shade.

The lofty maid, the dark-browed Tragic Muse
Lingered and loved the fountain of the river
As the day fainted.   Then the rising dews
Wetted the arrow Love drew from his quiver
And made it heavy-winged its flight refuse.
At half its range the shaft, with tremulous shiver
Struck full upon the breast of the great stream
And piercing deeply stirred love's first wild dream.

Up rose the mighty torrent in white mist
And in his strong wet arms the maid entwined,
Bathed her black tresses and her dark cheek kissed.
Clasping her to him, as though he would bind
Her heart to his, he bore her where he list,
To distant depths, wherein the ocean kind
Received their godlike loves in deep-sea room
Where waves are still and nameless beauties bloom.

She was our mother. Here, upon these rocks,
She brought us forth amid the ocean's roar,
And wrung the sea salt from her raven locks,
Singing to seaward down the sounding shore.
Here, where the wild sea-bird our music mocks,
She left us, through the sunset clouds to soar
High on white wings, in springing arch of flight
Toward the transcendent homes of heavenly light.

She taught our lips the strange entrancing strains
That draw men down to join the shadowy throng.
She taught us how to weave and wind wild chains
Of sounds about men's ears, sweet, soft and strong
She gave us of love's fire, that love's life drains,
She left us all her heaven-born gift of song.
Rest, mariners! The moon sinks to the deep
While we breathe songs and kisses through your sleep.

The moon already touched the low sea line, and
the great shadow of the yacht's sails fell upon the
darkening shore. Suddenly there was a stir in the
water and the long dark shape of a strangely-fash-
ioned vessel, dim and indistinct amid the half-light,
loomed up from the water, gliding swiftly and
making noiseless circles in the sea, as though pro-
pelled by an unseen power. Augustus felt an icy
chill run through his frame. A cool breeze began to
fill the sails of the cutter, and carried her slowly
away from the island. Chard grasped the helm
mechanically, gazing back at the faces of the Siren
sisters, and at the moving shadow of the ship, straining his ears to catch the last words of their song.

Once more their voices rose, full of a fateful, passionate temptation : —

The sweep and the splash of the strokes come nearer,
The dull quick knock of oars swung in the tholes,
Till the white faces gleam in the moonlight clearer
Of sailors who sell for our song their souls!

The dark ship looms in the brightness above us,
The long keel grates on the deadly strand,
The strong white bodies of men that would love us
Leap from the bow to the soft wet sand!

Our arms go round them, our cold lips wound them,
Our sweet song lulls them to rest and sleep.
With our breath, and the mist of our breath, we have drowned
    them,
Just as the moon sinks into the deep.

We have silver lips, and hearts of lead,
To kiss and caress till the sailor is dead,
To soothe him and breathe on his curly head,
To drain his blood till his soul is sped,
To blow the sea-foam o'er the dead man's bed,
When the stars are dark and the moon is fled
From the deep sea.

The wild strains died away like a dirge on the cool air as the yacht ran swiftly forward. The moon was gone, but another light was on the water. The east was already blushing, and the fair Dawn Maiden scattered her rose-leaves in the path of the coming morn.

In their deep chairs, Lady Brenda, Gwendoline and Diana sat motionless and pale, while Augustus, paler even than they, stood upright and held the helm.  But the shades of the dead men were gone, and the living were alone together in the cool peace of the stealing twilight.

THE END.

www.ingramcontent.com/pod-product-compliance
Lightning Source LLC
Chambersburg PA
CBHW030246030726
47493CB00023B/613